Time &

Patricia O'Reilly's fiction books are *Felicity's Wedding* (2001), *Once Upon a Summer* (2000). Her non-fiction books are *Dying with Love* (1992), *Writing for the Market* (1994), *Earning Your Living from Home* (1996) and *Working Mothers* (1997).

She is a writer and researcher, and has written extensively for Irish newspapers and magazines, and radio. She is a lecturer/trainer in various aspects of writing.

PATRICIA O'REILLY

Time & Destiny

Hodder

LIR

First published in Ireland in 2003 by Hodder Headline Ireland
First published in paperback in 2004 by Hodder Headline Ireland
A division of Hodder Headline

A Hodder/LIR paperback

1 3 5 7 9 10 8 6 4 2

Although this novel was inspired by the life of Eileen Gray, all characters in this publication are fictitious and any resemblance to real persons, living or dead, is purely coincidental.

A CIP catalogue record for this title is available from the British Library

ISBN 0 340 83152 9

Typeset in Plantin Light by Palimpsest Book Production Limited,
Polmont, Stirlingshire

Printed and bound by
Clays Ltd, St Ives plc

Hodder Headline's policy is to use papers that are natural, renewable and recyclable products and made from wood grown in sustainable forests. The logging and manufacturing processes are expected to conform to the environmental regulations of the country of origin

Hodder Headline Ireland
8 Castlecourt
Castleknock
Dublin 15
Ireland
A division of Hodder Headline
338 Euston Road
London NW1 3BH

This book is dedicated to Eileen Gray,
who, I suspect, would not approve.

'Avec le temps et la paille, les figues mûrissent' –
'With time and straw, the figs ripen.'

Old Provençal proverb

Prologue

It was one of those warm, almost breathless, Parisian summer afternoons. Bel, Colette and Jacques sat under the green-and-white striped awning of a pavement café, watching the world go by, sipping wine and saying little.

Below them stretched the cobblestoned pavements of the lower quay, glistening white in the heat, and the cool smoothness of the grey-green Seine. Down the promenade a boy watered horses and a lavender-seller plied her wares. In the middle of the river a commuter boat chugged past a barge, coloured posters gleamed on the bateau-mouche's square roof.

'Did you know, chérie, that the Eiffel Tower is three hundred metres high?' Jacques broke the silence to ask Bel. She knew that and much more about the Tower because she had taken a guided tour of the city the previous afternoon, but she would not spoil his pleasure by mentioning it.

Bel McDonagh was a typical rich young New Yorker of the 1920s bowing to her millionaire father's wishes and ambition by completing her education doing the circuit of cultural Europe but equally determined, as she put it, to experience life to the full. Now that she was in Paris, her aim was to sample real Parisian life in the raw.

During the day she dutifully visited museums, art galleries

and places of tourist interest. In the evenings, in the company of other Americans, she frequented smoky jazz basements and caught the occasional floor show at the Moulin Rouge or the Folies-Bergère. When the opportunity presented itself, she stayed up half the night, toying with a glass of absinthe and feeling utterly woman-of-the-world, as she played hands of piquet, quadrille and bezique in Left Bank gambling clubs.

She wore her plump, virginal youth carelessly, as though it were eternal, as though there was no such thing as ageing or loss of innocence.

Determined to return home dressed from head to toe in the height of French fashion, she met Jacques Doucet on her first visit to his salon to order some of his movie-star bias dresses which were this season's talking point among chic Parisians.

She was dazzled by his salon's gilt and cream rococo opulence, the gold-tipped scrolls curlicuing from every corner, and the curly-haired cherubs gambolling across the ceiling. Its air of church-like sanctity impressed her too, as did the grooming, charm and tiptoeing professionalism of his assistants.

As for the couturier himself, he was even more exactly as she imagined him. A tentative friendship, based on the unlikely attraction of opposites, developed between them.

A few weeks later, she wrote to her father saying that she was bowled over by the dresses which made her feel so elegant and quite Hollywood glamorous. He wrote back enclosing yet another draft for $1000 and urged her not to stint on herself. It was advice which Bel took to heart.

Initially, she was impressed by Jacques's European-ness, his aristocratic bearing and sophisticated lifestyle. Gradually, she came to appreciate his benevolence, the comfort of his dark whiskered face and kindly blue eyes. Recently, she had interpreted the occasional intimate way he called her chérie as a sign of his growing fondness towards her. It was a fact which she hugged to herself in romantic anticipation.

For his part, Jacques was intrigued by the heady combination of Bel, intrepid lone traveller, and apple-cheeked ingénue. There were not many such innocents in today's world, or if there were, they did not remain so for long in Paris. Her air of prosperous naïveté brought out in him a paternally protective streak which up to now had remained so well hidden that even he had not suspected its existence.

Colette, red hair wild, the sleeves of her raspberry pink blouse rolled up to reveal dimpled elbows, hated to be out of the spotlight. She showed indifference to her present company, and in the Eiffel Tower and its height, by deep sighs and by looking around distractedly in the hope of spotting more convivial companionship.

'Are you all right?' Jacques queried sympathetically.

A chance to complain about her ex-husband was too irresistible an invitation for Colette to pass up on.

'No, of course, I'm not all right. How could I be? Being dragged through the legalities of Willy still claiming my Claudine books as his. Lying. Pretending he wrote them. When every word is mine. Accepting literary credit and barrow loads of money.' She paused to light a Gauloise, to wallow in the sympathy oozing from both Jacques and Bel, and to stretch the drama of her life even further by adding with a sigh, 'As well as his constant affairs, all the time we were married.'

Jacques took a sip of wine. 'So I've heard.'

'Why did you put up with it?' Bel asked diffidently. She was quite overawed by Colette's blatant sexuality, larger-than-life personality and natural flamboyance.

Colette shrugged. 'Men. There's nothing to be done. He's French.' She paused, grinned wickedly and murmured, 'And if he could, I don't see why I couldn't.'

Bel's pansy eyes widened, though she supposed there was nothing unusual about someone like Colette having an affair. Even the elderly in Paris seemed to have afternoon liaisons.

She looked up the quay at the lavender-seller who had given up on sales and was wheeling her barrow upriver, the sun's yellow light shining on her bared muscular arms and on the orange of her kerchief.

Travel broadened the mind, Bel knew. Perhaps she had not yet journeyed far enough to be inured to what she was seeing and hearing. But never had she imagined anything like life in Paris. Or could it be, she wondered, that despite being an utterly modern American, there still lurked the disciplined residue of her Irish-Catholic heritage and upbringing? She hoped not. The life she planned for herself would not be hampered by such restrictions.

Jacques reached across the table and in a gesture of solidarity, touched the back of Bel's hand. To save her from further embarrassment, he felt obliged to change the subject from affairs which he knew, given any encouragement, Colette would discuss *ad nauseam* and in salacious detail. The unedited intricacies of her current liaison and Willy's behaviour were most certainly not for Bel's ears. Sometime, he decided, he would quietly and discreetly explain the situation to her.

'Eileen's late.' He looked around, hoping to see her tall figure come along the quay.

'But I'm here.' Bel, blonde curls bobbing, reminded him. She had not known that Eileen Gray was joining them. Her English title, design talent, aura of quiet glamour and adventurous spirit were the talk of Paris. From Colette's raised eyebrows, Bel knew her attempt at levity had fallen flat.

Jacques's expression and voice were all kindness. 'Forgive me, Bel. I'm not good company. I'm a bit distracted.'

'Jacques. Don't you know I need copious quantities of wine to drown my many sorrows?'

'Really Colette,' he said with a touch of asperity, though signalling the waiter for another bottle.

'You're a right old woman. Always worrying about Eileen,' announced Colette, with a sly look at Bel.

'I've reason to. She's flying with that aviator Lecointe.'

'Not the record-breaking Sadi Lecointe?' screeched Colette.

'The same,' said Jacques. 'And worse than that, she's trying to persuade him to give her lessons.'

'Just recently he's broken the record at two hundred and five miles an hour,' informed Colette breathlessly.

'And,' said Jacques sternly, 'that Englishman friend of hers, Charles Rolls, who introduced her to flying, broke records too. Don't you remember, doing that round trip from Dover to Calais? And where's he?' He paused for effect before answering his own question. 'Dead and buried.'

'I've flown too, you know,' boasted Colette. 'When I was reporting for *Le Matin* during the war. It was horrific. Absolutely terrifying. Quite the most petrifying experience of my life.'

Neither Jacques nor Bel commented. Colette's superlatived dramatics seldom required a reply.

But Colette would not be ignored. 'Jacques, as a friend, may I offer you a word of advice?'

Jacques, an amused smile playing around his lips, nodded.

'Don't fall any further in love with Eileen.'

For a moment, only a moment, it seemed as though her remark had penetrated Jacques's sophistication.

Bel wondered how Colette could go on with such nonsense.

Quickly Jacques retaliated. 'An overactive imagination is, no doubt, a necessary requisite for a writer.'

'But surely you know, Eileen and Damia are quite inseparable these days.' With a flourish, Colette lit up a fresh cigarette.

'I didn't know you smoked.'

'It helps my nerves. And, Jacques, don't try to change the subject.'

'I'm not. So Eileen's friendly with Marie-Louise Damien, the cabaret artist?' He shrugged. 'So what?'

'So that's her real name? How do you know?'

'Eileen and I have seen her show. She's good.' Jacques allowed himself a smug smile as he topped up their glasses of wine.

But Colette would not be deterred. 'Ah. But have you seen her performance up and down the Champs-Elysées with her pet panther in her open top automobile?'

'No, I missed that.'

'A pity. Because on occasions Eileen has been known to join her.' Colette informed slyly, taking a lingering drag of her cigarette.

'Well, Eileen is the original free spirit,' Jacques stated categorically.

'Given the chance, aren't we all?'

'I'm not too sure. I don't consider myself a free spirit and, I'm sure, Bel doesn't either.'

'No,' said Bel, with more than a tinge of regret. She was following the conversation avidly. Though she would like to be classified as a free spirit, right now she considered it more romantically beneficial to align herself with Jacques.

Colette would not be deterred. 'Eileen and Damia aren't common knowledge.'

'So?' Jacques shrugged. 'Why should they be?'

'You know how reticent Eileen is.'

'She's entitled to her privacy. We all are.'

'Privacy is so bourgeoisie.'

'Nonsense. Eileen is vital, talented and full of fun and yet she's all the more appealing – and indeed, mysterious – because of her natural reserve.'

'She has a flaring temper,' Colette interjected.

'And great inner strength,' announced Jacques.

Colette peered over his shoulder and announced, 'And here comes the paragon of inner strength now. And, you'll be glad to know, looking none the worst after her flight.'

Jacques swivelled around and watched the tall elegant navy-suited figure move gracefully along the quay. 'What exquisite tailoring. Eileen dresses with such understated elegance.'

Even though her outfit was this season's latest, a Breton suit by Lavin, Bel felt fussy and fat in her short braided jacket, white organdie collar and fluttering red ribbon.

'I prefer clothes with a bit of flamboyance myself,' said Colette.

'So I've noticed.'

Colette made a fruitless attempt at tidying her blouse into the waistband of her red skirt.

Even before Eileen had drawn up alongside their table, Jacques was on his feet. 'Come. Sit down. Have a glass of wine. Tell us about your flight.'

The excitement of flying had Eileen sparkling vivaciously and put colour into the usual pale of her cheeks. 'It's indescribable,' she said, sitting into the chair Jacques had pulled out. 'Quite wonderful. Such freedom. Up there with the birds. It's so much better than ballooning. Imagine, we went at more than a hundred miles an hour. And our height was at least two hundred feet.'

'Did you have a lesson, get to fly yourself?' Despite herself, Colette was impressed.

Peeling off her navy gloves, Eileen answered. 'No. Would you believe, Sadi refused to let me take the controls?'

'Well this whole business of air locomotion is extraordinarily dangerous. And particularly for a woman . . .' Jacques began rather ponderously.

'We're no longer living in the dark ages. We must move with the times. Flying's still a relatively new invention and, of course, there are bound to be minor problems, though now that parachutes have been perfected, it's as safe as motoring.' Eileen's half smile took the admonition from her firmly spoken words.

Bel watched the softness of Jacques's eyes and the smile playing around his lips as Eileen spoke. For a moment, but only the briefest of moments, she wondered could Colette be right. Then her youthfully optimistic nature re-asserted itself and she shrugged off the ridiculousness of the idea of Jacques being in love with someone as old as Eileen Gray.

'Well, I'm glad you didn't fly,' Jacques said.

'Oh, but I shall.'

'Nonsense. It's much too dangerous. Nobody'll give you instruction.'

'Bet they will if she uses her title. I should know how titles open all sorts of doors,' Colette stated categorically.

'Your connections are nothing to boast about,' said Jacques firmly.

'I never use my title. It's quite unimportant to me. Imagine calling myself an Honourable.'

'A title's good for business, particularly in Paris,' Jacques said quietly. 'You do realise that, Eileen?'

'Maybe. But, no.'

Silence stretched between the four of them. Colette made a *moue* of disgust. Jacques looked calm and dignified. Eileen watched the river, as though mesmerised by its languid nibbling movements. Bel glanced from one to the other.

'What's your latest project?' Jacques asked Eileen.

Eileen pulled back her eyes from the water. 'Right now, I'm not working on anything particular, though I assure you, I'm far from idle.' She gave a little laugh. 'I'm in the weighty process of thinking.'

'And what has you thinking so deeply?' Jacques asked, a teasing tone entering his voice.

'That I'd like to do a screen. A lacquer screen. Something allegorical or mythological. Ancient figurines. On a red background, I think.' She took out from an efficient briefcase-like bag a roll of tobacco and a packet of papers. Competently, she rolled a cigarette and accepted Jacques's light.

'So, what's stopping you, chérie?'

This was the first time that Bel had noticed Jacques address Eileen as chérie. She decided it was a slip of his tongue.

'All kinds of problems.'

'So? Problems exist to be mastered. If I hadn't believed in my bias collection, I wouldn't have presented.'

'You must have known that was destined for success. The dresses were so feminine. So flattering. Creations of which Proust's heroines dreamed . . .' Eileen murmured dreamily.

'Oh, stop thinking. Just go for it, Eileen,' said Colette airily. 'And you never know, you too and your screen may be immortalised in literature.'

Eileen sighed. 'Lacquer-work is different. There're so many technical difficulties to be surmounted.'

These bantering nuances were incomprehensible to Bel. But then she did not know that Marcel Proust had mentioned Jacques's gowns in his latest novel. She felt left out of their conversation, though she refused to be excluded. 'What difficulties?' she asked Eileen.

'Lacquer problems, as I said.' Eileen's antipathy towards Bel was barely veiled.

Bel felt her insides curdle in misery. She had been raised, not only with the privileges of wealth, but surrounded by her father's supportive love and approval, and she was unused to such discourtesy.

Jacques looked from Eileen to Bel and back again and asked quietly, 'So, why don't you clarify the mystery of this lacquering for us?'

Eileen's hands fluttered in explanation, her fingers were slender, her nails perfect pink white-tipped ovals and the aroma from her tobacco was like incense. 'A screen such as I'm thinking of would require up to twenty coats of perfect lacquer. Each coat can take up to three days to dry and in between there's all that rubbing down.'

She paused for a shallow puff from her cigarette. 'As I know only too well, from start to completion, the smallest piece of lacquer-work can take nine months. At any stage something can go wrong which means scrapping the whole project. And I've still to come up with the design,' she finished with a roll of her eyes and a dramatic wail.

'So. Give yourself time, the design will come, the technicalities will fall into place and you'll create your screen.' Jacques squinted towards the nibbling river. 'Already I can see it in my mind's eye and I promise you it's a work of art.'

Bel too looked up along the quay. The lavender-seller was long out of sight and the boy tending the horses had gone too.

Eileen brought her hands together and gave a little clap. A full-blown smile transformed her normally solemn expression to a delightful mischievousness. 'All right. It has to be destiny. You've persuaded me, Jacques. I'll do the screen. And I'll call it *Le Destin*.'

'*Le Destin*. That sounds a good name. It's strong. And it'll look well written, too,' Colette concurred. 'Name is so important.'

Right then Bel decided to change the spelling of her name to Belle. That, she thought, would look better when written than Bel. But not until she returned to New York.

Jacques smiled at Eileen and said softly, 'And after *Le Destin*, all Paris and beyond will flock to your gallery. The gallery by which you will leave your mark on the world.'

'What gallery, Jacques? You tease me about my dream.'

Chapter 1

Only half past three and already the shallow November light is thinning and the day faltering.

The woman senses the change in her bones and the chill of premature dusk creeps into her soul. She is tall, grey-haired, grimly thin in both face and body, all knuckle-distorted fingers and thick glasses with large lenses framed in heavy tortoise-shell.

The older she grows, the more she is affected by what she calls her twilight mood. Involuntarily she shivers, draws the slate-coloured chenille wrap more closely around her shoulders and nestles into its warmth.

But only briefly. She refuses to give in to decrepitude.

Easing out of the leather and chrome armchair, she settles the soles of her black-laced shoes firmly and carefully on the wooden floor, before pulling herself upright while feeling for the walking stick propped, as always, to her right hand side. Grasping the handle firmly and ensuring the steady suction of rubber ferrule on board, she makes her slow way towards the window.

It seems to her that swirls and wisps of fog, God's smoky breath as they called fog as children, impede her view, though these days she cannot be certain. She sighs. Existence in a monochromatic blur.

Still, she supposes, she should be grateful that time has not impaired her memory nor her ability to create. Her work is what she will be remembered by. Already she has begun the process of ensuring that nothing remains of her private life, that all personal records, photographs and papers will be destroyed.

Moving sideways to her drawing table, she shuffles through a stack of blueprints and sketches. She pulls one to the top. Head bent low, large magnifying glass in operation, her face lights up as she relives the design and creation of *Le Destin*.

Behind her the door opens quietly and Brigid enters. She is middle-aged, with an ample ripe body. Fine wrinkles fan out from her mouth and soft shadows lurk beneath her eyes.

'What're you doing here in the dark and cold, Miss? Come into the salon where it's warm.' While talking she tries to assess her employer's mood. She is still unsure as to whether or not she will tell her about that French reporter from *Le Matin*, the one who rang yesterday looking for an interview.

Eileen Gray does not turn around, does not acknowledge Brigid's presence, just keeps moving her magnifying glass up, down and across the sketch.

'What are you doing?' Brigid is standing behind her now.

'Looking at this.'

'But you can't see proper.' Brigid has the disconcerting habit of stating the obvious.

'Looking has nothing to do with seeing.'

Brigid gives an inward moan. Miss Gray has been acting contrary ever since she started on that business of clearing out and burning those old papers of hers. 'Can I help?' Brigid's voice reverts to soft and cajoling. Despite occasional lapses into minor irritability, she is innately kind and a born carer.

Usually Eileen responds to Brigid's gentleness, but not today. 'The way these drawings and sketches are, it's impossible to find anything. I'd like you to put them in order. Correctly catalogued. In job and date sequence. And as soon as possible. Please.'

'I'll do my best,' Brigid assures, stifling another moan and tucking her flyaway hair behind her ears. 'Come on into the salon. Out of this barn of a place.'

From years of experience she knows no good comes out of Miss Gray rooting around among those old drawings of hers, getting upset and coming up with all sorts of daft ideas. Job and date sequence, indeed. Drat. Brigid is not even sure what that means.

'I like it here. It reminds me of the nursery in Brownswood. That was spacious too.'

'I know.'

'I keep forgetting.'

'You never remember that I come from the old place.'

'I do. But these days my memory is selective.'

'I wouldn't worry about it,' Brigid replies hastily, again unsure of what Miss Gray means but determined to jolly her out of going down misery road, as she calls it. 'Nothing we can do about such things. Come on. I'll read you the newspaper.'

'Which one?'

Brigid breaths in relief. It looks as though Miss Gray might forget about cataloguing. 'Yesterday's *Times* over from London.'

Brigid does not read from choice. She particularly hates having to read aloud and, to minimise her discomfort, she does so sitting at a table, with the paper spread out in front of her.

As her stubby index finger laboriously picks out word after word and phrase after phrase, her voice, monotonously relaying the information, ignores both the natural cadence of the writing and any form of punctuation. Her concentration is so great and the effort of getting the words off the paper and into Miss Gray's head, as she thinks of the process, is so arduous that she has virtually no comprehension of the meaning of what she is so painstakingly stringing together.

Equally, Eileen, from her youth a keen follower of both national and international news and current affairs, finds it difficult to draw intent out of Brigid's torturously droning reportage.

In this matter of newspaper reading, both feel they do the other the favour.

Brigid is half way into a piece about French couturier Jacques Doucet's estate being up for auction when she realises what she is reading and the probable implications for Miss Gray. Great friends she and Monsieur Doucet were. For weeks after learning of his death last year, she stumbled around pale-faced, not sleeping and refusing to eat.

Brigid stops mid-word, which happens to be her excruciating pronunciation of *Destin.* A shiver of premonition, a footstep over her grave, as her mother, Lord rest her, would have said. *Destin*? Wasn't that the drawing Miss Gray was looking at?

'Continue.' Eileen's voice is at its most imperious.

Brigid realises that either her lady's mind has been wandering or else she has not absorbed the meaning of the story, probably a little of both and, sure, isn't that as well, she decides, giving her a tender look.

She squints at the clock on the mantelpiece. 'Look at

the time. Here, let me make you tea. You've missed your afternoon cup.'

To Brigid's relief, Eileen nods. She likes the symbolism of afternoon tea and the memories it brings back, even if these days it is only a cup.

No way, Brigid decides on her way to the big warm comfortable kitchen which she has made her domain, will she now say anything to Miss Gray about that reporter. From her limited knowledge of people from newspapers, she suspects he will want to talk about this auction. There is no point in upsetting Miss Gray. What happens to Monsieur Doucet's belongings is of no concern to her. What she does not know will not trouble her.

Waiting for the tea, Eileen allows her mind to drift. Her driftings are pleasant, as she remembers her first impressions of Paris. Its modernity, brightness and vitality. Such a contrast to the old-fashioned staidness of fog-filled London.

It was the summer of 1900. The year of L'Exposition Universelle. A world record breaker by being the largest exhibition of its kind ever mounted. Showplace for the best of international, commercial, historical and artistic exhibits.

The city, decked out in its best raiment, acted host with pride and in style.

While fascinated by all the various innovations and teeming ideas – its most celebrated pavilion, and Eileen's favourite, was the Palace of Electricity whose facade opened in a fan illuminated by 5,700 light bulbs – the memories Eileen carried with her on her reluctant return to London were lingering sensory impressionist smudges of sight, sound, smell, taste and touch.

High graceful buildings with curved balconies smothered in trailing mauve wisteria and tumbling scarlet geraniums.

Dream-like misty street lamps of black wrought iron.

Clip-clop. The comforting sound and swaying movement of the three-horse omnibuses, with their pervasive smell of horse dung.

Boulevards lined with fragrant French limes, horse chestnuts in pink blossom and slim and stately poplar trees.

The titillating taste bud delights of quenelles and quiches, coquilles and croissants. Beaujolais and Beaune. Chablis and Champagne.

The bim, bom, boom of the cathedral bells of Notre Dame, resonating the name of your loved one, so it was said.

And as for style. The classically elegant appeal of the women's pastel hems in luxurious foulard sweeping the pavements, their flat hats, piled high with tulle, feathers and flowers, balanced as though by magic on upswept hairstyles. They were escorted by cane-swirling men with twirled moustaches, dashingly flamboyant in gaily striped flannel jackets, narrow ties, wing collars and straw boaters.

As though it were only yesterday, she can not only picture, but feel the way she was then.

Liberation saturating her bones.

Young, strong-willed, vibrant and full of life.

Emancipated enough to insist on returning to live on her own in Paris.

Believing that memories cling to possessions, she came with the minimum of personal memorabilia, determined to leave her past behind and to make a new life.

Here in this, the city of love, on the River Seine, this

magical place of combusting creativity, designers and theatres, restaurants and parks, she knew she would be able to identify her artistic strengths and to forge her career, to live her life as she chose and to escape the stifling attention, restraints and demands of both English society and her family.

On one of those daffodil days, more than seven decades ago, with nothing more in mind than wandering and soaking up atmosphere, outside the gold-tipped railings of the Louvre, she crossed the Seine. On the Pont Neuf, she paused to watch the passage of the grey-green water which in the spring sunlight looked as though it were sprinkled with a multitude of diamonds.

Reaching the Left Bank, she walked a few hundred yards along the Quai Malaquais, bustling with the stalls of second-hand booksellers. Drawn by nothing more than the curiosity of a new place, she turned into the Saint-Germain-des-Prés district by rue Bonaparte.

The street, nestling comfortably in the shadow of its fifteenth-century church, was flanked by discreet shop-fronts selling exquisite jewellery and rare antiques, interspersed with elegantly proportioned eighteenth-century hôtels, each tucked behind its own high stone wall and equally high wooden gate.

The gateway of number 21 was not only open, but a large red-and-white notice proclaimed the second floor apartment available for rent.

Though not consciously looking, instantly she knew she had found her Parisian base and her new home. Reached by a wide sweeping staircase, the apartment was comprised of six large high-ceilinged rooms, three with floor-length windows looking out onto a cobblestoned inner courtyard.

Standing by one of the urns, full of trailing variegated ivy, she gave several whoops of joy and even executed a couple of steps of a jig. Such behaviour was alien to her and, she suspected, out of place in this sedate neighbourhood, though she presumed nobody watched from behind the shuttered windows.

A few weeks later, she and her belongings were installed, and she set about putting her imprint on her new home which she was entranced to learn was the old *hôtel particulier* of the Marquis de Cyr.

Her quiet charm resulted in the owner agreeing to the removal of a pair of gilded mirrors, as well as the balcony in front of a glassed-in gallery. But all her pleas for getting rid of the 'pâtisseries', the French nickname for the ceiling plaster mouldings, fell on deaf ears.

Seven decades later they are still in place though, courtesy of Mama who came up with the money without as much as a murmur of dissent, she was able to buy the property after three years. She smiles in amused reminiscence. The impatient passion of youth. But in those days there was more to her life than the pursuit of tasteless pâtisseries.

She had an appetite whetted and primed for adventure; inner creativity champing for release; artistic dreams fighting for expression and a self-confessed addiction for motoring, flying and any other innovation which caught her fancy.

She considered it a real coup to be one of the first women in Paris to acquire a driving licence, and that evening she threw a celebratory supper. A few months later she bought a Chenard Walker, against whose gleaming black paint work she broke open a magnum of champagne. During the 1914–18 war, she nominated her car for ambulance service with the proviso that she would drive, and her claim to be the fastest ambulance in town remained undisputed.

As for all forms of flying, she was hooked from the beginning. Her 'baptême de l'air', as the French call it, was in a balloon with Charles Rolls. Well she remembers the mystical silence of gliding out from the English flats of Romney Marsh. After her inaugural aeroplane flight near Marseilles she took lessons, became an accomplished pilot, clocked up hundreds of air miles and was one of the first passengers to fly from Acapulco to Mexico City.

What wonders she has seen. What accomplishments she has achieved. What transformations she has experienced. And yet of recent days there is an unfinished ache within her.

'Life can be lonely. Without work or people or anything much happening,' she remarks on Brigid's return with the tea and two chocolate fingers. Eileen loves chocolate. The tea is cupped, milked, sugared and stirred. With a wave of her arm, she gestures that it be placed on the cork-topped table in front of her.

With the deterioration of her sight, many of the finer and less fine points of living, including eating and drinking, even an event as simple as afternoon tea, have had to be modified. Brigid has long since dispensed with the finesse of trolleys, cloth-covered trays, teapots, milk jugs, sugar bowls, spoons and strainers, though it is unlikely she will ever to stoop to handing her lady a mug.

Still, the process of watching her drink is fraught with tension. First there is the agonising negotiation of cup to lips, the refined sips, then her frustrated sucking in of breath as clatteringly she seeks to return cup to its indentation on the saucer. Afterwards she eats the biscuits calmly in slow, nibbling bites.

'I'm always here. You know that.' Brigid has taken up her stance between the chair and the door. No way will she tempt fate and Miss Gray by going near the table with its invitingly spread-out newspaper.

'I know.'

As happens occasionally, Brigid takes the initiative, chides her employer as though she is a recalcitrant child. 'What's up with you? What has you bothering about those old drawings?'

Having no comprehension of the intricacies and heartache of creative talent, she has never been in awe of either Miss Gray's reputation or of the work she carries out.

'Sometimes, like now and for the past while, I feel so alone.' Dusk has turned to night, the only light in the room comes from the floor lamp pooling over the newspaper. Not that Eileen is overly aware of the darkness.

'You're not alone. You've me.'

'I know. But I've an urge to talk to a kindred spirit about my work.'

Eileen craves a brief return – she is sure she would be happy with just the one – to the heady excitement of discussing with like-minded people the creative fulfilment of design, the thrill of sourcing obscure materials, working with sub-contractors, the pitfalls of outside manufacturing, the grateful clients and the difficult clients, the nerve-racking mounting of exhibitions and, of course, selling – though the latter always came low on her list of priorities – and what degenerated into the final heart-stopping suspense of waiting to read in magazines and newspapers the opinions of critics and reviewers.

'You can always talk to me. You did when there was nobody else.'

Eileen remembers. And only too well. Those dark days and nights. Black times. Without Brigid's constant and innocent presence pulling her back from the abyss of despair, she is certain she would have descended into madness or death. While it is years since the subject has been mentioned between them, until her dying day, she knows, she will not forget and, as always, she is uncomfortable with the ignominy and pain of remembrance.

'Remember, Brigid, a long time ago, we agreed that matter was closed.'

'That was decided by you.' As occasionally occurs within their relationship, servant assumes the role of master, becomes the dominant force. 'And when I'd served my purpose.'

For Brigid, those were uneasy times. Even thinking about them brings her out in a cold sweat.

In this gloaming light she cannot see her employer's face.

Perhaps it is as well.

If the room were better lit, probably, Brigid would not have dared speak out. 'We shouldn't have cut ourselves off from everyone. Living like hermits. Loneliness can turn a person's head. A right *amadán* I was, to stay.'

Eileen's answer is derisory but it is a protective rather than a cruel mechanism, 'You cannot understand either loneliness nor the workings of the creative mind. And anyway where would you go? Who'd have you?'

Brigid smiles a plump-cheeked mysterious smile which she knows Miss Gray cannot see. She has a secret of her own.

Her five-year-old secret is in the portly shape of a suitor. Pierre is a baker and a widower, the proprietor of a bright warm bakeshop around the corner in rue Visconti, so cosy that it reminds her of the old kitchen in Brownswood Manor. Here, the aroma of sweet smoky ham vies with creamy cheeses with thick yellow and red wax skins, and the warm baking smell of rolls, plaits, baguettes and croissants.

Pierre murmurs about l'amour, which she knows is the French for love. In turn, his attention has given her confidence and a new sort of courage. She feels protected by his masculine bulkiness – so much more natural than Miss Gray's bony female slenderness – and flattered by his kisses, and whispered words of tenderness. He is the only man who has ever held, much less kissed, her.

Sometimes she wonders about moving in with him, not that he has ever mentioned it. As man and wife, of course. No way would she live in sin; she shakes her head at the thought. But she is well into her fifties and has spent more than forty years in Miss Gray's employ. She supposes she would be mad to even contemplate leaving here. But if Pierre were to bring up the subject, she would like to be prepared.

As always, Brigid's fleeting dream of a life with Pierre passes. It comes and goes with titillating regularity. For now, Brigid, the carer, returns. 'Why not invite some of your friends around?'

'Because they're all either dead or doting. There's nobody left. That's what happens when you live too long.'

Chapter 2

Belle comes awake slowly, gives a languid cat-stretch, opens first one eye, then the other. Gradually and joyously she absorbs her surroundings. She is in New York, in her apartment, with Jack just a few steps down the corridor.

She allows herself some moments of sensuous luxuriating in the soft peach of the room, savouring the warmth and comfort of her bed, enjoying the serene sounds of silence and the way the flimsy drapes on the windows suffuse the November light with radiance.

A shiver of delicious anticipation runs through her at the thought of the next few days.

Time to get up.

Preparing to face the day, any day, is not a simple matter for Belle Fagan. Over the years a complex set of morning ablutions has overtaken her. As well as showering and moisturising, there is deep breathing, bending and stretching, followed by the application of meticulous make-up and choosing clothes appropriate to her social commitments or charity work of the day. Belle keeps determinedly busy.

Her bandbox image which she wears like a mask has been cultivated and modified over the years. It owes little to nature, much to the skill of various beauticians, but most of all to her own disciplined dedication in her eternal quest for the holy grail of groomed perfection.

Tall and dark with an appealing manner, Jack Devine is that potent mixture of dreamer and analyser, with the ability to creatively link seemingly unrelated thoughts.

He lives and works in an elegant apartment of flying buttresses a few blocks from Central Park. It is his grandmother's apartment. With the exception of her bedroom and various locked desks and cabinets of family papers, he has the place to himself. Except when she makes one of her visits.

Thinking of which he hears the tip tap of her heels along the parquet of the hallway, making for him in his great-grandfather Dan's den. She had arrived and retired by the time he got back from last night's reception to mark the Kandinsky exhibition in the Guggenheim Museum.

'Morning, darling. 'Fraid I've overslept horribly.'

He rises from the cranberry-coloured sofa which he is sharing with his mandatory morning stack of home and international newspapers. Grandmother and grandson embrace warmly, a genuine body to body hug. They love each other deeply and unequivocally. He drops a kiss on the top of her head.

'Well, you're certainly worth waiting for.' The compliment is sincere. At nearly seventy, Belle is a remarkably pretty woman. Blonde, slender and immaculately groomed. The passage of her time has been kind.

'I hope you didn't wait breakfast,' she murmurs into the pale blue cashmere of his sweater. As always when seeing him, her heart turns over at his dear familiarity.

'Don't worry Gran, I ate ages ago.'

'You'd cereal? Something solid?'

'Yes,' he lies. As usual, he had breakfasted on black coffee and his thoughts. 'The rest will do you good.'

'New York's not a place for resting,' says Belle virtuously. She constantly disputes suggestions about taking life easy. And as for age, particularly her own, she never discusses it. 'There's something special about here. A particular energy. Don't you think?'

'Oh, I don't know. The trouble with cities as big and as modern as New York is that there's no relationship between people.'

'But, darling, there is. Of course, there is.' Belle, slender wrists jangling bracelets, stands uncertainly but stylishly in this season's grainy grey wool cardigan, matching knee-length knitted skirt and soft pink blouse with a floppy pussy-cat bow.

These 'philosophical expoundings', as she calls them, that Jack goes on with upset her. Over the years she has become an expert at changing subjects and at avoiding unpleasantness. Her eyes catch a diverting flutter of movement from outside the window. 'I didn't know pigeons could fly so high. Ten stories up sure is high, isn't it?'

'Yes, Gran. I suppose at this height they find an artificial centrality.' Jack knows what he has said is gibberish to her, though to him it makes a daft sort of sense.

'I suppose,' she agrees uncertainly. 'Still, you'd think they'd stay nearer the ground.'

'Who?'

'The pigeons.'

'I guess they know you're up here. And they came to see you.' The fans of laughter wrinkling at the outer corner of Jack's eyes work overtime.

Belle smiles too, relieved the subject has been successfully deflected. 'Oh. Jack. You haven't changed and I hope you never will. From the time you were a small child, always one for the little jokes.' She pauses for a moment before asking with calculated indifference, 'Are you busy today?'

Jack knows at what she is hinting. When seeking his company she is as transparent as a moonstruck teenager, pride and love spinning behind her eyes. Still, time spent with her is small repayment for all she has done for him; she will only be in town until the end of the week and she is fun to be with – witty, humorous and quite inexhaustible.

'Right now I want to go through the newspapers. Then, I've a few administrative things to deal with and some phone calls to make. And after that, if you're free, I thought we'd lunch. We've a booking in The Four Seasons. And, as you know, tonight we're off to *Gigi*.'

Belle's eyes light up and she gives a skimpy laugh under which she tries to hide large feelings. Her favourite restaurant and a Parisian musical. All in the one day. It is almost too much. But even more important is spending time with Jack. Quality time, as she believes it is now called.

'Free. Sure I'm free, Jack. Don't you know I only come to New York to be with you.'

That he knows. But he keeps up the pretence and she loves him for it that she is still part of a swinging social circle. 'And to shop and to dine and do the theatres and to meet up with all your old boyfriends.'

She laughs, raises a hand as though to forestall his further listing of her imaginary misdemeanours and indiscretions.

He continues, 'And to check on your apartment and, of course, to make sure I'm not entertaining hordes of unsuitable women and holding wild coke parties.'

'No, but some day, I'm hoping to find Elvira Elliott back and permanently in residence.' Now why had she said that?

The look he gives her is bleak. 'Regretfully, Gran, that's unlikely. We blew it. I blew it.'

The blueness of Jack's eyes that glow, sadden, dance and animate his every expression has always undone Belle's resolutions about not giving in to his every whim and being firmer with him. She consoles herself by remembering the positive benefits of knowing you are cared for and loved, as recently listed in *Cosmopolitan*. Belle loves magazines, their features on fashion and beauty tips, and she assiduously follows the advice of various agony aunts.

'What you get up to here is your business,' she says without meaning it, but trying to recoup their earlier banter. Since his birth, his life has been her life, his happiness her happiness and his business her business. 'I'm pleased for you to have the use of the apartment. Places need to be lived in.'

Jack wishes his grandmother would practice what she preaches. After all he will be twenty-eight on his next birthday but from the way she goes on, anyone would think he was the child and she his mother.

Not that his mother, Patsy, as she insists on being called, was ever maternal. She was too tied up with her charity works and fund-raisings to be interested in either him or his sisters.

Before she returns home, his grandmother, he knows, will root through his underwear drawers, check on his socks and shirts, explore the contents of his icebox and nose around among the bottles in his cocktail cabinet.

'I'll make coffee.'

'Don't forget your cereal,' he jokes. 'This morning's special is hamster-pellets of All Bran.'

'Oh, Jack. You're dreadful. Will you have a coffee?'

'No, I'll get on with things here. The dining room's all yours.' Jack hopes, but without too much optimism, that she will take his hint, have breakfast in there and leave him undisturbed to get on with the morning's business.

In the small yellow and white kitchen, Belle juices an orange which she sips slowly while waiting for the coffee to perk. Through the window, the atmosphere is jewel-bright and the sky so blue that she can almost feel the tang of it on her tongue. Today is a day for savouring.

She dithers. Will she? Won't she? Yes, she will. Why shouldn't she join Jack? But she will take her coffee in silence.

Still decorated in the heavy maroons, rich mahogany and tasselled and fringed curtains of the twenties, for Belle the den holds her father's presence like a talisman.

In quiet and rare moments, Jack is certain that he too has sensed old Dan McDonagh's rather comforting snort of disapproval at his lifestyle and even the occasional waft of his Havana cigar.

'It's beautiful outside,' Belle remarks, depositing the immaculately appointed tray on a low Regency tea-table in front of Jack.

She pours two coffees, sugars Jack's with a flat spoonful, stirs. As she passes over his cup, her eyes rest on a title that she knows better than herself. 'I don't believe it. That newspaper?'

Jack grins. 'So now you've discovered my guilty secret. Before I take you to lunch, you'll have to cross your heart and hope to die that you'll never reveal what you've just seen.'

Belle ignores his banter. 'But why? After all you said and how hard you fought to extricate yourself?'

How can he even begin to explain the hurt of his father's rejection because of his refusal to go into the family business.

'Curiosity. Wondering how my heritage is progressing. Isn't there an old Irish saying about blood being thicker than water?'

Belle tucks into the far corner of the sofa with her coffee. She thought Jack had finished with all that family angst and was getting on with his life, happy with his antique business.

She had made it financially possible for him to be free, to do as he wished, and her faith in him has paid dividends. From personal experience, she knows there are occasions when a line has to be drawn under the past. She also knows that re-visiting above that line can be painful and non-productive.

'Sometimes, Jack, we must stick to our past decisions so that we can live in the present and plan for the future.' Even to herself she sounds sanctimonious.

Jack guffaws. 'Good God, you sound just like those preacher fellows on television.'

'I don't know what you're talking about,' she says with as much dignity as she can muster. She is far from flattered at his comparison.

He winks before retreating behind the bulk of *The New York Times*.

'Any news?' she asks after a while of sipping and over-active worrying about Jack and his future.

'No, of course not,' he teases. 'Don't you know all papers are just full of nothing words?'

'Oh, Jack.'

'Only joking. They're full of Nixon. What else? These days he is the only news.'

'I never thought he'd get in for a second term. And so well too.'

The McDonagh family had taken a keen interest in politics since the mid-nineteen hundreds when Belle's grandfather, Tim Pat, newly arrived from Ireland in the wake of the Famine, became one of the leading activists in promoting coast to coast railroads. Early on he learned that the successful playing of the American political game was the key to achieving his objectives and the path to riches.

The Fagans and Devines, also refugees from the Famine, who married into the McDonaghs, became equally wealth-conscious and equally astute power-game players. The three families evolved into a class of Irish Mafia which looked out for and after its own.

'You're not the only one who didn't think Nixon'd get in,' Jack tells Belle. 'It's a real landslide victory. He's still on about promising to achieve peace in Vietnam with honour not surrender.'

'I'm sure he's doing his best,' Belle soothes. Whatever her personal opinion, she is a firm believer in the dictum that he who is in power should be obeyed.

'There're hints that the damage done by the American bombing to the North Vietnam economy will force Hanoi to agree to a cease-fire.' Jack glances down at the paper. 'It says here that Henry Kissinger is in Paris working on it.'

'I never trusted him. All that corrugated hair.'

Jack laughs. As he turns the page to the European news section, Belle's eye is drawn to a name. A name she never expected to see featured in *The New York Times*. The shock to her system is enormous.

'What's this here about . . . ?' Unable to say the words or to absorb the sense of the print, she points.

Jack follows her finger, 'Yves Saint Laurent. Don't tell me he's another of your admirers?'

Jack folds the section of the paper to more manageable size and scans the small news item. 'I don't believe it. Saint Laurent has paid $36,000 for a lacquered screen. It says here it's a record price for a modern piece of furniture. There must be a lot of money in women's fashion. $36,000. Whew.'

'No, not him. It's . . .' Belle cannot bring herself to say the name.

Jack continues reading, then announces, 'It's *Le Destin* by Eileen Gray. I've only recently come across her work. It's quite amazing . . .' he trails off, aware of Belle's stillness and ragged breathing. 'What is it, Gran?'

'That piece. What else does it say?'

'That's it. Nothing more. Basically it's just about this Doucet's estate being auctioned off.'

'Good God. Is he dead?'

'Well and truly. According to this, he died last year.'

He senses rather than feels her deflate. Again he asks, 'What is it, Gran?'

She stands up. 'Nothing, really. Jacques's death is a bit of a shock. When I was in Paris, he made several outfits for me.' Upright, she feels more in control.

'You sure you're okay?' Jack thinks her response to the death of a dress designer, even a French one, a bit extreme.

She nods, one ragged breath follows the other, and in

between floats an image of a whiskered face with cerulean eyes. Willpower and the discipline of years steadies her breathing, though her body feels as if it were made of zinging harp strings, her insides shake as with ague and her mind flashes with brief abstracts of memory.

Jigsaw-style micro-second images from more than fifty years ago form and re-form, weave in and out through the maroon walls in front of her, dart backwards and forwards around the shelves of books and glass-cased models of locomotives, slide up and down between the gilded picture frames.

Jack is towering over her. 'What is it?' he repeats, worried by the greyness of her face.

'Nothing. Don't fuss, darling. Just a touch of dizziness.'

'Come on. Sit down.'

She gives a self-deprecating smile, checks that the bow of her blouse is correctly tied. For the first time, he notices that she looks her age and inappropriately girlish with pearlised pink lips and baby-blue eye-shadow.

How could she ever explain to Jack?

Despite the Four Season's impressive walnut-panelled surroundings, immaculate place settings, elaborate floral arrangements and the perfection of the crab cakes with their dressing of lobster sauce, Belle has little appetite, but she makes an effort for Jack's sake.

She feels she owes him an explanation for what she sees as her lapse of self control. 'To tell the truth, darling, Jacques Doucet's death is quite a shock. I've always thought of him as invincible.'

'Nobody's invincible,' Jack says from the vantage of youth

and the profound experience of having witnessed the death of his paternal grandmother. 'We all have to die.'

'He must have lived to a fine age. He was quite the mature man about town when I was in Paris.'

'You actually knew him?' Jack is relieved to see a touch of colour return to Belle's cheeks and the re-emergence of her chatty self. He has often thought that an element of sadness lurks beneath her smooth-browed concern for him and the family, and her light-hearted chatter about fashion and socialising. 'I thought you only wore his clothes?'

His grandmother has always been reticent about her time in Europe.

'I knew him well. I was one of his best customers. His bias dresses were all the rage when I was in Paris.'

'I can imagine you. Dressed in the latest fashion. Attending all the in-places. Flapper fun. I wish I'd been born then.'

'Nonsense. You'd have hated it. You're a thoroughly modern American.' She prims her lips.

Unsure of the reason for her irritation but not wanting to cause her further upset, Jack asks, 'Did you socialise with this Jacques Doucet?'

'A little.' Her eyes fill.

'And who else?' Jack rushes in. The dining room of the Four Seasons's is not a venue for tears.

It is so long ago. Her time in Paris is encapsulated into a blur of socialising, shopping and sightseeing. People are not stored in her memory bank.

Though triggered by Jack's question, from the mists of the past, ghosts of insubstantial personalities emerge. Belle was reared to be impressed by important people.

'Sergey Diaghilev, the Russian ballet impresario. Claude

Monet, you know, the painter, and that English writer, Somerset Maugham. As well as various designers, dancers and actors.' As far as she can remember those were the people being talked about, some of whom she met in passing; others she spent time with at openings, receptions or dinners. 'I guess, what your father would call creative newsworthies. Oh, and, of course, Colette, who wrote *Gigi*. She was everywhere.'

This remembering has made Belle uncomfortable. 'I'm so looking forward to the show tonight.'

'Me too.' Jack smiles his heartbreaking smile.

'You know the story of *Gigi* is based on Yola Letelier, the wife of a French newspaper proprietor.'

'No, I didn't.'

'Yes, she and Queen Elizabeth – the queen mother – were great friends.'

Jack looks sceptical.

'Yola had an affair with Lord Louis Mountbatten that went on for years.'

Jack looks even more sceptical. 'I've never even heard of him.'

Unfazed by Jacques's lack of social nous, Belle continues. 'The Mountbattens always stayed with them when they were in Paris. Mistresses and lovers were an accepted part of life for the aristocracy.'

Jack laughs, 'Belle McDonagh and gang. You must have been in your element.'

Belle laughs too, as much in relief that she has succeeded in changing the subject from her time in Paris, as at her grandson's blithe belief in her popularity. But Jack is not that easily diverted.

He asks the question that has been burning him. 'It said in

the paper that Doucet collected the works of Eileen Gray. No doubt you came across her too?'

A few months ago at an executor's sale, Jack had picked up a chrome-and-black leather chair. Later he learned it was called the *Transat*, catalogued as a modern classic and designed by Eileen Gray.

His enquiries in American fine arts circles about her and her works fell on barren ground. From his contacts in Europe, he received sketchy impressions of an elusive has-been, long out of favour and fashion.

Intrigued by the lack of available information and with his appetite thoroughly whetted, Jack put in a request to the research librarian who served his father's stable of titles. The following week, she summoned him and he spent a fruitful and fascinating morning going through the English language press clippings on Eileen Gray. Later, he would have the foreign features translated.

The first write-up on her was in the English edition of *Vogue* magazine, dated August 1917; dozens more followed in such diverse publications as London's *Daily Mail* and *Good Furniture Magazine*, the *Chicago Tribune* and the *New York Herald.*

The early features and profiles lauded her work – lacquer, furniture and interior design – and eulogised her and her aristocratic background and talent. Then overnight, it seemed, press attitude changed. Coverage became scanty and critical. From the index it was obvious that interest in Gray's works eased off from the 1930s onwards.

But as far as Jack was concerned, the real find of the morning was the two profile publicity photographs. They showed Eileen Gray with shingled hair, a style since adolescence that he has found singularly erotic. In one she is serious, looking into the far distance. He particularly liked the other in which she is smiling, a secret smile, head tilted, elegant hands held to her face, the pale cuffs and collar of her shirt diffusing light on her features.

Sitting at the rickety desk, within a green pool of light in the small office tucked away to the back of the building, Jack fell in love, as much with Eileen Gray as with her work, which he sensed was ripe for revival. In the trade Jack was regarded as having a good, if young, nose.

During lunch, he has updated his thinking.

Saint Laurent's record-breaking purchase of *Le Destin* has received international newspaper coverage. What makes print today will be televised and on radio tomorrow. Within a few weeks Eileen Gray and her work will be the subject of documentaries, magazine features, architectural and interior design analysis and erudite commentary.

The discovery that she is still alive is the biggest bonus of all; the *New York Times* reportage of her as a recluse in Paris he refuses to regard as a problem.

Belle pushes her unfinished plate to the side. 'Eileen Gray. Now that name rings a bell.'

'So it should. I reckon she'd have been well known when you were in Paris. Think, Gran. What can you remember about her?'

'She'd a title.'

Trust Gran.

'And . . .'

'She was odd. Irish, I think.'

'Anything else? What about her work? Come on, you must remember something.'

Belle stares into the distance. Stalling for time. Uneasy with crowding memories. She takes a sip of wine, she needs its fortification. Reluctantly, she admits, 'I believe she did some pieces for Jacques.'

The plan that Jack has been mulling over for the past few hours has ripened. 'I'm going to Paris. To meet this Eileen Gray and to hear her story.'

'Jack. Don't.'

'Why not?'

'Leave well alone. Your life is here.' Even as she speaks, she suspects her words are falling on deaf ears.

She is right. Jack is not listening, he is in dreamer mode. 'I guess Dad'd change his tune if I got him an exclusive. 'The Eileen Gray Story.' The woman behind the legend. What do you think, isn't that a good title?'

Belle is transported back to her earlier awful feeling. That feeling as though her body is made of harp strings, but now Jack is the one trilling his fingers across them from side to side, causing them to reverberate with memories, zinging memories echoing and re-echoing. She feels weak and powerless. 'You realise he'd take that as a sign of your capitulation.'

Jack knows his father still clings to the hope that he will 'come to his senses', and continue the tradition of the three previous generations of Devines whose ambition for power and hunger for wealth have resulted in today's successful chain of newspapers.

He looks fondly at his grandmother, 'You know, I'll never make a newspaper man.'

'I know that. But I wouldn't under-estimate your father.'

After lunch, Jack puts Belle in a cab to take her back to

the apartment and disappears on some mysterious errand of his own.

Cities have special and different smells for Belle. London reeked of damp and rotting wood. Paris was scented delicately with garlic and Gauloise. New York is of transformers and electric trains.

She has not been out of the States since her European tour. Bless her husband Mick, but he was more into Gaelic games than travel, and if he were to go anywhere, he used to say with childlike fervour, it would be back to Ireland. Back to Ireland! And not one of the family returned since their ignominious poverty-stricken exit some hundred and twenty years previously.

He plotted the journey often enough though, and during those bursts of enthusiasm he spent hours poured over maps and airline and liner schedules. He planned his visit with such excitement that she used to wonder could he face the reality of the poverty and emigration being reported from Ireland during the 1950s, and especially from his home place of Connemara.

When cancer intervened, she was devastated, and when he died her only solace was that he had been spared the shattering of his dreams. He is dead fifteen years and not a day goes by that she does not miss him and grieve for him.

Her cab driver, a skinny Puerto Rican with a greasy cap, hurtles through the streets and honking traffic at breakneck speed while ranting about America's defeat in the United Nations on 'the two Chinas'.

Shoulders shrugging, hands gesticulating inches from the wheel, swirling around in determined eye contact, he is particularly incensed at their delegate George Bush's comment that the decision was 'a moment of infamy', and demands of her, 'Now whadda ya think of that?'

Belle makes a series of non-committal murmurs; she has never before come across a cabbie interested in international current affairs. She is grateful when they draw up outside her apartment block.

The elevator glides silkily upwards and, after divesting herself of her grey fox jacket, touching up her lipstick and tidying her hair, she makes for the den and curls into her father's chair.

This is her consolation zone, her comfort blanket, the place where Dan McDonagh held out his arms and calmed her on her hysterical return from Paris; where without a word of recrimination, two months later he sat her on his lap, as though she were still a child, and urged her to accept Mick Fagan's proposal of marriage.

Mick, a straight-talking, ruddy-cheeked, self-made man of Irish background, was in construction. He was a business acquaintance of her father's, fifteen years her senior and enormously wealthy. 'It'd be for the best, lass,' Dan said. 'Best for all of us. As time will tell.'

Has time told? Or hasn't it? She does not know. But she does know that she never had an opportunity to know what might have been.

Jack strides into the den, a determined air about him, triumphantly waving a copy of *Le Matin.*

'Look, Gran, this is the screen that Yves Saint Laurent bought. *Le Destin.*'

The reproduction is newspaper grainy and almost indistinguishable.

'Now, if you'll excuse me, I've to ring Paris.' Jack looks at his watch. 'With the time difference, I don't want to leave it too late.' Kindly, he suggests, 'Why don't you take a little nap?'

As Belle opens her mouth to protest – she would much prefer to be party to what is going on – Jack adds firmly, 'You'll enjoy tonight all the better.'

She feels she is has no choice but to retire to her room where unseeingly she flicks through the latest edition of *Vogue*.

Chapter 3

'A man rang while you were resting,' Brigid informs Eileen.

'Who was it?'

'A Mr Devine . . . I think.' Catching sight of the raised eyebrows, she hastily adds, 'It's all written down.' Miss Gray has always been dead fussy about messages.

'Devine? From where?'

'He didn't say. But he sounded American.'

'Well, what did he want?'

'To call on you.'

'What did you tell him?'

'What I always say. That you don't receive visitors.'

'You did right. Though it's flattering, people wanting to visit. What's his particular interest?'

'What d'you mean?'

'Why did he want to see me?' Eileen enunciates slowly.

'He said something about modern antiques.'

Unable to bear the tension any longer, Belle gives up on *Vogue*. She slips into a soft pink Foxford robe, adjusts the shade of her lipstick to match, runs a comb through her hair and touches her signature Chanel perfume to wrists and throat.

Correctly groomed, the world is a more manageable place.

Not a sound is to be heard from the den. She taps lightly and walks in. Jack is seated behind the desk, head in hands. He looks up and bursts out, 'She doesn't take phone calls. She won't see me. Imagine, Eileen Gray doesn't have any visitors.'

'Well, you did say she was a recluse. And there's no use behaving like a spoilt child.'

'Yes, but . . .'

'You didn't talk to her, then?' She states what seems obvious, but she has to be sure.

Jack shakes his head and Belle feels as though a load has been lifted off her shoulders, though like a stab through her middle, she feels his disappointment. Now that he will not be visiting Eileen Gray, she can afford to be generous with her memory. As she had tried to rest, long-forgotten incidents from her time in Paris had crowded back through *Vogue*'s pages of jewel-coloured velvet Christmas party-wear.

'I was there, darling. On that day.'

'You were where?' Jack is torn between distraction, politeness and annoyance.

'I was there when Jacques encouraged Eileen to create that.' Belle points to the picture of *Le Destin* still spread out on the desk in front of Jack.

'Why didn't you tell me this before?'

'I'd forgotten.'

She was there, and what an innocent she had been. So wrapped up in Jacques and the sexual nuances of that warm, almost breathless, Parisian afternoon that the talk of *Le Destin* had scarcely registered.

A few days later, when Jacques invited her for dinner, she

was ecstatic. Dinner à deux. Perhaps he was going to declare himself, to ask her to marry him. Of course he was. Should she write to her father? No, she would wait until she had something positive to report. She had planned to dispense with her virginity during this tour. So far, no luck, though the way things were progressing, she was beginning to be optimistic.

She spent long hours considering what to wear and eventually settled on one of Jacques's dresses in shimmering off-white. Her chemise and knickers were of the finest ivory silk satin and her sheerest of stockings were held up by a dainty suspender belt, trimmed with tiny pink rosebuds. As for her shoes, their toes were pointed, their heels high and their ankle strap flattering.

In anticipation, she even had her nails professionally manicured and could not resist confiding about Jacques to the manicurist who was flatteringly interested in Bel's aspirations.

Bel was not into all this liberated suffragette nonsense that was all the go when she was in London. She wanted to marry, to settle down and to raise a family. When she did, it would be for love, the kind of love portrayed by smouldering-eyed lovers in the movies coming out of Hollywood. And she was enough of her father's daughter to know the importance of money and position.

If she were to model herself on anyone, it would be on the glamorous movie star Gloria Swanson who, it was reputed, never wore the same dress twice and who had married a genuine European marquis.

Bel had been raised in a predominantly male atmosphere and the only men she knew were of her father's generation.

She had no contact with men of her own age, no experience of dating or courtship, but in matters of the heart, she was certain that Jacques, at least twenty years her senior, met all her criteria.

For his education of Bel, as he thought of this dinner, Jacques choose La Tour d'Argent both for its view of Notre Dame from its glassed-in dining room and for its menu.

After they had given their order, he leaned towards her across the table.

The time has arrived she thought, her heart beating furiously, her head full of engagement rings, glad that she and her hands were looking their best. Diamonds, she wondered, or perhaps a sapphire or a ruby, though she liked emeralds too.

'Sometimes for protection,' began Jacques, 'innocence needs to be educated.'

With difficulty Bel pulled herself back from her contemplation of precious stones. Innocence? What was Jacques talking about? Tonight she felt anything but innocent. But in true Hollywood style, she cupped her chin in her hand, ran her tongue around her lips and looked deep into his eyes to listen.

Quietly and without a trace of dramatics, as was his way, he clarified and amplified on the meaning of Colette's conversation while they had waited for Eileen to return from her flying trip.

As Bel listened, her eyes widened. She had not known Colette's affair was with the Marquise de Belbeuf.

'She's a transvestite lesbian,' Jacques said. 'Prefers to be known as Uncle Max, though most people called her Missy.'

Bel floundered to understand. Before arriving in Europe she had not come across homosexuality, nor even heard of lesbianism, and Jacques had quite a job explaining to her the meaning of transvestism.

Her education sure was taking a different direction from what her father had anticipated.

Over her initial shock at someone she knew behaving like *that*, she decided this definitely was life in the raw. Tucking into her starter of feuilleté filled with asparagus, she felt very sophisticated to be dining with the man she loved while discussing such matters.

Jacques then spelled out the story behind the scandal at the Moulin Rouge which had rocked Paris and which, in his opinion, perfectly illustrated Colette's lively, if morally reprehensible attitude.

Colette had appeared in a play titled *Madame la Marquise de Mornay*, partnered by the author, the Marquise de Belbeuf herself. When the two ladies kissed passionately at the end of a sketch, the Marquise's husband, who was in the audience, called the police and had the theatre closed down.

When Bel had absorbed both the humour and depravity of Colette's conduct, she made what she hoped was a sophisticated, woman-of-the-world remark. 'I feel sorry for Willy, despite his dishonourable behaviour over the Claudine books.'

Jacques waited until they had been served and had tasted the house speciality of pink lamb with its accompaniment of summer vegetables before saying quietly, 'I wouldn't waste my sympathy on him. Do you know the meaning of the term "green fruits"?'

Bel shook her head and delved into a green side-salad.

'Young children. Willy has sex with children. Both girls and boys.'

Bel was so horrified that she stopped eating, dropped her fork with a clatter and forgot about sophistication and precious stones. Same-sex relationships were one thing, she supposed, even if unimaginable. But sex with children . . . ? She had not known such things happened and, for a long time afterwards, she presumed they only occurred in places like Paris.

'Willy's behaviour is a well-known secret,' Jacques explained. 'And while it's not condoned, he's a powerful man, with friends in high places.' Something about tonight had him uneasy. Perhaps he should have left Bel's innocence intact. She was luminously young. But he wanted to finish what he had started. 'Invariably, the children he abuses are from deprived backgrounds whose parents lack the education and money to bring the matter to court.'

'So he gets away with it?' Bel was horrified. She had heard or read somewhere that losing one's virginity relaxed one's perspective on morality. Perhaps her reaction to Willy's behaviour would be less extreme, more mature, if she were not still a virgin. She did not think so and she sure hoped not.

Jacques shrugged. 'On occasions Willy has paid compensation to the families.' He leaned across and touched her hand. 'The world can be hard place, chérie.'

Jacques's goodness and kindness put her in mind of her father, and she thought of how comfortable he was to be with and how handsome he looked in dark broadcloth, a gleaming white shirt and diamond cufflinks. And she just loved the curl of his beard.

Perhaps it was the intimacy of their dinner, the sexual

content of his disclosures or too much wine. Perhaps it was too much hope or too many stars in the sky, but during the short walk back to her hotel, Bel was able to persuade herself that the evening had been an unqualified success and that Jacques had almost proposed. She took his protective hand under her elbow as further evidence of his affection.

Bel was like that. She could find a sliver of silver in the darkest of clouds. She spent the next days recalling to mind every word, every sentence, analysing obsessively not only the meaning of Jacques's words, but also interpreting his various facial expressions.

Until then Jacques had only ever thought of Bel in a daughterly role and he never suspected that she viewed him as anything more than paternally protective. Throughout dinner he was flattered at her luminous eyes, moist lips and, despite the subject matter, the way she hung on his every word. For the first time he noticed in Bel's eyes that look of interest that never lies.

Why, he wondered, couldn't Eileen be as softly pliable? But then she would not be Eileen.

He remembered Colette's numerous innuendoes about Bel being attracted to him and, as he turned the key in the door of his apartment, he gave a little hop, skip and a jump.

Bel may have put on layers of sophistication to protect herself from the world but should he wish, her attitude had given him permission to peel them away, one by tender one. He thought of her live, young skin against his taut, mature one the cones of her feet like soft ribbing beneath his thumbs, her cupped calves, the smoothness of each raised knee, the overmuscles of her thighs and satin whisperings beneath their luxurious stealth.

The evening Jacques and Bel dined together, Eileen had planned a liaison of her own.

Marcel Dubois was an aspiring writer, twenty-two years old, who claimed friendship with Gide, Proust and Rodin. Pale-skinned, he had curling walnut hair and candid hazel eyes. Intelligent and lucid beyond his years, sipping wine in the Café de Flore, he listed his hates as clichés, stupidity and pedantry.

Eileen was as fascinated by the looseness of his youthful joints and his cub-like pliancy as she was by his freedom from religion, mystique or morals.

'He has no wish or need to conform, he lives outside society, surrounded by the dogs and cats he picks up in the streets,' she told Colette, who continuously fell in and out of love with indiscriminate enthusiasm, and considered being in the throes of a passionate relationship as important as her morning coffee and croissant.

Colette was delighted at Eileen's interest in someone other than Damia. Despite not being privy to its intricacies, she had long filed that relationship under lost causes. Jacques was in love with Eileen and while she seemed to care deeply for him, they appeared stalemated. Colette believed that Eileen committing passionately to Marcel would 'loosen her up', as she inelegantly put it.

Marcel and Eileen tiptoed around each other for weeks. He called her a 'marginal soul' and publicly confessed to a liking for marginal souls, with auburn hair and Mona Lisa smiles.

Equally publicly, she sang praises of his voice, gestures and especially his nostrils. Privately, she fantasised about the heat radiating through his scalp and cheeks.

Eventually, according to him, she asked him to call on her, 'at eleven o'clock tonight, to talk of love'.

His amorous expectations were shattered when Eileen called down to him in the courtyard that she was indisposed with a headache. Afterwards, she said if he was really interested and cared enough, he would have persisted beyond her excuse.

'I think I'd forgotten about *Le Destin*,' Belle says to Jack. 'Until it came up this morning.'

'I find it hard to believe it was Doucet who inspired Eileen Gray to this,' says Jack sceptically, running the palm of his hand over the surface of the screen, gently touching the profile of the youth carrying the shrouded old man, and with the tip of his index finger caressingly outlining the slight third figure, seeking in the greyness of reproduction to capture the mood and texture of the screen.

'It most certainly was,' insists his grandmother. 'And I visited her workroom.'

'You what?' Jack yelps.

'You heard,' says Belle sternly, the way she used to when he was a child and not paying attention.

'Why?'

'To buy your great-grandfather a piece of lacquer.'

That afternoon Bel tagged along, purely to be in Jacques's company.

'I'm worried about Eileen working and living in this atmosphere,' Jacques confided to Colette. 'Lacquering is messy. It can't be healthy breathing in all that dust and chemicals. And as for her animals . . .'

'Eileen can't resist a stray. She always has two or three cats and dogs in the most deplorable condition. Mangy coats and festering eyes. And she loves them back to health.'

'Can't be good for her well-being. Though she's doing wonderful work. Simple. And very delicate.'

'I find her current pieces too plain. I prefer more decoration.'

'I'm going to buy something for my father,' Bel said.

'Good idea.' Jacques was enthusiastic.

Eileen professed herself delighted with Jacques's gift of chocolate, though she did not seem in the least pleased with her callers. Understandable, in the circumstances, Bel decided. She would not want to be caught out either looking grubby, shiny-faced, with her hair a bird's nest mess, wearing that awful smock and those dreadful socks.

For the occasion, Bel had dressed in white, her blonde curls bobbing around the edges of a flowerpot hat of picot straw, trimmed with black cock-feathers and blood-red roses.

Eileen had a habit of eating chocolate with endearing gluttony both when she was depressed and when she was elated. Enthusiastically she ripped open the package, and broke off two squares which she popped into her mouth before passing the bar to the others.

Bel and Colette each took a piece. Jacques waved away the bar of chocolate.

'It's not fair, the way you can eat and remain so thin. Look at Bel and myself.' Colette prodded her middle and Bel, mortified by her comment, waited for an assurance of her slenderness from either Jacques or Eileen or both. When none was forthcoming, she dropped to the floor the chocolate she was nibbling at and put herself on an immediate diet.

Colette, who had the ability to make herself instantly at home, was hunkered down in the dusty grime of the floor examining the most elaborately decorated table Bel had ever seen. 'Now this is quite wonderful,' she exclaimed.

'Yes, it's gorgeous,' Bel ran a hand gingerly over its top. No way was she going to get her dress dirty. 'What is it?' she asked Eileen.

'A table.'

Bel flushed.

'Greek-inspired and called the *Lotus*. In dark green lacquer, decorated with ivory lotus flowers – hence the name – and amber rings and silken ropes,' proudly Jacques recited. 'Right, Eileen?'

'Right, Jacques. Though I'm not all that sure about it?' Eileen addressed him, a question in her voice. 'The design looked streamlined on paper but during manufacture, it seems to have taken on a persona of its own. I think it's too fussy.'

'Decor is becoming more flamboyant,' Colette insisted. 'And you're leaning towards minimalism.'

'Minimalism appeals to me.'

'Looking at your work in progress, I take your point.' Jacques was walking around microscopically examining and fondling various pieces.

'I'm trying,' Eileen, following him, explained, 'to simplify the figurative with geometric designs and to dispense with those ghastly drapes and curves of Art Nouveau which are everywhere.'

'Oh, no,' wailed Colette. 'How could you, Eileen? It all sounds deadly boring. As boring as this.' She picked up a small lacquered tea-bowl, its simplicity of design enhanced by its black luminosity.

Jacques took the bowl off Colette, ran his index finger around its perimeter and brought it to the window where he examined it thoroughly.

'Exquisite. Eileen, this is truly exquisite. I suspect minimalism is due for revival. You're ahead of the trend and going in the right commercial direction.'

'I'm not interested in being commercial, as you well know.'

'So you say. But you will. We have to be commercial. In these competitive times, it's the measure by which our success is judged.'

'Not in Eileen's case,' said Colette, running her fingers through the amber rings of the *Lotus* table and speaking as though Eileen was not present. 'She's independently wealthy and unlike the rest of us, doesn't have to sell on to make a profit so that she can put a roof over her head and food on the table.'

'Colette, really.' Eileen was outraged.

'It's true,' said Colette defiantly.

Thinking to diffuse the developing situation, Bel said, 'I'd like to buy the *Lotus* table. As a gift for my father.'

'It's not for sale,' said Eileen firmly in her most clipped, most cut-glass accent.

'Well, one of those little bowls then?'

'They're not for sale either.'

Eileen's antipathy towards Bel quite amazed Jacques. It was so unlike her. He whispered to Bel, 'Perhaps on another occasion, chérie. Eileen, may I wash my hands?'

'I suppose your bathroom's still a mess, full of bits and pieces and clouds of steam?' teased Colette.

'You know it has to be,' said Eileen coolly. She hated when Colette breached what she considered to be the boundary of their friendship, particularly in front of a stranger like Bel McDonagh. 'Lacquer must dry in a humid atmosphere. And the only place that can be achieved is in the bathroom and by keeping the taps running.'

When Jacques returned, he raised his eyebrows to Eileen.

'I know. I know,' she said. 'When I get this lacquering business sorted, I'm going to have the most wonderful bathroom in the world. Minimalistic, grey and chrome. With the thickest of white towels and one of those powerful new showers.'

'No doubt the towels monogrammed, "The Hon".'

'No, Colette. Just EG,' said Eileen, who until now, had not considered having towels monogrammed.

'Will I ring for afternoon tea?'

Bel thought Colette very brave.

'There's nobody here.'

'Where's Tranquille?' Colette asked.

'I let her go last week.'

'You what . . . ?'

'Let her go. She was most untranquil.'

'And the month before it was Modeste.'

'I didn't like her.'

'You don't have to like servants . . .'

'Where's Madame Berger?' The apartment was in a worse state than Jacques had ever seen it. Covered in dust, smelling of unknown and unhealthy chemicals and animals, and littered with indescribable debris.

'She has the afternoon off.'

'The afternoon off?' Colette sounded outraged.

'Yes, her uncle or . . . somebody's ill. I'm not sure. It doesn't matter.'

'Yes it does. Give servants an inch and they'll take a mile.'

'You remind me of my mother, she used to say the same about the staff in Brownswood.'

'And where's Sugawara?' Jacques enquired. From the beginning he had been highly critical of Eileen turning a room of her apartment into a lacquer laboratory, as he labelled it, and even more critical of her installing her teacher – and a male Japanese at that – in her home.

'Oh, he's gone out somewhere,' said Eileen airily. 'Occasionally we get on each other's nerves. He hates to be shouted at.'

Jacques laughed heartily. 'Eileen, you're quite incorrigible.'

'Well, isn't it all in the name of art?' she asked gaily, removing her smock. She looked around vaguely. 'Now, there must be wine . . . somewhere . . . I wonder . . . ?

Eileen was beginning to roll down the sleeves of her blouse only to be halted by Colette's shriek, 'What's that?'

'Nothing.' Eileen hastily covered her arms and buttoned the cuffs of her blouse firmly.

'A red rash like that, nothing? I don't think so.' Jacques moved nearer Eileen, his face all concerned enquiry, he took her hands in his. 'Look. And there's the beginning of it on the backs of your hands.'

Eileen put the offending hands behind her back. 'Oh, it's nothing. Just lacquer disease. Goes with the territory. Sooner or later all lacquerists catch it.'

'Lacquer disease. Is there a cure?' Colette looked nervously at her own smooth white hands and arms. At the best of times, she was a bit of a hypochondriac.

'It can be difficult to heal. Eventually I'll get used to it. The babies of Japanese lacquerists have leaves from the lacquer tree put in their first bath to keep them immune.'

'Good God,' said Jacques.

Colette lifted the watch she wore on a thin gold chain around her neck. 'I'd no idea it was so late, I'm afraid I'll have to go. Another appointment.' She backed out of the room.

When she had left, Eileen laughed gaily. 'She's afraid she'll catch my rash.'

Jacques was not amused. 'This is an unhealthy environment. Eileen, you'll have to have at least one servant to keep the place clean.'

'Please, don't lecture. I can't bear it.'

'I'll organise someone for you.' He reached into his pocket, took out a leather bound notebook and slim gold pencil. Taking the sting out of his admonishment, he joked 'Now, Mademoiselle, your requirements?'

Bel felt so superfluous that she did not even bother listening to what Eileen was saying. She should have left with Colette but she had hung on hoping Jacques would invite her for dinner. She thought it quite ridiculous that someone of Eileen's age could not hire her own servants.

Jacques made a few notes. 'Servant in the process of being organised. And you must find other premises for lacquering. As I keep telling you, it's an unhealthy occupation.'

'I suppose you're right. But think of the upheaval. Working out of here's so handy. Everything under the one roof.' She gave a gusty sigh.

'You look worn out, the way I feel when I'm putting together my collections. You've been flat out on lacquer projects for over a year, now. Allow me to help you, chérie?'

Eileen nodded gratefully.

Bel felt even more superfluous.

'I'll have a look around. See if there's anything suitable to rent in the area.'

'Jacques, would you? That'd be wonderful.' She gave him a brief hug and Bel averted her eyes.

Jacques put away his notebook. 'Come on. I'll take the two of you for an early dinner.'

Bel hated Eileen when she accepted with that half smile of hers. She hated her even more when she appeared looking stunning in a buttery silk shirtwaister and a string of amber beads.

By now, despite Bel's best efforts, her white dress was decidedly grubby.

'What did you get great-granddad?' Jack looks around the den as though hoping to spot an Eileen Gray original.

'Nothing.'

'Why?'

'She'd nothing he'd have wanted.'

'To hell with it, I'm going to call her again. I'll not give up.' He looks at his watch. 'It's too late now. Tomorrow morning first thing. Though with the time difference, I'm probably going to have to wait until the afternoon.' His voice lightens. 'Enough of that. You and I are going to have a wonderful time at *Gigi*. And let's start right now with a glass of champagne.'

As Belle dresses for the theatre, the burden of the day's happenings weighs heavily on her shoulders. Jack's dogged determination reminds her of her father. Dan McDonagh never gave up either.

Chapter 4

The floor has bumpy red tiles and the walls are muddy green, adorned with pictures tracing the progress of Christ from pudgy baby to tortured man, as well as Saint Patrick in all his mitred and green-vestmented glory. A variety of scapulars ward off the devil, fronds of blessed palm protect from fire, but none of the many Saint Brigid's crosses dotted around the kitchen have fulfilled their promise of fecundity.

Faithfully, each February another cross arrives from Enniscorthy. For twenty of the forty-odd years Brigid has spent in Paris, believing fervently in the powers of her namesake, she has prayed furiously for a man, marriage, and a home, but above all for babies, lots of babies.

The dawning awareness that her time had run out and that all the crosses in the world could not now grant her motherhood was slow and bitter, though Pierre's attitude has her somewhat mollified. His daughter and two sons are grown up and he has no further interest in either babies or children. Only you, he tells her, looking lingeringly into her eyes.

The sturdy range is Brigid's favourite piece of equipment. Complete with chimney crane, pot hooks and hangers for the long handled frying pans, griddle plates, kettle, metal pots and cauldron, it is a replica of the one in Brownswood. Nothing, she believes, beats the flavour of bread baked in the range. Pierre can keep his new-fangled electric ovens.

This morning she is baking a loaf of Irish soda bread for him.

She puts the flour into a large bowl, sprinkles in a generous teaspoon of bread soda and, making a well in the centre, approximates the amount of buttermilk which she has nurtured at the side of the range until it is of jelly consistency. After a good stir, she removes the mixture from the bowl, sprinkles flour on the table and sets about kneading.

Her knuckles are deep in the dough when the phone rings. Drat. And this early. It is scarcely nine o'clock. Brigid hates being disturbed when she is baking, particularly a loaf as important as this. Another few minutes and she would have the bread in the oven.

These times three phone calls within three days is quite remarkable. Often from one end of the week to the other, the instrument sits on its little lacquer table in the hallway, silent and accusingly.

Please God, she prays, don't let it be that reporter again.

Sloughing off the dough from her hands, she wipes the residue on the blue-and-white striped roller-towel.

She hopes this interruption will not cause deterioration in the bread's raising agent. She wants to prove to Pierre that Irish soda bread is as good, if not better, than its French counterparts which, she has to admit, she enjoys, topped with wedges of pale cream cheese, washed down with Pierre's favourite red *vin ordinaire*.

He has opened her eyes in so many ways. Introduced her to so many new experiences. Her favourite is the market in Courbevoie, tucked away between the church and a street of little shops. It is even better than fair day in Enniscorthy.

It is only about three miles from the Arc de Triomphe,

but on the day Brigid visited, she felt as though she were hours away from both the city and her responsibilities. She and Pierre found terracotta pots of tall green aspidistras and exotic rubber plants from Madagascar, a stall selling lengths of cobwebby antique lace and slabs of fragrant gritty lavender soap.

They held hands there, too, for the first time. She felt self-conscious but his hand felt so right and so welcome in hers that she gave it a little squeeze and he smiled happily.

Giving her hands a further perfunctory wipe on her apron, she lifts the receiver, 'Allo. Ou est ici?' Her French is excruciating, her accent almost unfathomable. But within a few days of arriving in Paris she realised that survival necessitated trying to speak the language.

What is it with the French and their refusal to speak anything but their native tongue? The Irish too would have favoured keeping Gaelic but they had no say in the matter and were forced to adopt the English language. Brigid harbours a sneaking admiration for the determination and dedication of the French.

She lets out a sigh of relief at the voice on the other end of the telephone, speaking English, though with an American accent. It is that Mr Devine again. She listens. Then answers, 'No that is not possible. As I said yesterday, Miss Gray does not receive visitors.'

From the workroom comes an imperious, 'Who is it?' And when Brigid does not answer immediately, the querulous demand, 'Come here.' Miss Gray is still being contrary.

'One moment, please,' Brigid says to the phone.

Eileen, magnifying glass in active service, is minutely examining skeins of dyed wool laid out on her work bench.

They share space with swatches of floor covering, swags of material and samples of leather and wood.

Northern sunlight pours in the window suffusing woman and samples with cruel clarity.

Brigid feels a rush of compassion for the sad lonely figure of her lady. How frail her body has become, how strong her spirit remains. 'It's that Mr Jack Devine again.'

'What does he want?'

'Same as yesterday. To visit you.'

'Oh. All right. I'll see him. Today. After my rest.'

Brigid is amazed. 'Miss Gray. Are you sure?'

'Yes. Just tell him.'

'Will I say you'll only talk about your work?'

'Yes, of course. You should know that by now.'

Miss Gray's refusal to talk of her personal life is a stipulation which for as far back as Brigid can remember has to be made clear to all newcomers. Not that for a long time now, with the exception of this Mr Devine and, Brigid supposes, that newspaper reporter, there is anyone who wants to visit, much less to ask questions.

'Remember, I did see that writer, Mr Chatwin. Mr Bruce Chatwin. And that was all right.'

Brigid had forgotten. Despite him being a reporter, that visit a few years previously, had been more than all right. It was as though they had always known each other. 'The unification of two soul mates,' Miss Gray said afterwards.

Bruce Chatwin, who charmed an interview out of her for *The Sunday Times*, had that ease of manner, rarely encountered but never forgotten. He was tall and slender, handsome as well. 'I've always wanted to go there,' he said, hands behind his back, studying a map of Patagonia, painted in gouache.

'Me too,' Eileen replied. She was ninety at the time. With the passage of years and the deterioration of her sight, she had been forced to become an armchair traveller. But, typically, she was an enthusiastic one. 'Please go. And do think of me.'

She liked to believe he took her advice. He resigned from *The Sunday Times*, with a laconic telegram stating, 'Have gone to Patagonia'. Six months later he returned with the framework of a book which, published as *In Patagonia,* was the beginning of his literary career.

Brigid returns to the phone. 'Mr Devine, Miss Gray says you may come this afternoon at five . . .'

The phone speaks and she chuckles. Positively chuckles. The sound is all the more amazing as it is a long time since chuckles have been part of this household.

'What's going on?' Eileen calls. Nowadays she can be as obsessed with the minutiae of domesticity as previously she was with her work.

Changed times. Brigid remembers her locked deep into some project, refusing invitations and receiving no visitors. Demanding total silence, oblivious to food, not bothering to sleep and, if not reminded, forgetting to bathe or even to change her clothes.

Curiosity and impatience having got the better of Eileen, she comes to the doorway of her workroom, leaning heavily on one of her walking sticks. She has several solid sticks of clouded malacca with crooked handles and large rubber tips which cling reassuringly to the ground. These sticks dangle comfortingly from various vantage points of door handles, cupboards, chairs and windowsills.

'One moment, Mr Devine, sir.' Still half-chuckling, Brigid

puts her hand over the mouthpiece. 'He's still in America, Miss.'

'Oh, I see.' Eileen feels thwarted. Within the space of a few moments she had visualised with enjoyment the whole intellectual and social spectrum of entertaining this Mr Devine. She so craved outside stimulus. This concept of modern antiques, she finds interesting. 'When will he be here?'

'The day after tomorrow. Thursday.'

'He may come on Friday.'

Brigid relays the message, gives him the address and replaces the receiver.

Hoping that prior to the visit Miss Gray will not have her embarking on a flurry of cleaning and catering, Brigid returns to the kitchen.

She re-kneads the flabby dough, shapes the mixture into a circle, cuts a cross on its top, sticks the knife into each of the quarters to make an escape route for the steam, though her mother always insisted it was to let out the little people. Hoping for the best, she tucks the loaf securely into the bread oven, and covers its lid with hot coals. It will be done in about an hour's time.

As a child propped between the forked branches of an old apple tree in Brownswood's orchard, Brigid fantasised about leaving Enniscorthy. No way did she want to end up a servant like her mother. From babyhood, she had heard talk of the changes around the place when Miss Ethel had married Master Henry Tufnell Campbell, long before she was born.

Even though she had never been further than Wexford town, she dreamed of living in a big city and those dreams were nurtured by Hollywood life as portrayed on the screen in the Roxy cinema. Wistfully, she wished she looked, even a little, like Betty Grable, and she was passionately in love with Cary Grant.

Given the opportunity, not that she expected opportunity, she would like to be a nurse before she married and had lots of babies. She had made enquiries from the school master who knew everything, and discovered that training was free in the big hospitals in London.

Her mother, when she told her, said she was getting above herself and that nursing in a place like London was not for the likes of them.

'Miss Eileen will be kind to you,' her mother comforted Brigid the evening the master made his announcement that she was to join his sister-in-law's household in Paris.

Brigid was scared. Paris. Where she knew nobody. And as a servant. She travelled by bus, boat, train, boat again and finally the underground Metro which terrified her. Two afternoons later, she presented herself at 21 rue Bonaparte, carrying her meagre possessions in a shabby valise, wearing her everyday dress under her only coat and well-worn shoes.

Cook sat her at a corner of the kitchen table, told her to be quiet, that the mistress would be with her shortly and then she disappeared. The kitchen was warm with dark walls gleaming with copper pans.

It seemed to Brigid that she had waited for ever when the door opened. A slender lady with cropped hair, dressed in a grey skirt and a cream blouse, entered, followed by what Brigid presumed to be a gentleman in formal black and with dark hair brushed back from his forehead.

Brigid stood up, looked from one to the other, 'Good

evening, Ma'am,' she said to the woman, and 'Good evening, Sir,' to the man she presumed to be the woman's husband.

Eileen stood awkwardly, as always, unsure of how to go about this business of acquiring a servant.

Brigid waited expectantly.

'Can you cook?' Eileen asked, oblivious to the fact that the terms of her cook's engagement was that she would do all the household cooking and have total authority in the kitchen.

Brigid had never even boiled a pot of water. The older women, including her mother, terrified of losing their positions, jealously queened over the kitchen in Brownswood. Brigid wondered should she pretend. But falsehoods were not her way. 'No,' she answered, 'I can't cook.'

'Can you iron?' Eileen tried. She knew the laundering of the silk blouses she so favoured was both difficult and time-consuming.

Brigid shook her head. That was a skilled operation done by a woman who cycled out to the Manor once a week from town.

'Have you ever cleaned?'

Brigid smiled sadly, shrugged. No. She had never been trained in any form of housework.

This interview had turned into a nightmare. She would be sent home, back to County Wexford. The shame of such an expulsion on her and her family would be nearly as bad as being returned by the sisters from the convent as being unsuitable for the taking of the veil as a nun.

Her last hope of getting the position evaporated and she thought in the fading light of having to face that terrifying journey on the Metro again.

Beginning to turn away, she thought she heard, 'Well, how

about giving it a try?' She wondered was she so desperate that even her ears were deceiving her.

When she realised the implication of the question, Brigid's face broke into an ear-splitting smile. That night, lying on a bench near the range, she fought sleep in case when she woke up, she would discover that getting the job had only been a wonderful dream.

The 'husband' she found out next morning from Cook, was called Fräulein Bloch.

Now that Jack's visit to Paris and Eileen Gray is confirmed, Belle wonders how her father would have handled the situation. She supposes he would again employ his philosophy of time-telling.

As she, Mick and Dan sat over the ritual Friday-night dinners, in his gentle but determined way Dan, stroking his beard, often spoke of the importance of facing up to the difficulties of life and what he called 'rectification' to the best advantage of all concerned and then, as he put it, letting sleeping dogs lie.

The whiskey decanter making its appearance on the table was his cue for the ceremony of his cigar. Opening the heavy wooden thermidor, he fiddled lengthily and painstakingly, uncharacteristically making complex the simple act of cutting and lighting. With tobacco tip glowing redly, he enjoyed what he called, his 'thinking silence' – a silence which neither Belle nor Mick would dream of interrupting. Inhaling and exhaling, Dan's internal debate emerged in punctuating puffs of smoke.

Some minutes later he would shrug out of his jacket, loosen his neck tie, remove the top stud from his collar, untie the laces of his boots and, legs crossed, would relax into business, political and Church debate, discussion or conversation.

He and Mick, who never disagreed about anything, would span their chosen subjects, touch glasses, intone '*Sláinte*' and look indulgently at Belle. She was certain that her father and her husband held no secrets from each other.

She gave birth to a daughter on Saint Patrick's Day. Mick, face ruddier than ever, whooped with delight, even though she knew he had hoped for a son. He suggested naming her Patsy. Belle, relieved to have the birth behind her, went along with his choice.

Despite the valiant efforts of her husband, and the none-too-subtle urgings of her father, both hell-bent on assuring the future of their respective dynasties, and of Belle's assurance that she was doing her best, she failed to conceive again.

It was a fact of life which did not surprise her.

On each occasion when Mick came to her bed, she was reminded of the last time she had seen Jacques.

When she awoke sometime during that night – her last in Paris – her hotel room bore Jacques's imprint. But he was gone. She was not surprised. Time was short. He would have so many arrangements to make.

Next morning, with her time running out, when he had not returned, she telephoned his apartment and his salon. His manservant did not know of his whereabouts and his chief couturière whom she had dealt with on numerous occasions could not nor would not help.

There was no reply from Colette's apartment.

From Eileen's maid she learned that Miss Gray was not to be disturbed. But at least Eileen Gray was there. Bel had her driver take her to rue Bonaparte. The maid did her best. But Bel was not her father's daughter for nothing. She wriggled past her, up the stairs and into the workroom.

Eileen and Jacques were seated in front of the fire on either side of a low table on which sat an open box of chocolate truffles. Their compatibility coated them in impenetrability. She sat, feet tucked up under her, a cigarette dangling from between her fingers. He, in the process of lifting a coffee cup to his lips, dashed it back to its saucer.

'How dare you,' Eileen said in her cut-glass voice. 'Come here uninvited.'

'Why are you here?' Jacques asked, half-rising.

Bel, who had scrutinised his every facial expression, analysed his tones of voice and evaluated each of his gestures, knew then what she should have realised weeks previously.

Her dreams crashed and shattered around her.

Colette had been right.

After her return from Europe, Bel's weeks were full of big, sad, lonely spaces packed with denial. Until her father squeezed the truth from her and forced her to face her situation. He set the wheels of rectification in motion and ensured they were implemented.

And so it had remained for fifty years.

But now the boundaries are changed. Should she take the family into her confidence? She shudders at the idea. Not only would it irrevocably damage what she and her father sought to protect but, she is certain, and glad to have reached the conclusion, it would serve no purpose.

She wonders about Jack. Occasionally, at the back of her mind, lurks the notion that he should know. But no. She cannot, she will not. And for one of the few times in her life, she is unable to find the smallest sliver of silver in her cloud of fear.

The past cannot be undone. The past cannot be undone, she repeats like a mantra. Her father instilled that into her. She can almost physically feel the line that she and he had drawn under her European tour being slowly but definitely erased. How she wishes he were still alive, sitting behind his desk, with the calming aroma of his cigar emanating from the den.

Brigid's worst fears are realised. Miss Gray instigates a mad flurry of tidying, cleaning and polishing for Friday.

With Brigid poised up the ladder cleaning blinds, Eileen debates, 'We'll have champagne and olives. Or tea? I do like a proper afternoon tea. And we never have it now. Or perhaps Mr Devine would prefer cocktails? Americans drink cocktails, don't they?'

'I couldn't say.' This heavy cleaning is no joke.

'They do. Concoctions with names like Manhattans and Screwdrivers. Whiskey and vodka vulgarly dressed up. With sugared glasses and those ghastly red glacé cherries. Even swivel sticks and paper umbrellas.' She shakes her head in bemusement. 'No wonder Americans have so little culture.'

Brigid tackles the struts of a chair with an oiled cloth. She has not seen her employer so animated in years. 'You don't think much of Americans, do you?'

In Enniscorthy during the 1930s, '40s and '50s, the food and clothes parcels, not to mention the envelopes of dollars sent home by American emigrants, had pulled many a family back from the borders of hunger and poverty.

'I've never had reason to,' Eileen says, as always when the subject of Americans is raised, remembering her father.

Chapter 5

At half past ten on Friday morning Jack waits in the lobby of his hotel for a car and driver to take him on what he shudders to think of as the typical American tour of Paris. The only reason he can justify it is by the shortness of his stay.

Earlier he tried to imagine Queen Victoria, King George VI and the Duke and Duchess of Windsor who, according to the hotel brochure were regular habitués, breakfasting next to him in the marble-floored, silk-panelled and gold-leafed dining room but, in the end, he decided they would be more likely to dine in their respective suites.

During these lateral imaginings, he feasted on two large milky coffees and, to his amazement, two unbelievably light, melt-in-the-mouth croissants liberally smeared with butter and apricot conserve.

It is a mostly grey morning though, as often happens at the beginning of a winter day, occasional flashes of sunlight, low and polarized, find their way through the clouds to linger caressingly on buildings and boulevards.

His car is a gleaming black Citroën and his peak-capped driver is the quiet rather than chatty type, though when he does speak it is in informed, perfectly modulated English.

With Jack seated beside him, he turns out of rue de Rivoli into the impressive Place de la Concorde, with its spouting fountains and Egyptian obelisk. 'Site of Louis XVI and Marie Antoinette's execution, 1793,' he intones. Next, he drives up the majestic Champs-Elysées, the spine of western Paris, to the Etoile and the powerful Arc de Triomphe, commenting laconically, 'Greek temple style. Built 1806 to 1836 to commemorate Napoleon's victories.' And on to the Eiffel Tower, 'The tallest building in the world when it was constructed. For the Exposition of 1889.'

From his initial impressions coming in from the airport yesterday and driving the streets this morning, Jack decides that the contrast between New York and Paris is non-quantifiable.

New York is a young city of screaming sirens, aggressive advertising, fast cars, excessive drugs and high fashion. Under the street lights, young faces strain into masks of old age, and old faces pleat second childhood. The looming architecture is of exaggerated dimensions.

Paris, on the other hand, is handsomely secure in its maturity and its victorious history. Its air is one of quiet affluence and easy sophistication; its people are confident, its architecture elegant. With the exception of the Eiffel Tower, which he labels hideous, its famous landmarks strike chord after chord of design compatibility, each so aesthetically harmonious that Jack's breath catches and his eyes prick.

Here there is no question of conflict about architecture scoring off nature, or nature scoring off architecture. Here is utter harmony. This city feels like home. He knows exactly what that English poet meant when he wrote about the beauty of the world making him sad.

As they head towards the Île de la Cité, the heart of Paris

and Notre Dame, Jack dispenses with his driver. History for him is emotional, with the power to move. Desperately, here this morning, he wants to be moved and to feel. Even if he sees but a fraction of the sights and does not learn another date, he prefers his own walking company. Immediately he feels freer, looser, less of a tourist.

Along a length of the Right Bank he strolls, past displays of eye-catching and not so eye-catching paintings. Some are surprisingly good, some appallingly bad. They come in every shape, size, composition and subject. Water colours, acrylics, oils, inks, chalk and charcoal.

Notre Dame's Gothic exterior is more beautiful than he imagined a cathedral could be. Inside the dimness of the church, a flare of candles mark the statue of the Virgin Mary. Perched on a chair, listening to the silence, the immense stone silence, hollow and reverent, an urn for music, he finds himself thinking of Elvira.

After lighting a long taper candle, he prays in the flickering gloom for he knows not what. He wishes she were here with him, sharing these experiences.

For as long as he can remember, Jack has liked women, loved women. But he has only once been in love.

While still in his teens, he realised that the majority of girls he dated were operating on a different wave length to him; they were looking for a relationship that eventually would lead towards marriage, whereas he only wanted the fun socialising of now. Neither past, nor future, all he wanted then was the present.

Having no wish to operate under false pretences, at the beginning of each new relationship – and there were many – usually over a romantic meal, he explained that he was not in the market for commitment. Despite this, invariably, his dates presumed they would be the one to change him.

As each relationship inexorably dwindled towards ending, he ensured an amicable parting, usually helped along with a goodbye piece of jewellery. His diplomatic behaviour has resulted in an eclectic bevy of women friends.

From the beginning, his feelings towards Elvira were different.

It was as though a thunderbolt hit him when he first sighted her, quite literally, as the song says, across a crowded room. Ethereal and ephemeral, she stood unadorned by any form of jewellery, in a simple black strapless dress, on the edge of the crowd, barely sipping from a glass of red wine.

She was in the company of an older distinguished-looking man, his dark head marquisited with silver, bent protectively towards her. He envied that man.

The occasion was New York City Ballet's end of season party, a fashion jungle with women dressed in this season's puffball skirts in ice-cream colours and killer stiletto heels, while their men's uniform was blue pinstriped ventless suits and two-tone power shirts.

The event, Jack decided from cynical sideline observation, had more to do with materialism, ostentation and obsession with money than with the true creativity which idealistically, he felt, should govern dance.

In thoroughly bad form, he carped away to himself, as though he and Modern Antiques were not a dollar-sign-headed corporation. He had spent his day lucratively at an out-of-town viewing, driving back to the city in the dark, the trail of headlamp beams marking out the snarled freeways like an illuminated street map, while at eye level the downtown skyscrapers showed off their spotlit profiles against the inky sky.

Sirens day and night. Cars faster and faster. Advertisements more aggressive. Vertiginous glass façades reflecting building upon building. Ruthless building without consideration of setting, well-being or ecology.

Musing, he made a city series of random connections, delighted with his bullet-point links of instant buzz and contradictory beauty. The theatrical sophistication of Broadway and the raw creativity of Greenwich Village; the Afro, Mohican and pre-Raphaelite hairstyles that stalked the streets and the myriad of multiracial idiosyncrasies provided a heady eclectic mix. Not forgetting the powerlessness of pungent poverty when measured against the scented luxury of wealth.

A dash back to his apartment, a quick shower and an even quicker change of clothes and there he was, under sufferance, at the Lincoln Center, bored and reluctant, representing both his mother and grandmother.

Occasionally, when Belle was unable to get up to New York for one of her functions, she asked him to deputise. Jack considered it a small price to pay for her generosity. But that evening was one of his small-minded times, though his annoyance was directed more towards his mother than his grandmother.

Dammit, Patsy was an active fundraiser for the ballet and it is she, not he, who should be here. Her excuse was involvement in an even more worthy operatic evening that she could not get out of, arranged months ahead of the ballet, she wailed dramatically, before blowing three smoke rings into the air. And he had known that she was, if not actually lying, certainly bending the truth.

When the man talking to this ethereal being turned his head, Jack recognised philanthropist Sam Lang, host of this evening's party.

Making his way through the throng to pay his, Patsy's and Belle's respects, he worked the crowd professionally, his head full of masculine words drenched in smoke and feminine chat rising melodically against the clink of vodka over ice, saying hello here, waving there, touching an occasional shoulder, planning on how to wangle an introduction.

He need not have worried. Sam presented her immediately and instantly turned into the crowd. The hand Elvira Elliott placed in Jack's was long cool and bony, and he could feel the faintest trembling of her fingers in his palm. Close up, she was thistledown light, with clouds of dark hair, fondant eyes and a rosebud mouth.

He glanced down at their clasped hands and then at her feet which were knobbed, bony and splayed, incongruous in delicately strapped low-heeled sandals. With those feet, she had to be a dancer.

He wished he had paid more attention to this evening's performance. *Serenade* it was called. The programme notes described it as an American-style production in the European tradition. He considered it pretentious. Art masquerading as art for the sake of money.

He did not speak for some seconds. Nor did she. Not a word, not a greeting, not a pleasantry passed between them. And when finally he looked into Elvira's face, his blue eyes locking with her green, he felt as though his breath was being sucked out of his body.

Sam Lang was busy hand-clasping, hugging and accepting effusive greetings and giving and receiving wild compliments. Networking at its most insincere. Jack thought if Sam could not actually see, he must at the very least be aware of the thick silence of soul-mate lust lurking between Elvira and himself.

With a wry smile, Elvira broke eye contact and with her head to one side, watched Sam for a few moments. Intently. Jack heard her murmur, 'Oh Lord, forgive us our platitudes as we forgive them their clichés.' And then, as though to take the fondness out of her comment, she gave a throaty chuckle.

She looked at him, met his eyes again, raised an eyebrow and they grinned conspiratorially.

'I'm pleased to make your acquaintance,' he finally said. 'Very pleased.'

'Are you a dancer?'

'No, of course not.' He was amused. He could imagine his father's outrage at the suggestion. Antiques were bad enough, but in Paddy Devine's book a son a dancer would be the limit. 'Why do you ask?'

'I saw you looking at my feet.'

Over the following months, Jack and Elvira fell in love. Madly, passionately and sublimely in love. The luxury of their love was time, closeness, talking or reading together, body fitting against body, knees and arms, legs and hands, falling asleep together, domesticating the darkness with each other's presence.

Their love changed their very idea of themselves. Their heads and hands and torsos, the sensitive ends of their fingers, their legs and feet, their hearts and brains and their bodies.

Their time together remains with Jack as shards of bittersweet memories. Much as they wanted each other. For always and ever, they swore. Commitment terrified them. Each would have liked to change but neither was willing to make the gesture.

Jack had met his match.

Their parting was not easy. But they had reached that point of no-return in their relationship when there was no staying in the present; they must either go forward to the future or revert to the past. They thought, wondered and analysed. With pain outweighing pleasure, they tortured themselves and each other.

It was Sunday. Early evening. November light fading to a violet sunset. Together they prepared their meal. In wordless harmony, she assembled and dressed a green salad, while he laid the table and watched salmon poach. Then she spoke, softly, so softly that he had to strain to hear. 'I slept with Sam Lang.'

He could not have heard correctly. 'You what?'

She repeated, her voice even lower. 'I slept with Sam. Last week. When you were away.'

He said nothing. He could not.

Using the wooden servers they had bought together in Macy's she tossed the salad. Ragged leaves of iceberg lettuce, tears of chicory, strips of green peppers, medallions of cucumber, all coated to oily perfection.

But he has to know. 'Why?'

She was crying, head bent, tears dripping into the salad bowl. 'To see how I felt about you. To see if I wanted to spend the rest of my life with you. To make a commitment to you.'

'And what did you decide?' His voice was cold as ice. He remembered the marquisited head bent protectively towards Elvira. He should have known. Related and unrelated thoughts flew in all directions.

By now she was sobbing so much that he had difficulty making out her words. Yes she wanted to be with him for always. She was committed to him for ever.

'Well, I feel differently. In the circumstances I'm sure you understand.'

Head held high, she left the kitchen still carrying the servers.

Jack stored their various shared memories in separate frames for easy recall and returned to the life he had known before meeting Elvira. He presumes she did the same. She is the only woman whom he truly loved, yet she is the only woman whom he allowed to leave without either token or contact.

No matter how hard he tries, he cannot eradicate his last sight of her proud tear-stained face as she walked out of his apartment, away from him. And his own awful empty feeling when he woke the following morning. And the morning after and the morning after . . .

Eventually curiosity impels Jack towards Saint-Germain-des-Prés. He crosses the Seine and enters the district via rue Guénégaud, dark and narrow, with six-storey high buildings.

He wanders a warren of little streets with exotic sounding names and when the weather changes for the worst, he shelters under an archway, impervious to the howling wind, amused by large graffitti letters proclaiming 'Libertie! Equalitie! Sexualitie!'.

On the move again, he finds a rough tenderness at the way

the mist-slicked streets seem to drag at him. He is particularly touched by the determined artistry of one newspaper that wraps itself around his feet in exotic desperation, as though binding him to this place.

As he enters the little cobblestoned square dominated by, according to his guide book, one of the oldest churches in Paris, and plane trees looking as though they have grown undisturbed for ever, fresh howls of wind and squalls of rain have him running for shelter to the Café de Flore. From inside, he watches as outside, umbrellas sprout like black mushrooms.

Again, according to Jack's guide book, this café was a regular haunt of Jean-Paul Sartre's during World War II. His principal liking for it, he later wrote, was that it had a stove for warmth, a Metro across the square for transport and no Germans to bother him.

During Jack's student days, he liked to think he identified with Sartre's belief that hell was other people. In his case, he regularly and glibly announced, to gales of peer laughter, it was his parents.

The place cannot have changed much, Jack decides, taking in the art deco decor, mirrors and light fittings, the well-worn coffee-and-cream mosaic floor, simple marble staircase and slim brass banister.

He stretches an espresso to infinity.

Outside the storm rages. It is a rattling storm. Wave upon battering wave of it dispensing angry bursts of thunder and pencil thin daggers of lightning. Starting. Pausing. Stopping. A psychedelically staged crescendo of an orchestra gone mad. More bolts of lightning, more cracks of thunder, followed by a short burst of torrential rain. Then it is over.

Through the window he watches as though by magic, a watery pre-dusk sun appear and the square swarms with activity. Entwined lovers with long hair and black clothes; chic women, with equally chic dogs on colourful leads; men wearing well-cut dark suits or co-ordinating casuals with a groomed aplomb un-encountered in New York.

Leaving the café, he backtracks the winter streets trying to place the location of a flower shop he had come across in his earlier wanderings. Suddenly it looms out of the dusk.

Its brightly-lit window is full of out-of-season flowers – cathedral spires of blue delphiniums, pyramid honeycombs of pink and purple lupins, pom-poms of golden yellow dahlias, translucent white clarkia, trails of mauve wisteria and masses of headily scented blowzy roses in scarlet, crimson, tangerine and lemon.

He loves flowers, and keeps two large Waterford glass vases of fresh blooms in his office. Now he stands, looking around, unsure of what one brings an icon.

Then tucked into a corner, he sees them. Simple. Unpretentiously elegant. Long-stemmed tiny cream roses, in tight bud, surrounded by a halo of glistening green leaves.

To the delight of the owner, an amazingly stylish stork-shaped woman with an upswept hairdo, he buys the lot.

As he makes his way back to the square, he feels as though he is moving in a dream-like sequence, grey swirling wraiths of ghosts from the past, surrounding and protecting him. A glance at his watch shows he still has time before identifying the Gray apartment.

He lingers, soaking up the atmosphere, while running through the format of his interview and moving the tape recorder, insisted on by his father, from Burberry to inside pocket of sports jacket.

Finally he wanders down rue Bonaparte with its fairy-tale shop fronts with mysterious and romantic-sounding names like Besson, Galerie Sebastien, Arthus and Nobelle.

The antique shops sell bundles of curve-bladed ivory-handled knives; carved mahogany marble-topped wash stands; plates, decorated with startled looking fish and improbable species of flowers; imaginative occasional chairs and bundles of starched crisp crochet-trimmed linen.

A tall screen of collages comprised of faded sepia photographs, calligraphed verses, scraps of ribbon and fabric, rather like child's scrap book, stands towards the back of one window. He wonders at the love and memories that went into its construction.

The galleries are full of elongated and oblique statuary in bronze and stone, surrealistic wall hangings, ancient tapestries and framed and unframed paintings.

An antiquarian book store displays worthy titles like *Figures de la Passion*, *Women who Ruled the World* and *Art Nouveaux Designs at the Paris Salons 1895–1914*. Peering through fogged glass, he makes out leather-bound, gilt-edged, pocket-sized books, a first edition of the La Fontaine Fables and a selection of the works of Racine. Towards the front of the window is a letter from Colette in a dashing hand on bright blue paper with an address in rue Jacob, a street he is certain he came across during his travels; propped beside the letter is a framed engraving of La Fayette alongside a document with the meticulous signature of a neat man. A note from Flaubert is in spikey, sloping upwards writing, sliding off the right-hand side of the page. Someone in a hurry, Jack decides.

Talking of which . . .

A quick look at his watch confirms that he is running out of time. On his way down the street, he sees an open gate and is unable to resist entering the twilit elegance of the courtyard, a place of trailing plants, paved and gravel paths and stone urns lit by lozenges of light from wrought iron lampposts.

Feeling like a trespasser but compulsively lured, he takes in the beauty of the shuttered building, its classical eighteenth-century proportions, enhanced by buttery cream paint. A small blue and white porcelain plaque proclaims it to be number 21.

Afterwards, he maintained that Eileen Gray's apartment found him.

At three minutes to five, taking fortifying breaths of self-hood, he climbs the outside steps, his imagination on over-drive, his sense of anticipation deliciously honed.

Now that he has reached this point, he is equally excited at the prospects of meeting Eileen Gray, seeing examples of her work and getting this profile which will prove to his father that if he so chose, he could handle the macho newspaper business.

When Jack bearded him in his office, Paddy Devine knew nothing more of Eileen Gray than the information contained in the one column, two-inch European News sidebar of Tuesday's paper. Initially he had been sceptical of his son's proposal, thinking there had to be a catch, insisting that interviewing was more than asking a few questions and writing up copy to high-school-essay standard.

Jack refused to budge, 'For once in your life, give me a fair hearing and a chance.'

With his father a captive audience, he pleaded his case with passion, citing the scoop factor, as well as the international social and artistic significance of the revival of her work. He answered his father's probing journalistic questions fluently and promised to look into sourcing photographs.

'Go for it, so,' Paddy was amazed to hear himself say.

Jack felt as though he were one of his seasoned reporters and guaranteed to get his story.

As Belle had suspected, Paddy took Jack's proposal as a sign of capitulation. The young whelp. He knew a son of his would come around in the end. After all, didn't his veins run with printer's ink.

Already Paddy was plotting discreet disentanglement of Jack from Modern Antiques. He would set him up here with a title, an office, a generous salary and a flexible expense account package, but he would ensure that he learned the business from the ground up. By God, he would.

For now, he made do with handing him a tape recorder. Jack waved it away.

'Accuracy is one of the first and most important attributes of journalism,' Paddy told his son. 'Use it.' He was relieved when Jack, after a quick look at the operating procedure, pocketed it without argument.

'We'll talk when you get back.' Father walked son to the door, approval radiating from his every pore.

What samples of her work, Jack wonders, will Eileen Gray have on display? His appetite is thoroughly whetted by her press clippings.

Screens. No doubt, the most interesting examples of lacquer, brick and cork.

Tables, of course; he would love to see the tasselled *Lotus*, the round black-topped, the small ivory one with two drawers, examples from the slender-legged series popular during the late twenties.

Chairs. Particularly the *Siren.* A variety of those she has designed for more than five decades, many now copied under licence and others which have become collectors' pieces.

Her gouaches will decorate the walls and, most definitely, the floors will be resplendent with her abstract rugs.

Brigid is in thoroughly bad form. The whole of Friday morning was spent with Miss Gray fussing over those fiddly canapé things, with her ideas for filling and decoration growing more elaborate by the minute – and not a decent bite to be got from the lot of them. All talk and hindrance her lady is on the rare occasions she ventures into the kitchen.

Just as she was breathing a sigh of relief and rinsing off the chopping board, Miss Gray insisted on a selection of chocolate pastries from Rumpelmayer's.

Brigid took the opportunity to pay a fleeting visit to Pierre. His bakeshop was so cosy, he was so warm and loving and full of compliments, that she left him even more reluctantly than usual to return to her life in the chilly apartment.

This afternoon though, for the first time, she saw Pierre as he is, settled in his ways with a grown family, a good business, a comfortable relationship with her and a contented life. Even if he were to ask her to marry, and she doubts he ever will, she could not, would not, leave her lady. Much as, on occasions, Miss Gray drives her to distraction, she loves and cares deeply for her.

Brigid gives a last sigh for the life she never had. A nurse in London. A wife with a man of her own. A mother surrounded by babies and toddlers. A home. What is she? When she thinks of it, nothing more than servant-companion to a difficult old lady. What has she achieved? Nothing. And these days, barely a word of thanks or appreciation does she get.

Seldom lost for an omen to suit whatever the occasion, Brigid takes Miss Gray's contrariness, her own out-of-sorts feeling and this afternoon's storm as ominous portents of this Mr Devine's visit. By now she has elevated him to a status not far short of Lucifer himself.

Chapter 6

Belle opens the white louvred double doors of her closet. Despite her clothes being hung, racked and drawered in colour and outfit co-ordination, she is in a quandary.

This season there is no leading right fashion look, which upsets her, as she favours definite guidelines, rather than the less sartorially certain hit-and-miss of do-it-yourself. She was intrigued to read somewhere recently that every style, even those in bad taste, adds to the vocabulary of the fashionable woman, though not for one moment does she subscribe to that theory.

Despite being considerably younger and blonde rather than dark-haired, she has always received as a compliment her likeness to the Duchess of Windsor. Many years ago, she took to heart Wallis Simpson's philosophy of never complaining or never explaining. And in her secret heart of hearts Belle has always envied her for getting her man.

Shattered and all as she is at learning of Jacques's death, she is enormously pleased to discover he never married.

She should return to Bellport. Instead of hanging on here while Jack is in Paris.

Bellport.

Shortly after their marriage, she and Mick had driven out from the city on a mean November weekend of sharp winds and spitting snow.

'Bellport, my Belle, it's a perfect name and a perfect place for our vacation home. Great for our boys. Our sons.' Mick had touched her burgeoning bump and she had not known how to reply. Being Belle she stayed quiet. 'While we're here, I'll take a look at available properties.'

That there were no properties obviously for sale in no way disappointed nor deterred Mick. Like her father, once an idea took hold, he never gave up until he had translated it into achievement. Rambling the small unpretentious town, they came upon tea-rooms, of the kind Belle remembered from her visit to England, all wooden panelling, blazing fire, copper utensils and check table cloths.

Her new husband was not the tea-room type, though he was still at the stage of being enchanted by and pandering to the prettiness, frivolity and extravagance of his young wife. His wonder and delight at her pregnancy made him amenable about unimportant things in a way that was not natural to him. The major decisions of their life, Belle was beginning to realise and not really to mind, he would always handle and probably without consultation with her.

She had swapped paternal control for husband control. It was not what she had planned for her life, but circumstances had well and truly quashed her ambitions – Paris had become as unreal as a dream – and she had retreated back to the security of the known with relief.

Mick and she were the only customers in the tea-shop and, mostly in silence, they drank steaming cups of Earl Grey and ate English crumpets smothered in whipped cream and strawberry jam.

Mick cross-examined the waitress about houses for sale. When she looked at him blankly, he requested the owner.

Eventually, the manageress, who had red hair and a jaunty smile, arrived at their table and when she told them that she knew of no such properties for sale, explaining proprietarily that places around here stayed within the family, Belle hoped Mick would be satisfied but, again, suspected the opposite.

Afterwards they strolled the seafront, clawing their way into the teeth of the wind, while above them seagulls arced and screamed.

Looming in the distance, Mick spotted the outline of a building. Nearer, it turned out to be a rambling clapboard two-storey cottage sprawling on to the beach. Mick hurried them towards it. Hands behind his back, he stood looking up at it for a considerable length of time and after walking its perimeter, to Belle's mortification, he insisted on knocking.

The heavy wrought iron knocker seemed to echo emptily through the house.

'Come on,' she tugged at his sleeve. 'There's nobody in.'

It was beginning to grow dark, the wind had dropped, and the air was full of birds, their wings whopping by, invisible, but close as a whisper and with the drifts of sea mist, she found the place spooky. This pregnancy had made her sensitive to atmosphere and vulnerable to all kinds of imaginings.

Mick pressed his face against the stained glass panel of the door which depicted a ship in full sail.

Suddenly, the inside silence was broken by a pulling of bolts and a removal of chains. Mick stepped briskly backwards and the door swung slowly open.

The man who stood before them lit by the light from the hallway was tall, slender and delicate-looking with hair exploding in a dandelion-like corona of white frizz. He had a worried expression and was wearing a maroon velvet smoking-jacket and a black woolly muffler.

In the face of Mick's enthusiasm, he stood no chance but Belle never knew how they ended up in his stiflingly hot parlour.

He was George Tuthill whose ancestor Captain John had built the fisherman's cottage in the mid-nineteenth century. He seemed singularly lacking in curiosity as to their reasons for being here but he was obviously delighted with their company and he turned out to be a gracious host.

Belle watched as his long slender tremoring fingers poured three minuscule glasses of sherry, before he drew in close to the roaring blaze of the log fire, adjusting his muffler, as though permanently cold. Mick joined him, sitting opposite and he pulled in a chair between them for her.

Belle, who throughout her pregnancy felt uncomfortable in the heat, moved towards the back of the room, while idly listening to their conversation.

Through the un-curtained window, she could hear the heavy indrawn breath of receding water dragging at the shingle, followed by the brief collapsing climax of the thud of breakers.

Mick, who thrived in male company, was entranced with the opportunity of giving his Irish *piseogs* an airing and George, his frail voice interspersed with a barking cough, matched him with tales of the derring-does of his sea-faring ancestors. Impersonal stories that told nothing about either man.

The beginning of their bonding was the discovery that both their ancestors came from the township of Clifden. Mick held forth on going back, bringing his sons. If George had similar aspirations, he said nothing.

Belle's stomach rumbled for food; she was constantly hungry and the sherry sitting stingingly and heart-burningly somewhere in her middle added to her discomfort. She thought longingly of the dinner menu she had seen written up in the lobby of their hotel – clam chowder, broiled scrod with creamed potatoes and apple pie.

The tenor of conversation changed. Mick was cutting a deal. From the sound of it, a slow deal. Belle, who knew her husband's reputation, felt this time he had met his match. Surely George Tuthill was too well established and too old-money to be swayed.

It was unbelievable that Mick believed he could walk in and buy a property just because it took his fancy. But she was proved wrong. Mick was an ardent advocate and George, it appeared, was more than willing to be swayed.

He opened up and once started there was no stopping the floodgates of his life story. Between the lines of his impersonal telling, Belle read the heartbreak. He was a bachelor, the end of his line and now that he was in the last stages of consumption, he could rest easy if, as he put it, the house found a good family. He glanced shyly down the room at Belle's middle.

The only stipulation to the sale was that the portrait of the whiskered Captain which dominated the chimney breast must remain. Family tradition had it that it would be unlucky to move him from his final resting-place.

Belle shivered. Stipulations from the grave unnerved her. But she said nothing. In the few short months of her marriage, while neither happy nor unhappy, she had become used to making the best of what life offered, even down to accepting dry crackers for dinner. Though, sometime in the distant future, she still hoped for this cloud full of silver linings.

The men in Belle's life. Past and present.

Jack is so right when he insists his father wants him in his image and likeness.

That is something Belle has known from the day he was born. From even before his conception. Though a generation late, the boy arrived at last. As, eventually, she knew he would.

The remainder of the family saw his coming as the securing their dynasty.

Belle saw it as the timeless inevitability of destiny.

Her heart tearing out of her, she looked at the perfection of the tiny dark-haired boy child lying in his frilled crib, and she had known as surely as if she had given birth to him that he was flesh of her flesh and blood of her blood. She reached in and with her right index finger touched his cheek.

'What'll you call him?' she asked Patsy and Paddy, cuddling together on the hospital bed, just now looking the loving couple they were not, nor ever had been.

'I don't know. I was so sure it'd be another girl, I thought it'd be unlucky to choose a boy's name.'

Such a remark was typical of Patsy. Never committing herself, never presuming the best. Even from the time she was a little girl wearing smocked dresses and bows in her hair, she had a pessimistic streak.

'We'll call him Patrick, of course,' Paddy said, jumping up

from the bed, rubbing his hands in glee, his untidy six-foot bulk dwarfing the small private room, 'Haven't I waited long enough for him.'

'No, you won't. We won't,' Patsy's voice was raised and she sat up straighter in the bed. So much for harmonious coupledom. The baby stirred uneasily, as though upset by his parents' conflict, and he set up a thin wail. 'I'm sick of all this going-on about being Irish and bog-trotting names. We're American, not Irish. And, seeing as I did all the work, and was sick for the whole nine months, don't you think I should've some say in the matter?'

She looked to her mother for confirmation but Belle and she had never had a close relationship. Indeed, their relationship was non-existent. Always had been.

To her constant shame, from the moment of her daughter's birth Belle had felt little warmth towards her. Oh, she had gone through the motions of bringing her up, giving her the best, ensuring her welfare, all the while consoling herself that Mick's passion for their daughter more than made up for her attitude.

Amazingly, in the sterile hospital room with its aseptic green blinds, vinyl floor and crisply laundered bed linen, some obscure psychological adjustment metamorphosed and she felt her love for her grandson spill over to embrace her daughter.

Paddy interjected, 'With Patrick, he'd be called after both of us.'

Patsy fired back, 'And what about your four daughters? You'd none of this going on about their names. Nothing about calling any of them after us.'

Belle could not believe that any wife would speak so to her

husband, especially her own daughter who had never heard her parents raise their voices.

'Well, they were girls.'

'Girls,' Patsy shrieked. 'Don't girls count for anything?'

Paddy looked startled. 'They do. Of course they do.' For one who made his living by communication, there were occasions, particularly when dealing with Patsy, when he could be amazingly obtuse and insensitive.

Patsy was relentless. 'Did you trouble yourself choosing their names? Did you take any interest in them? No, you didn't,' she answered herself. 'Mary Lou, Betty Ann, Sally and Annabel,' she recited, as though he did not know the names of his daughters. 'You didn't care. You were too busy. Always waiting for the boy.'

Belle, unable to believe what she was hearing, amazed by Patsy's lack of control, clutched at her handbag for comfort.

Paddy looked even more startled. He was used to Patsy's outbursts but nothing had prepared him for the venom of this. Of course, he loved his daughters and, of course, he wanted a son. And yes, with the birth of each baby, he had hoped it would be the boy. Wasn't it only natural?

As though from a distance, Belle breaking her policy of non-interference in her daughter and son-in-law's lives, heard herself say, 'How about calling him Jack?'

Paddy looked at his wife. 'Jack Fagan. Jack Fagan,' head nodding, he rolled the name around.

Patsy sat up even straighter, looked into the bassinet. 'Jack. Jack,' she said.

'Jack Fagan,' went Paddy again, after a quick check that his wife approved. 'It has quite a ring it. Doesn't it? Last year Jack Kennedy saved the crew of his torpedo boat. If Jack's a good enough name for the Kennedys, it should be good enough for us too.'

'Jack. After Jack Kennedy, of course. Mummy, you're a genius.' Patsy was all smiles. 'Isn't she, Paddy?'

'I think we're in business,' said Paddy, disappointed that his name would not be carried into posterity, but relieved that his wife, who prided herself on her all-American attitude, would not insist on calling his heir something like Herb or Burt or Al.

As she watched Jack grow from baby to toddler and from boy to man, Belle frequently felt the guardian-like presence of her father.

Through the imagined waft of his Havana, she heard his comfortable Irish murmurings about throwbacks and about traits skipping a generation.

She is so frightened at what may be stirred up by Jack going to Paris. She hates the way fragmented memories tug at her skirts of recall. Goading and prodding as though seeking response, the same way as she remembers pestering her father as a small child, trying to compensate for the mother she had never known.

This mother who, before dying, and even before Bel was born, so her father told her, had whispered, 'Call her Annabel for me.' She never tired of hearing the story, never wondered at its ending had she been a boy.

During the christening of her granddaughter Annabel, Belle had murmured a prayer of gratitude and grief to her long dead mother and in the process felt strangely comforted. Now she wonders and is ashamed at the youthful vanity that had her changing the spelling of her name.

Secrets ruin families she heard a chat-show hostess with thick eyebrows and a beehive hairdo, remark recently on day-time television. Belle knows it to be true. But after all this time can she face the consequences of her carefully constructed existence, like a house of cards, tumbling down around her ears?

This morning when she had woken her four-poster bed seemed vast and pretentious and the peach decor of the room appeared contrived and over-done.

In the avocado bathroom, she caught an unrehearsed sight of herself and for a fleeting moment wondered at the identity of the raddled woman with the morning face and bruised pansy eyes in the too-youthful coffee-and-cream floating negligee.

To avoid further confrontation with her mirrored image, she quickly stepped into the shower. But even the force of its water and the addition of scented unguents with their promises of a permanently moisturised body as well as irresistible desirability did nothing to restore her good humour.

A moisturised nearly seventy-year-old is laughable. A contradiction in terms, she finds herself thinking. It is the kind of clever remark Jack makes. And as for desire, it is so long since that has featured in her life she cannot even remember what it feels like. Yes, she can. She had never forgotten. But she does not remember. She will not allow herself to.

Face gleaming with day-cream, she dithers over her outfit. Sweater and trousers? Skirted two-piece? Light wool suit? Day dress?

With the dawning awareness that her choice of clothes will make no difference to anything or anyone, in a panic she settles on a moss green skirt and a slim-fitting top.

She will feel better with make-up. She always does. But not today. Confronted by the back-lit magnifying mirror, specially installed to ensure faultless application, she is horrified at the crêpe of her eyelids, at the furrows leading to her mouth and at the map of wrinkles above her upper lip. For the first time in her adult life, she leaves the sanctity of her bedroom without her mask of cosmetics.

Since learning of Jacques's death, Belle has had flashes of her real self, her true self, the intrepid young being who existed before she erected her series of protective barriers. The uselessness of her father's precautions and the awful burden he placed on her eat at her.

Pity wells within her. Pity for herself. For her life. And the awful mess her father made of it. Correction. The mess that she allowed her father to make of her life. Despite all his assurances about time telling, time has told Belle nothing. There. She has thought it. Not said it.

Spraying Chanel cologne high in the air and walking into its mist, she doubts she ever will say it.

Not even in a whisper to herself.

Chapter 7

Brigid is disconcerted to discover that Mr Devine is more Gabriel than Lucifer and quite a sight for sore eyes, an Irish expression that readily trips off her tongue, but which around Miss Gray she keeps in tight check. And all those roses. Pity, she thinks, they are so small and so wishy-washy.

Jack has a habit of linking and assessing new surroundings and people. Servant, he presumes, as his door-opener is wearing a white apron.

Hallway. Disappointing. Draughty and unadorned – except for telephone table. Where he is divested of coat and bid to wait while presumed servant enters a door along the corridor. On her return, she motions him to follow.

Salon. Certainly not the showcase he had envisaged. From his position at the doorway, it is the person who dominates, not the simply furnished room.

Eileen Gray, again, he presumes, in classical Whistler's Mother pose, though without the head covering, seated on what he recognises as one of her signature white leather-and-chrome chairs. The *Bibendum*.

Shattering staccato details rather than his usual panoramic images assail him.

He should have known. Of course, he should have. Naturally, she is old. Next-door-to-death old. A veritable female

Methuselah. Subconsciously, he had absurdly presumed that someone capable of designing and creating such magnificent pieces would remain forever frozen in her prime.

His awareness of old age as the natural precursor to dying dates back to the summer he was ten and to the death of his paternal grandmother. She lived upstate and he only saw her twice a year, once when he and his father visited in spring and once during fall when she came to New York to stay with them.

While he knew she was old-woman-elderly, in a way his grandmother Belle was not, slow-moving, thin and frowning with sparse grey hair, black clothes and a lonely dignified manner, he did not associate her with dying. Indeed, he did not associate anyone he knew with ever dying.

That mid-morning summer, he stood looking out of the tiny-paned window of her bedroom. The world outside was unreal. The spotlight of breezy sunshine coming in under the ceiling of cloud was the dream light of no familiar hour of the day. It was the first time he had been in his grandmother's bedroom.

Its walls were covered in faded pink roses, the size of saucers, and hung with the paraphernalia of the Roman Catholic religion. The wooden floor was rag-rugged and the furniture was old, solid and well-polished with protective crochet doilies under the various statues and bottles of holy water.

No sound, except for the torturous drawn-out rasping of her breathing, breached the silence. No frogs. No crickets. No distant train whistles. No squelching automobile tyres on the roadway.

It was as though the universe held its breath, awaiting her next breath.

His parents and himself were on 'watch duty', his father's phrase. Earlier his aunts and uncles, dressed in dark clothes and wearing long faces, had been in and out of the bedroom. Then, for a while, he had heard them tiptoeing around downstairs.

They were gone for now, pleased to abdicate responsibility and to pass on their vigil, if only for a few hours. Paddy fretted that a breaking lead story would not be edited to his exacting standard in time to meet the paper's print deadline. Patsy, irritated at missing a fund-raising lunch, tutted and muttered about it not even being her mother.

Eventually, the two of them left Jack in charge as though it were some rare treat, his father talking about 'responsibility' and his mother instructing him to listen to his Grandma's breathing and to call them if he noticed any change. He heard his parents bickering over the phone, their voices drifting upwards from the airless hallway with its dark wood panelling and bottle-green patterned carpet.

Jack did not know how to be in charge of a dying grandmother, particularly one he hardly knew, but feeling he should do something other than stand and stare, his childish fingers plucked and smoothed the patchwork comforter around the foot of her bed.

He did not want to venture too near the thin, yellow-faced, sunken-eyed creature propped high on the bundle of pillows. He found it scary that she bore so little resemblance to the person who on her last visit a few months ago had taken such an interest in his grades and impressed on him the importance of schooling. 'Education is freedom,' she said. 'With education, you can go anywhere, do anything.'

When it seemed to him that she had not taken a breath in

ages, he risked a sideways look, hoping he would be able to justify calling his parents and handing back this responsibility. He was startled to find her eyes open, staring at him, though without recognition he thought.

Then her tortured breathing rasped again, teeth whistling, nostrils pinching, eyelids fluttering, narrow chest rising and falling. She smiled, a terrifying smile of blackened inner lips and a grey swollen tongue, and he was moved to a pity that had him holding her hand, before progressing to stroking it.

She whispered something. He could not be sure, but it sounded like, 'Don't want to die.' And he looked at her with new compassion. All the time, she kept breathing, her rattling lungs speaking with every breath, 'Not yet', watching him, as she took one agonising gasp after another, 'Not yet,' watching him as the gap between each pant lengthened, 'Not yet.'

Just as he was wondering about giving her a drink or dampening her lips – the knowledge that she needed fluid came from nowhere and yet it had to be from somewhere – like a miracle, what felt like a drop of water fell on his hand. It was followed quickly by another and yet another.

They were drops, all right. But not of water. They were tears.

Grandma was crying, silent, lean tears rolling down her cheeks. Then she smiled again and she gave a little sigh and this time he smiled back and he leaned in closer to stroke her cheek which felt like dried paper.

He thinks he, too, was crying when she drew her last breath.

It was a gentle breath, more of a sigh of resignation, and he knew she had died in peace and he hoped that eventually she would get to this heaven place she was always talking about. But right now, he wanted her back.

He was not frightened. He felt death all around, as some sort of benign presence, peacefully in the room, its fluttering shadow still gently hovering around his Grandma.

He did not think of God. Not then. But afterwards when he thought about that morning, he knew He was there. As a child, he had wished there was a God in their home. But Patsy was relentlessly secular. She believed to be American was quite enough. Paddy, who was indifferent to anything which did not influence his beloved newspapers, found it easier to follow her lead.

Jack sat on the edge of the bed watching this woman who had been his father's mother, fascinated at how, now with the life gone out of her, the lines of tension softened and eased from her features.

He heard Patsy's heels clattering up the stairs. She came into the room, a lit cigarette trailing smoke from between her fingers, and started screaming and kept on screaming.

Even through her racket, he heard his father replace the phone with a loud thunk and thump up the stairs, shouting, 'What's wrong?'

Jack said, 'Nothing,' as his father came through the doorway.

'What do you mean, "nothing"?' Patsy yelled, 'Your grandmother's dead.'

Still, Jack saw nothing wrong with that. She was going to die. Going to die that day. His aunts and uncles and parents not only said it, they wished her death done with. It would be a happy release, they said. She had died. Now it was over. To pretend otherwise was hypocritical. QED, as his geometry master wrote on the board under a completed theorem.

Jack watched as his father stood helplessly, head bowed, his great bulk seeming to cave in on itself. Never before had he seen him so vulnerable and so out of control. He wanted to go to him, to wrap his arms around his waist and to hug and be hugged in return.

But he remained seated on the side of the bed.

Patsy said something about it being for the best. Her voice was gentle, soft and kindly in a way it seldom was.

A moment later his father slipped thumb and forefinger into the breast pocket of his jacket and took out two coins. Shiny Irish half pennies. He gave them a perfunctory rub of his handkerchief, motioned Jack off the bed, leaned in, closed Grandma's eyes by running the palm of his hand down her face, before placing the coins, one on each of her eyelids.

Jack thought it terrible thing to do.

Paddy stood back for a moment, as though admiring his handiwork. Then he took a handkerchief from his pocket, carefully he smoothed it out, folded it into a triangle, doubled it over and repeated the process again and again until he was left with a long strip which he placed under her chin, brought up over her ears and around her head where he tied it in a rabbit's ear knot.

Jack thought that an even more terrible thing to do and he felt sad for Grandma's loss of dignity.

In the meantime Patsy, cigarette extinguished, hands flapping, haphazardly sprinkled Lourdes water on the bed, splashing in a way she would not have dared if Grandma could see her.

She capped the fluted bottle and returned it to the top of the chest of drawers, though not on its doily.

Next she turned her attention to the window, pulling at the handle.

'What are you doing?' Jack asked.

'Opening the window.' With a heave it flew open.

'Why?' Even though Grandma was dead, it was breezy outside and Jack did not like to think of her lying in a draught.

'To let the spirit out.'

'What spirit?' Jack looked around nervously, knowing his mother, half expecting a Hallowe'en type ghoul to materialise from a corner of the room or out of the big closet with its mirrored front.

'Your Grandma's spirit.'

That was okay. That was to do with God. Though? 'Wouldn't it be nice to keep her with us? For a while anyway.'

'Do you hear that, Paddy? Keep your mother's spirit with us! You've a daft son.'

'Don't worry, Patsy. Nor you Ma,' he addressed the figure in the bed. 'If it's the last thing I do, I'll make a man of him.'

At that point Jack became frightened of old age, its downward slide to death, but mostly the awfulness of what other people could do to you after you had died. And, if you were a child, before you died.

When the fragile figure on the white chair turns towards him, Jack is confronted by a caricature of the woman in the photographs, with the addition of thick disfiguring bottle-end glasses.

It seems as though stillness extends forever between them,

yet it must be only a few seconds, until Jack hears the servant say, 'Miss Gray, this is Mr Devine.'

Eileen Gray, though still looking in his direction, appears impervious to his presence.

The social niceties pounded into him during childhood come to his rescue.

'This is a pleasure. At last we meet. And these are for you.' From behind his back he produces with a flourish the exquisitely assembled roses, crackling in their clear cellophane wrapping.

She says nothing, but he reads the slight inclination of her head as acknowledgement. He places the roses on the sofa which is chrome-limbed and covered in dark blue tweed, and gazes around. 'Look at this place? So airy and modern. Clean lines and in such an old building. That spread in *Vogue* didn't do it justice.'

In Eileen's experience, Americans are the only nation who consider it their right to pass personal remarks on anything that takes their fancy and she is no longer impressed by what has been written about her decades ago. 'You're well informed, Mr Devine,' she says dryly. 'But don't think I'm taken in by flattery.'

Jack refuses to be put off. He settles himself opposite, and banteringly replies, 'I guess you've been flattered by the greatest minds of this century.'

'Yes, Mr Devine, I presume I have. And those who visited had the courtesy to wait to be invited before sitting.'

Whoops. Jack is amazed at her quick-witted strength. Hard to credit that she must be twenty years his grandmother's senior.

He decides he will play Eileen Gray along. Slowly. Flatter

her, draw her out. Say nothing about the profile. Her defensive attitude is not conducive to explanations nor to producing the tape recorder. Perhaps later her mood will mellow.

He had planned to be up front about this interview. To fill her in on its background. To make it a joint effort. But not now. He does a quick re-think of his strategy and decides to say nothing. But he is uncomfortable. Subterfuge and this sort of pretence is not his way.

He wonders about mentioning his grandmother. He was sure such a connection would be an icebreaker, but when put to her, as only Belle could, she had been passively resistant. And he suspects Eileen Gray could be equally unreceptive.

Jack stretches out his long legs, 'Tell me, Eileen, how do you fill your days?'

Another space filled with stillness seems to expand forever until he wonders if she heard his question.

She sits up straighter, touches her thick, still curly hair, its natural greyness softening her features.

'You may address me as Miss Gray.' Her tone is the personification of politeness.

From the sideline, Brigid is sadly aware of her mistress's determination to keep control. At her age, she should be taking things easy, resting, not putting herself through this.

Jack feels like a small boy with his hand caught in the cookie jar but he determines to recoup. When he speaks again his tone is deferential. 'Miss Gray, may I ask again. 'How do you fill your days?' The words are out for the second time before he realises it is hardly a question on which a journalistic scoop will be built.

She sits a little straighter, answers proudly and concisely. 'By remembering my designs and by creating more.' Jack breathes easier. 'My designs have stretched me to my creative limits. And I know they have succeeded because they have stood the test of time. To borrow your phrase. Become modern antiques.'

'How does an item become a modern antique?' Jack asks. He has often wondered at the co-relationship between design, materials, timing and the fickleness of the various markets.

She thinks for a moment. 'I believe it to be primarily a matter of multi-directional and multi-functional design. After that, it's up to the buying public.'

Trying to remember her precise words, he casts around for a suitably intelligent follow-up question but all he comes out with is, 'I guess in your day, you met everyone of importance.' Dammit. From what he can recall from his notes, that question came much further down his list.

'And when, Mr Devine, would you consider my day?'

Fragile as it was, he has broken their rapport. 'I didn't mean . . .'

Dryly she says, 'I'm sure you didn't.'

'We Americans are big into VIPs.' He tries the jocose route.

'And what are VIPs?'

'Very important people. Like yourself.'

Her gnarled hands flutter. 'It's my work that's important. Not me. Nor who I am. Or who I've met. My designs were my light. Whereas I always thought of my personal life as being in the shadows.'

'Your designs – your light. Your personal life shadowed. I like it.'

What she is saying makes sense. He too, as a child and as an adult since the break-up with Elvira, feels his personal life to be shadowed.

Quotes such as these, will give an added an authentic edge to his profile. But no way will he remember them verbatim.

He will have to risk the recorder. With those thick glasses, her sight must be poor. From the pocket of his jacket he eases out the machine.

'Mr Devine, what's that you have?' It is that damned servant. Some servant to behave in this manner!

He turns around, glares at her, she looks back at him, fat and unblinking, and repeats the question.

Eileen agitates. 'What is it, Brigid, what's wrong?'

'It's just a little tape recorder,' Jack soothes. 'To take notes. I didn't think you'd mind.'

'Miss Gray will not permit.'

Eileen interjects, 'Absolutely not, Mr Devine.'

'Perhaps it would be better if Mr Devine were to leave?'

Even in America, the supposed land of the free, subordinates did not speak out like this.

Again that nerve-racking stillness stretches between the two of them.

Eileen regrets the impetuosity of her invitation. Craving company and the opportunity to discuss her work, she viewed the timing of Jack Devine's second phone call as fate and she has always admired perseverance.

Finally Eileen speaks but it is Brigid she addresses. 'Mr Devine may remain. On the understanding that there will be no taping.'

'And Miss Gray will only talk about her work,' interjects Brigid severely.

Jack holds up his hands, in a sign of peace. 'Okay. Okay.' Keeping it light, he makes a big production of fully returning the machine to his pocket but positioning it so that he will be able to easily access the On button.

No way can he afford to give up on those quotes.

Sitting a little straighter in her chair, Eileen slips into the role of hostess. 'Now, Brigid, you may fetch the wine.' When Brigid leaves the room, with a suspicious backward glance at Jack, Eileen graciously asks, 'Tell me, Mr Devine, do you have a favourite piece of mine?

'Jack, please. It's what my family and friends call me.'

Eileen returns to autocratic mode, it is one of the ways she ensures control and covers up the feelings of vulnerability which advancing age has brought in its droves. 'And I'm more comfortable with formality.' Her accent is cut glass and her statement has such finality that Jack feels his heart sink. He has got off on the wrong foot.

But could there ever be a right foot with somebody like her, a woman of such power and talent? She must have been wonderfully vital and dynamic, superb company in her day. Wicked, too, if crossed, he suspects.

'Point taken, Miss Gray.' He puts a definite emphasis on his last two words. 'I came across your work when I bought one of your Transaat chairs some months ago. But since seeing *Le Destin* – though only a photograph and a bad reproduction, at that, I'm fascinated and I'd sure love to hear how you came to create it.'

Even though he uses his grandmother's terminology of creation, he doubts the accuracy of her recall.

Eileen pauses, smiles in reminiscence, pleats at the grey rug across her knees. 'Yes, *Le Destin* was a creation. And you're the only person who has ever said so. Probably, other than my friend, Jacques Doucet, who has ever realised it.

I had the idea for the screen, but it was he who encouraged me.'

Jack breathes a sigh of relief. Back on track. But he is listening so intently trying to remember quotes that he is missing out on essence of Eileen's content. He has to record. He reaches into his pocket and surreptitiously switches on.

'My lacquer period, as I think of it, was one of the most rewarding times of my life. The forerunner to everything else. It was then I discovered that to create anything, one must first question everything.'

'Mmm. Questioning everything before you create. Interesting. I never heard it put quite that way before.'

That quote is strong enough to open his profile.

'I understand lacquering is a difficult and complicated process.' It was a statement more than a question.

'Well, I had Sugawara. He taught me all I know.'

'Yes, of course, the Japanese artist.'

Eileen looks at her guest with interest. She has never suffered what she considers fools gladly. 'You're well informed, Mr Devine.'

'As I said, I've been a fan of your work since the day I first discovered it. And you must be pleased at the record set by *Le Destin*.'

Brigid, standing in the doorway with the tray, catches her breath.

Drat.

She should have known.

She had known that no good would come out of this Mr Devine's visit.

What does he want, causing upset like this. Her hope that, perhaps, Miss Gray will not register the information is dashed.

'What are you talking about?'

'Jacques Doucet's estate.' Jack looks puzzled. 'Surely you knew, the screen was auctioned at the beginning of the week? It's because of the news coverage the story received in America that I learned of you and your whereabouts,' he finishes not quite truthfully.

Eileen's sharp intake of breath and deathly paleness reminds him of his grandmother's reaction.

He wonders at the profound effect of Jacques Doucet on these two such different women.

Chapter 8

Within a few weeks, Jacques found premises for a lacquering workshop on the top floor of a building on rue Guénégaud, within easy walking distance of Eileen's apartment.

With his usual calm acceptance of what life offered, Sugawara moved without comment. But Eileen bubbled. She saw the move as yet another step towards artistic fulfilment. She was as enthusiastic about the building, area and benefits of relocation as though it were she who had not only thought up the idea but made the arrangements.

Unsure of what she wanted from her life but irrevocably drawn towards the artistic, Eileen Gray was one of the first women to enrol in the Slade School of Fine Arts in Chelsea. After just a few lectures and classes, she realised it was not for her.

'I hate the place, Mama. Just hate it.'

Startled by her daughter's venom, Eveleen looked up from her embroidery frame where she was satin-stitching a parrot with red, blue and yellow plumage. 'Why?' she asked calmly. Calmness, she had learned, was the best way to deal with her impetuous youngest.

'Everything's wrong. It's too formal, the tutors are pretentious, the students are unfriendly. And I've no talent,' she finished on a wail.

Eveleen stifled a smile of relief, pleased Eileen would not be following in her father's footsteps. She hoped that with this painting nonsense out of her system, Eileen might conform, might take her place in society. 'So what will you do?'

'Move to Paris. Find my artistic direction,' said Eileen loftily, gathering up her portfolio, various sketch pads and a bundle of pencils and paint brushes.

The thought of Eileen loose in Paris was much worse than Eileen attending classes at the Slade. Stalling for time, Eveleen executed a neat back stitch before slowly cutting the thread. One wing completed. Next she would tackle the parrot's beak which she would work in varying shades of grey. 'That's not possible.' Even as she spoke, she knew that everything and anything was possible in Eileen's world.

During her first months in Paris, Eileen did nothing more strenuous than soak up atmosphere, wander the streets, attend exhibitions of painting, sculpture, ceramics and textiles, and dine with friends.

She was certain that sooner or later, artistic inspiration would strike and when it did not, she travelled to more exhibitions in Germany, Holland and Switzerland.

Her muse did appear. But it was more of a gradual awakening than the bolt out of the blue she had anticipated.

Decorative art.

It was like coming home.

She threw herself into the process of familiarisation, analysing concept, design and execution; soaking up articles and photographs in journals, devouring textbooks, and talking to the experts. The more she discovered the more she realised that it was the simple elegance of Japanese and Chinese lacquer work that attracted her.

There was so much for her to learn that she had no idea of where to start.

On an extended duty visit to London to see her mother, whose health had deteriorated, Eileen happened on an outlet in Dean Street. Surrounded by the artistic bustle of Chelsea, she looked in the sightless windows, then up at the black fascia board which announced in gold lettering that the premises was owned by a Mr D. Charles, specialist in the repair of antique lacquer screens.

Decorative art. Narrowed down to Japanese and Chinese lacquer work. What had been wishful thinking began to germinate and within minutes was a full-blown solution.

She grinned delightedly and executed a little jig of joy. While caring for her mother, she could serve her apprenticeship in lacquering. In the face of Eileen's determined eagerness, Mr Charles had little choice but to take her on.

After a year of grinding application, but during which her mother's health improved, Eileen was devastated to discover that she had merely acquired a working knowledge of the basics of lacquering. 'It's one thing to know how to do it, it's another thing to do it,' she wrote in despair to Jacques.

Refusing to be beaten, she returned to Paris armed with samples of materials and a list of contacts.

She engineered a meeting with Seizo Sugawara, a Japanese expert in lacquering, who had fallen so in love with Paris that he remained on after completion of his work for the 1900 Exposition.

'I want you to teach me the advanced techniques, innermost

secrets and creative intricacies of lacquering,' Eileen earnestly explained.

Politely and with a little bow, he informed her that such aspirations were not possible.

Undeterred, she persuaded him to take her on as a pupil, and she set up what she humorously referred to as the lacquer workshop, including a divan for him, in one room of her apartment.

'I was interested to discover that lacquer is the resin from the *Rhus verniciflua* or *Rhus succedanea* trees,' she announced during one of their first sessions. From childhood observations and from adult perceptions, she knew that knowledge was power.

Absorbed in painting a small panel, it was as though he did not hear her.

She tried again, this time speaking a little louder. Still he did not respond. His head stayed bowed to his task and from what she could see of his expression, it remained inscrutable.

That he was the deep speechless type, wrapped in his craft, an expert who went in for practical demonstration rather than wordy theory, rather pleased her. Yet she knew that for her to learn, she would have to find a way to unlock his knowledge and a means of breaking his silence.

Minutes ticked past before he spoke. Without raising his eyes from the simple black dish he was rubbing down prior to applying another coat of lacquer, he answered, 'Yes. And those trees grow only in the Far East.'

She sighed dramatically, determined to keep up her end of the conversation. 'So much knowledge to be acquired and so many problems to be overcome.'

Sugawara answered simply, 'Yes.'

Eileen would have liked a bit of encouragement and assurance but from the little she knew of the man, she suspected neither would be forthcoming. Now that she had his attention, she asked, 'What do you consider to be the main problems of lacquering?'

She sat on a small stool, arms wrapped around her knees.

Last night, during the small hours, she had woken up and in that drifting limbo between sleep and wakefulness, where truth is untarnished and reality crisp, she realised the enormity of the task she had set herself.

She wanted to bury her head under the clothes and go back to drawing Slade school nudes; tour the South of France in her new roadster; drift away in a balloon across the eternal skyscape; even return to London to live with her mother.

She got out of bed, wrapped herself in the swan's down duvet, walked to the window, pulled back the shutters, looked out through the downpour on her inner courtyard, thought of all the small worlds of rain on the glossy green leaves of her plants, and knew then that she could and would crack lacquering.

People and their motivations fascinated Eileen. She had that knack of making them feel important by finding their area of engrossment and drawing them out.

Sugawara was no exception. Despite his natural and national humility, he was flattered by this great lady's obeisance to both his craft and to himself.

'Impurities are the biggest problem,' he answered after only a short pause. 'But correct filtering removes imperfections.'

'Can lacquer be coloured?'

'Yes, once purified it can be left clear or mixed with colour pigments.'

She sighed with relief. This morning, the business of lacquering and the complexities of her relationship with Sugawara assumed a new manageability.

Gradually, she learned when to draw out Sugawara and when to leave him in silence to work.

Impulsive, dynamic and impatient by nature, on occasions she found the meticulous and detailed process of lacquering alien both to her and to the changing pace of western life of which she was an enthusiastic participant, though never again did she consider giving up.

Adopting the academic approach alongside the practical one, she filled page after page and notebook after notebook with information on the use of pumice stones, powdered stone, charcoal and other rubbing-down materials. She also recorded the processes of whitening wood, making plaster of Paris moulds and achieving textured surfaces.

So began months of intensive trial and error practising on small objects, such as bowls, plates, jars and panels in relief. Conscientiously, she charted her successes and failures, noting that lacquer applied too thickly rippled; discovering that the addition of natural dye resulted in a variety of different colours and tones. But no matter what combinations and variables she experimented with, blue, her favourite colour, eluded her.

The international experts maintained that as green always crept in and dominated, it was not possible to achieve a pure blue. With her usual stubbornness, Eileen persisted, testing and re-testing variations of powder and tube Prussian blue. Eventually, 'using a new chemical substance', as she later recorded – she refused to divulge further – she achieved a rich dark blue. Royal blue.

Though secretly pleased at her pioneering status, Eileen refused to be drawn into the commercial world of commissions and clients. Adamantly, she declined to execute the popular shiny pieces. Instead, she worked on designs of her choice and at her own pace.

In Paris lacquer, along with the flamboyant Art Nouveau and Tiffany styles, had become a fashionable passion.

It was a phenomenon which Eileen and Jacques frequently discussed.

One midday, strolling along the Champs-Elysées, escorted by her latest pack of yapping stray dogs, each with a colourful leather leash and matching diamanté studded collar, apropos of nothing, she remarked to him, 'I'm not interested in either dressing fashionably or in doing fashionable work, though I do consider myself quite passionate.'

She was dressed in classic Chanel. A slim-fitting frock in subtle aquamarine, its square neckline softened by her signature propeller scarf and favourite rope of pearls.

Jacques stopped mid-stride, amazed at the unexpected turn in conversation. 'Passionate? Really?'

She paused too, looked at him through her eyelashes from underneath the brim of her cloche. She could interpret his silences, read his gestures. As a child she had developed that skill. With Jacques she had effortlessly picked it up again, rather like an almost-forgotten musical instrument. Those endearing small gestures of his, inconspicuous to outsiders but filled with meaning for her. Throaty sounds, indicating pleasure or fatigue. The warm smile. 'Yes, I'm passionate.' She paused. 'Very passionate about my work.'

He laughed agreeably. He should have known. Eileen was a bit of a tease, but she was an innocent in the art of flirting.

She filled his thoughts. Despite her casual attitude towards relationships, he sensed smouldering passion and hoped some day it might ignite in his direction. He was experienced enough to bide his time. Changing the subject but not too much, he replied, 'I know. Personally, I've always thought style to be more your thing. But your dogs are the ultimate fashion symbols.'

'Hardly.'

'There aren't many dogs – even thoroughbreds – with such chic jackets. Designer materials and the best of fur.'

'Remnants and scraps,' she justified. 'Poor pets,' she hunkered down to address them. 'If Jacques had his way, you'd still be on the streets.'

They barked agreement, jumping around her, mouths opened in wide smiles and tails wagging in furious delight.

'Damn right. They would.' There was no malice in his tone but he often urged her, if she had to have dogs, to consider pedigrees. They walked a few yards further. Jacques broke their silence by, as usual, reverting to business. 'I advise you to take advantage of this trend for lacquer work. It won't last for ever. Be even a little passionately commercial.'

Eileen did not reply.

As usual, she went her own way. Her work remained distinctive, recognisable by its minimalistic austerity and low-key richness. Some was in traditional black, more in earthy browns and brilliant reds and, of course, blue.

On occasions, she added silver or gold leaf, inlaid mother-of-pearl, lapus lazli, coral and semi-precious stones before covering the whole with a fine coat of lacquer which, as she wrote into her notes, required to be the consistency of 'a thin coat of honey'.

Being Eileen and being volatile, she allowed herself the luxury of losing her temper and railing. She groused when lacquering's relentless pernicketiness got to her. 'I've to do twenty, sometimes forty coats and on the both sides to prevent warping,' she grumbled one crisp spring afternoon to Sugawara.

He paused, lifted his head and looked directly at her. 'I know. And that,' he said, 'is the cost of perfection. And it's small price to pay for the work you're doing.'

It was the greatest compliment Eileen had ever received, just as *Le Destin* was her greatest creation.

For almost a year, she searched for the perfect subject for her screen but it eluded her and she refused to settle for less.

Then, browsing without particular intent, on a warm afternoon, she came across a simply-framed pen and ink drawing hanging in the shadows in a little-known gallery in Montmartre. After the briefest of glances, she knew she had found her subject.

It was neither allegorical nor mythological.

The drawing was of a madman incarcerated in La Salpetrière hospital; it was unsigned, though it was dated July 1892.

The humanity of the man's insanity and his pain touched her emotions in the way she knew would release her creativity.

Sitting in the gallery's only chair, notebook resting on navy-skirted knee, she sketched a quick likeness. Then, her head reeling with ideas and images, instead of wandering back at leisure to her apartment as was her custom, she got the Metro for speed. But that afternoon it took for ever.

In the hot summer silence of her workroom, she rested

the sketch on her easel and stepped back in pencil-tapping assessment.

Within a few seconds, she had it.

Visual inspiration on feverish boil, she clipped in a fresh sheet of paper, and with broad strokes, she outlined two figures.

Nude figures.

With the addition of a few more strokes, one shape became a slight youth who of his own volition seemed to dance off the page, the other was sturdier, probably older, the sensible one; it was to him that she designated the task of carrying the man from La Salpetrière, as proprietarily she thought of him, and whom she delicately wrapped in a pencilled shroud.

Dead, she knew, he was beyond pain, but clothed, she felt, he regained a modicum of the dignity denied him in life.

The images shimmered, as though pulsating with lives as independent as she willed her own. Powerful silhouettes, heightened by the minimalistic simplicity of design. Ordinary, yet esoteric.

She was returned to the present by the bim, bom, boom of Notre Dame. Midnight. Unknown and unaware to her, breathless afternoon had evolved to sultry twilight before finally settling into stifling night.

She stood back and inhaled a hot breath of relief.

She exhaled in grateful slow motion.

It was as she wished.

Wearing that deep flush of creative contentment, she felt smile after smile break out around her lips. For a fleeting moment she wished she had someone with whom to celebrate but she quickly dismissed the idea as quite ridiculous.

The movement of the nude figures and the immobility

of the man from La Salpetrière would be immortalised in blue, highlighted with the merest suggestion of silver. As she had planned from thought stage, the background would be brilliant red and the reverse side of the screen would have abstracts of swirling lines.

Le Destin was a project long in creation but one which gave her the greatest of pleasure. Sometimes during the small hours of the night, alone in her workroom, lacking sleep, eyes blurring and focusing with difficulty, sustaining herself on squares of chocolate, it felt as though this screen was her life's purpose, as though from birth it had been her destiny.

She returned to the screen again and again, as a labour of love refining, redefining and improving design and colours, reluctant to see it completed.

Often she wondered would she ever be satisfied enough to let it go.

Her creativity, once harnessed, had flowed towards completion and, as Jacques had predicted at that quayside café, in the end, the technicalities which at thinking stage concerned her posed little problem.

From experience, she knew that the application of lacquer was the real skill test. Days of drying between each coat, and in between, the rubbing down which she did with a film of charcoal on the sensitive palm of her hand so that she could pick up on the slightest imperfection.

As the layers built up, the screen took on a further secret life of its own. Inward enhancement by outward luminosity.

Then one day it was finished and even she knew its perfection could not be improved upon.

'*Tempe à Paille*,' murmured Jacques, who had followed

every twist and convoluted turn of the process with faith and encouragement. And growing admiration and love for Eileen.

She turned to him, with her Mona Lisa smile, and wrinkled her nose. 'And what do you mean by that?'

'Time and straw,' he said. 'An old Provençal proverb about the fig needing time and straw to ripen.'

She hooted laughter. 'What am I, a fig? Or a piece of straw?'

He joined in her merriment.

'More like time and destiny, don't you think?'

He agreed. She had conquered her lacquer beast and reached a pinnacle of perfection he had not thought possible. For months she had been absorbed in the job; now the fun-loving Eileen had returned. Tonight they would celebrate.

With economical movements, she began tidying her tools, gathering the brushes for cleaning.

'Sign it,' said Jacques.

'You know I never sign my work.'

'And you know I don't buy unsigned pieces.'

'What do you mean?'

'What do you think I mean?'

She knew, but she did not want to hear. Now that *Le Destin* was completed, she was reluctant to part with it, though since leaving Brownswood she had trained herself to have no attachment to possessions. But this was different, this was a creation into which she had poured her very soul.

'Did you know the best lacquer brushes are made from the hair of Japanese fishermen?' she prevaricated.

'No, I didn't.'

She sighed. 'You want it?' She thought of it as a compliment. Not to her. But as a worthy epitaph for the man from La Salpetrière. Jacques was only interested in the acquisition of the most perfect and the most beautiful of possessions.

'I want to buy it. It is one of the most exquisite pieces I've ever seen. It will form the centrepiece of my new collection.'

'Your new collection?'

'Yes.' Despite his sophistication, on occasions Jacques could be like a little boy with a new spinning top. 'I'm going to clear out, sell on and concentrate on the best of modern.'

'Sell everything?'

'Yes. The lot.'

'Your paintings? Furniture? Porcelain?' Eileen was amazed. Among the cognoscenti, Jacques was almost as well known for amassing the best of eighteenth-century fine arts as he was for his twice-yearly fashion collection.

Jacques nodded. He ran the palm of his hand lovingly over the surface of the screen, lingering for a moment, protectively, on the shrouded old man, and with the tip of his index finger he outlined the slighter figure.

Despite her misgivings at parting with the screen, she knew he would be a worthy owner.

He turned to her. 'You must be so proud. This is the culmination of your career.'

The brain plays odd tricks. Draws incredible conclusions from the random linking of apparently unconnected thoughts.

Eileen looked into Jacques's eyes which were full of love. It was like finding the other half of her creative self, the perfect reflection. They were two souls who had discovered each other and in *Le Destin* become one.

Without him and *Le Destin*, she would only be a shadow of herself.

The knowledge unnerved her.

A question flickered at Jacques, lurked on his lips.

Jacques is going to ask you to marry him, Colette had stated in that dogmatic way of hers only last week.

Jacques hesitated and Eileen rushed in, 'I'm proud, really delighted with it.'

Jacques's moment was diffused.

She knew her next creative step should be a project that she would hold on to, which would indelibly leave her mark on the world. She had often thought how much she would like to build a house. A home for herself. But Jacques was saying, 'And now, chérie, the time has come for you to realise your dream and to open your own gallery.' He was right. Her dream was a gallery.

The idea of her building a house was preposterous.

Some days later she signed the screen and, when Jacques paid her fifteen hundred francs, the transaction felt sacred, rather like a betrothal contract.

Chapter 9

'Some wine, Mr Devine?'

After the initial shock of learning of the sale of *Le Destin* and the disposal of the remainder of Jacques's collection, Eileen has composed herself – hers is a less emotional, less dramatic a response than Belle's. While her childhood and natural reticence was a natural training ground for the repression of her feelings, over her lifetime she has further schooled herself to face up, to analyse and to accept.

While she still flew, regularly she took to the skies for therapy.

For a long time now, she has only been able to retreat upwards in her mind.

This afternoon, in her imagination, she returns to the skies. With Mr Devine sitting unsuspectingly opposite, she grieves for Jacques's death, for the disbursement of his collection and she finally accepts the permanent loss of *Le Destin*.

'Red, please,' Jack answers.

'A pastry?'

'Thanks, no, I don't have a sweet tooth. But I'll have some of these.' He reaches towards the tray of canapés with enthusiasm. The ducks' liver pâté on those curls of melba toast look particularly tasty. He takes three.

Brigid places a slice of truffle chocolate cake with a pastry fork on the table in front of Eileen who waves it away. 'No,' she says, 'I'll just have the wine.' With reduced sight, one learns to compromise, especially when eating in company. Brigid knows she will enjoy the cake later.

This meeting is not progressing as Jack had hoped. He finds Eileen wary, rigidly disciplined, as though waiting for some disaster to strike. The woman who created *Le Destin* has to have a soul. The recorder lies heavily in his pocket. He has turned it off, with just the few worthy quotations.

'I guessed wrong,' he says conversationally, munching on his last canapé.

'What do you mean?'

'I'd guessed afternoon tea. It's an institution with you British, isn't it?'

'I'm Irish. Not British.'

Whoops, Jack thought. I've done it again.

Despite being American – and Eileen supposes he cannot help that – there is something almost appealing about this Jack Devine.

Though he is right about the afternoon tea.

The ceremony of afternoon tea was an integral part of Eileen's childhood. Paper thin crustless cucumber and tomato sandwiches, tiny scones with strawberry jam and clotted cream, as well as fingers of porter cake.

As the youngest, she often accompanied her mother to the great houses around Enniscorthy. Wearing her best frock, boots and crochet stockings and with her hair dressed in fat auburn ringlets, she practised at being a model daughter, but still her mother ignored her.

Eventually, Eileen reached the stage where she would have found maternal attention disconcerting. While her mother and whomever she was visiting gossiped, she whiled away the time looking around at the different décors, furnishings, fabrics and artefacts, most of which she disliked for being too dark, too big and too heavy.

On her first visit to Miss Florence Corbett, she discovered that she favoured light, bright and minimalistic. It was the year after her father had left Brownswood to live permanently in Italy. Eileen was eleven.

Notwithstanding the economic importance of the Pounden family to Wexford county and their commitment, charity and dedication to the local community, as a woman seen as publicly abandoned by her husband, Eveleen had lost much of her former status.

Previously she had so many engagements that she could afford to politely decline Miss Corbett's twice-yearly invitations which now, in view of her non-existent social life, she was grateful to accept.

Miss Corbett was small, spry and sharp-featured, with dove-grey hair, keen blue eyes and the beginning of a tremor in her hands. Her history was unknown, though it was said she had been the mistress of the Lord Lieutenant up in Dublin Castle. But that was only rumour-mongering. Nobody in the town or surrounding parish knew anything about her.

One February afternoon, twenty-five years before Eveleen and Eileen came to tea, Florence appeared off the train at Enniscorthy station, as though out of nowhere. Standing on the platform, full of smoke and hissing steam, she looked around to get her bearings. Shivering as much from fear of the unknown as from the cold, she pulled her dark green cloak more closely around her and raised its hood in a futile effort at protection from the elements.

Snowflakes a shade lighter than the snow-coloured sky began to fall in quantity. With a manic rattle of wheels on tracks, the train left the station. Snow webbed and frosted the corners of the waiting room windows where she lingered, huddled over the tiny fire, one small valise at her feet. After an hour when nobody had come, she left the station.

Towards the west she could see the clouds breaking up and she took as a good omen the shades of lavender and robin's egg blue which marked the cutting edge of the latest cold front. Footsteps, including her own, stitched the pristine white snow and marked the tired twilight streets of the town.

She took up residence in the three-storey over basement red-brick house which waited in readiness. It had lain vacant for the previous two years, though for the past six months a fleet of carpenters, painters and wall paper hangers had been coming and going in a flurry of renovation and decoration, busy creating the perfect setting to accommodate both Miss Florence Corbett and the finest quality furnishings, carpets and drapes.

Once installed, she employed two girls from the town and opened her home to the local gentry and their wives who initially repaid her offer of hospitality by staying away in their droves. Eventually curiosity, and Florence's growing reputation as a hostess of discernment, got the better of the women, and her invitations began to be accepted.

At her musical afternoon teas, she played the pianoforte like an angel, made intelligent conversation and served the daintiest of sandwiches, the lightest of sponge cakes, the crumbliest of shortbread and the fruitiest of cakes. Her coffee was strong and aromatic and her tea smokily delicate.

Despite herself, all those years later, Eveleen was impressed and even more so when she learned that the baking and sandwich-making had been carried out by their hostess. In the early days of her marriage in Italy, Eveleen had found fulfilment in the intimacy of shopping, cooking, creating and eating.

Miss Corbett's house quite delighted Eileen. The drawing room had plain yellow walls, wooden floors, a minimum of pale furniture, untasseled, unpelmeted and unswagged curtains in deep, almost navy blue, a colour of which Eileen was inordinately fond, in a material, which to her unknowledgeable eyes, looked like a coarse wool. Later she discovered it was called tweed and originated in Scotland.

The overall impression was one of light airy spaciousness. It made her feel peaceful.

Miss Corbett's few ornaments were spaced and individually displayed to show them off to prime advantage. After a good look around, Eileen decided that her very favourite was rather like a soup plate, shiny black and unadorned, except for the hint of a trellis of the palest of pink flowers nestling between the soft green leaves which bordered its edge.

After staring transfixed for a while, she got up from her chair and walked over to where the plate hung on the wall. With hands clasped behind her back, she stood looking.

'You like it?' Miss Corbett asked, joining her.

'Yes,' she nodded, hating the way her ringlets and that silly bow on top of her head bounced each time she moved, though she was glad to be wearing her blue dress from Paris.

'Really, Eileen,' admonished Eveleen, her mouth tight. She

was curvily built, with high-cheekbones and fine eyes. 'Do remember your manners.'

'Oh, but I do, Mama. I do.'

For one of the few times in her life Eveleen was aware, really aware, of her youngest daughter as a person in her own right. Now in the early budding stages of womanhood, she would never be more beautiful nor more vulnerable.

In many ways, Eileen reminded Eveleen of her young self, though a stronger more complete version. She offered a silent wish that her daughter's life would be happy and fulfilled.

Eileen was cut from a different mould to her other children.

Like her maternal grandfather who never minced words, Eileen was recklessly honest. Straight and true like a young sapling, Eveleen thought. Even as a small child, when caught red-handed doing something forbidden, she would blurt out the truth rather than lie, prevaricate or justify.

This honesty factor was a childhood trait which Eveleen was certain would translate into the making of an adult of great integrity. Her daughter, she forecasted, would be a woman in her own right. Even recognising all of this, Eveleen still felt no warmth for Eileen.

'Would you like to eat your sandwiches off that plate?' Miss Corbett asked Eileen.

'Oh, yes, please.'

Only yesterday Sadie had complained to Eveleen of Eileen's refusal to eat either bread or eggs. Indeed, she had listed milk, meat and vegetables too, though she had remarked that if she got it, which she did not, Miss Eileen would eat chocolate 'until the cows came home'.

'What a well-behaved girl she is,' enthused Miss Corbett, reaching upwards on her tippy-toes.

Eveleen nodded unenthusiastically and wondered how soon they could make their escape. After a quick rub down the side of her skirt, their hostess put two egg sandwiches on the plate before handing it to Eileen who devoured them with gusto.

Recognising that conversation between the two adults was becoming increasingly stilted, Eileen waited until she had swallowed the last morsel of bread. Practising best manners, she thanked Miss Corbett. Then, running her thumb around the flowery border, she asked, 'It's china, isn't it? Real china?' She had a hunger to know, she collected information the way other girls of her age saved and stuck coloured scraps into scrapbooks.

Miss Corbett beamed. 'Yes, and it's more than a hundred years old. It's bone china. My grandmother's.' She stood with her back to the window, framed in the glow of low winter sunlight.

Eileen gave a thin shriek and dropped the plate. Bone china. Shattered shards scattered in all directions. A plate made from bones. Miss Corbett's grandmother's bones. She felt sick at the thought of actually eating egg sandwiches off an old lady's leg or perhaps her arm.

There is a familiarity about this Jack Devine that curls at the edges of Eileen's mind. She wishes she could see him clearly. His body language and general attitude remind her of somebody. The feeling is uncomfortable, like a niggling mental itch.

'Brigid, perhaps Mr Devine would like to see photographs of some of my completed projects.'

'May I ask is that one of your projects?' Jack points to a silver-framed photograph on the mantel.

'That's Jean Désert.'

'That's right, of course,' Jack remembers a feature about her gallery in the press clippings. In his initial sweep of the room the photograph of the low-slung building supported by Romanesque columns had looked familiar. 'Your retail outlet.'

'Yes, in rue du Fauborg-St-Honoré, one of the loveliest parts of Paris.'

As Jacques had so often said, having her own gallery was to be the realisation of Eileen's dream. Something by which she could leave her mark on the world.

'Why did you call it Jean Désert? Why not Eileen Gray?'

Eileen shrugs. 'What's in a name?' she asks Jack. It is the same question that she had asked Colette nearly fifty years ago.

Colette, hair newly hennaed, had been apoplectic, ranting at how difficult it was for women to be taken seriously in today's predominantly male workforce. And now here was someone of Eileen's design calibre and national, indeed growing international, reputation setting up a business and hiding behind a man's name. Throwing away an ideal opportunity to strike a blow for women's freedom and to assert herself.

'I am free and I don't need to assert myself,' Eileen had protested mildly. 'I take full responsibility for both my conscious and unconscious.' At the time she was deep into the theories of Carl Jung.

The philosophies of vociferous Paris-based feminists such as Gertrude Stein were not for her. She considered all this new-fangled going-on about liberation to be quite nonsensical. Liberation, she believed, was a state of mind, available to anyone who wanted it.

She was regularly invited and regularly refused invitations to various literary salons hosted by free-thinking influential women, many of whom were writers and artists, ahead of their time, playing a historically serious role in the early evolution of women's liberation.

'No, of course, you don't need to assert yourself. But still . . .'

'Have you seen them in the Café de Flore wearing black tailored suits with white gloves and white silk scarves. Sipping martinis?' Despite herself, Eileen was wound up.

'No, I haven't,' said Colette, intrigued, wondering were they there now. She hated to miss out on new trends, loved being at the centre of current happenings.

'Typical American show-offs,' said Eileen dismissively.

'Could be fun?'

'I can think of many other ways of having fun.'

'Was Jean Désert someone you knew?' Jack probes.

'Well . . . yes and no.' With a start, Eileen realises that, all those years ago, Colette had been right about naming the gallery. 'In the 1920s, it wasn't usual for women, other than dressmakers or milliners, to run businesses under their own name. Jacques suggested I use my title, but I decided against it. My compromise was to use a man's popular name. And I'd travelled the desert, even slept for several nights under the stars, and loved it. So, Jean Désert.'

When the perfect property in the perfect location came up for lease, opposite the newly built concert hall, the Salle Plyel, once again Eileen felt fate step in. The same fate which had procured her apartment and directed her towards the gallery in Montmartre where she had found her man from La Salpetrière.

'I'm going to paint the façade of the gallery black,' she told Jacques.

'The whole length of it? Are you sure?'

They were standing on the opposite side of the street looking across at the newly acquired building. 'Yes. Definitely.'

'It's very long.'

'I know. And to counteract its length, I'm going to widen the windows as much as possible.'

'Eileen, I don't think . . .' Jacques worried that she was approaching the business of this gallery with an artistic rather than a commercial attitude.

'You don't have to think, Jacques. I'm doing the thinking, I know what I'm doing.'

He doubted it, but he let her. He had little choice. Eileen was stubborn. When she got hold of an idea to do with her work, there was no reasoning with her. But then he was creative enough himself to have taken to heart that quotation of Epictetus about the enemy of excellence being the desire to please. No question of that being the case with Eileen.

She stood, totally absorbed, with clipboard making copious notes, as wrapped up in this project as she had been in lacquering. 'I'm going to frame the windows with white curtains. And lacquer most of the interior in white. And blue slabs of glass will bring light into the basement.'

The official opening of Jean Désert took place on a glorious May afternoon. It was a gilded occasion and Eileen was in high spirits. Perfectionist that she was, she had personally ensured that everything was impeccable. From the chilled champagne, to the designer canapés and the special order of chocolate petit fours from Rumplemeyer's.

Well pleased with the way the party was progressing, she moved into the street, champagne flute in one hand, cigarette in the other. Her tobacco, an aromatic Balkan and Turkish mixture, was sent over every few months from Morland's of London.

She stood watching the interior activity through the drifts of white curtaining, listening to the dip and swell of voices, words curling like blue smoke into the convivial atmosphere, trailing in their wake equal amounts flattery and criticism, she was sure, of her and of her gallery.

Among the rippling shadows of screens, chairs, tables and rugs, the shapes of the guests had blurred to the cat-lick figures of an Impressionist painting. She felt the happiness fairies from childhood hovering about her head.

Stepping back into the fug, she was greeted by an exuberant Colette dressed in her favourite shades of shocking pink.

Holding Eileen by both shoulders, Colette kissed her enthusiastically on both cheeks to the amusement of Jacques, who stood solidly and quietly watching and assessing and smiling.

'Eileen, darling, you're the success of the season,' gushed Colette in her socialising element.

'Thank you.' Eileen's voice was low, she hated having such obvious attention drawn to her in public. She looked particularly lovely in a slim-fitting turquoise dress, her opera length pearls and matching ear-studs.

Jacques moved forward. 'Congratulations, Eileen. Your dream come true. I drink a toast to you. What a wonderful job you've done with this place. You've totally converted me to the power of modernism.'

'And your animal rugs are quite divine,' Colette enthused. 'I'm going to get Willy to buy me one.'

Jacques was intrigued. 'Are you and he . . . ?'

Colette pealed laughter. 'Not really. Though we do have the occasional get-together.'

'That's generous of him,' said Eileen, thinking of Colette's constant rants about Willy.

'Well, lately I've been more than generous, as you put it, to him.' Her wanton look left no doubt as to the precise nature of their get-togethers.

Eileen looked around at her selection of rugs, each carefully and lovingly hand-picked. 'Which have you chosen?'

'A goat, of course. A grey one. What else.'

A flicker of amusement lurked around Eileen's lips, Jacques laughed outright and Colette delighted in being the centre of attention.

'Eileen, have you noticed, there are several reporters here? Even one from *The New York Times*?' Jacques asked.

'Not now. I couldn't bear it.' She was nervous of what the reporters might write.

When Eileen's name began to be known, on Jacques's advice, she made herself available for interviews with the international press.

She was a dream subject. Bright, vocal and knowledgeable. She came alive when discussing her work. Indeed, she was transformed to an uncharacteristic vivacity. All flashing eyes, waving hands and verbal passion.

The reporters loved her. She became their golden girl. Their aristocratic pin-up.

But before long her upper-class roots, penchant for flying and for fast cars and her unorthodox lifestyle became too much for the press to resist. As they pushed for more and more information, she considered their questioning about her private life not only intrusive but invasive. And said so. Also feeling the onus to protect her family from untoward publicity, quietly, without discussion with Jacques, she began to withdraw her accessibility.

'People like you and me, in the public eye, need the press,' Jacques stated firmly. 'To keep our names before our clients.'

'Perhaps. But our business should not be dependent on what reporters write.'

'But they're always so complimentary about you and your work.' As long as his name was correctly spelled, Jacques considered all press coverage good. He was envious at the amount Eileen had generated. And unsolicited at that.

Colette hated being on the periphery of other people's conversations. 'Eileen, you look wonderful. Your dress is divine.'

Eileen flushed. 'If you'll excuse me, I've many guests.' She began to move off.

Colette watched Eileen's discomfort with kindly Machiavellian pleasure. It amazed her how none of the principals were aware of the real drama being enacted around them.

'Jacques, did you give Eileen her dress?' she asked with blunt casualness.

'No. I did not.'

Jacques moved away too. Colette and her innuendoes annoyed him. What he wanted most of all was to be alone with Eileen. He had invited her for a celebratory dinner this evening but she had pleaded a previous engagement and had not proffered further information.

He ran his hand over the lacquered surface of a desk on which lay a necklace of amber with large oval beads. He recognised it as Eileen's, one she wore regularly. Looking around at the touches she had provided – a fan here, a cubist drawing there, a small silver tray elsewhere, he realised she had that rare gift of being able to turn a showroom into an intimate setting.

Colette, who had followed him, interrupted his thoughts. '*Merde*. I do believe I've committed a faux pas.'

Jacques did not even turn around. 'I don't know what you mean.'

'I think of myself as a perceptive observer of human nature . . .' she began.

But she had lost Jacques. His eyes were hungrily following Eileen as she moved competently among her guests.

While Eileen may not have been comfortable socialising within large groups, she was both adept and poised. She had confided to Colette that she preferred hostessing where she was in control, rather than being a guest where she was controlled.

Breeding achieved such proficiency, Colette believed. Despite her continuing success, fame and increasingly high profile, at times she felt her humble background forcibly. This was one of those times.

Suddenly, she was fiercely jealous of Eileen. Her upper-class background. Baroness mother, provider of unlimited funds for her various ventures. Her work and her success.

But most of all, Colette realised in a moment of sudden and sad insight, she envied the way Jacques cared for Eileen, truly loved her. Together they exuded an air of untouchable compatibility and togetherness. Nobody had ever loved her in that unconditionally pure way.

No wonder nothing permanent had come out of Eileen's embryonic relationships with the other men and women who had let their interest be known.

Colette wanted to lash out, to destroy Jacques's perception of Eileen.

'What an interesting ménage of guests we are,' she nudged Jacques. 'You in love with Eileen. Eileen in love with Damia. And me in love with . . .'

'What a ridiculous hypothesis. And you're still going on with that nonsense about Damia and Eileen. You really shouldn't spread rumour.'

'Not hypothesis. Proven fact, my dear Jacques,' lied Colette looking at him flirtatiously from under her eyelids. Not that she fancied Jacques, but she flirted on automatic. 'What about Eileen's dress?'

Dress? It had niggled at Jacques. But, of course. Now he understood what Colette was getting at. It was Damia who had bought it. His couturière had spoken to him about swatches of material sent for approval, the telephone order and the unusual request of making up from measurements. Not that he particularly minded. After all, business was business.

But . . . Damia buying Eileen a dress? He preferred not to think of the connotations.

He returned to positive track. In view of the importance of this opening, he should have made Eileen a gift of a dress. He determined to rectify that at the next appropriate occasion. Pity she is so independent.

Not for a moment would he believe Colette's insinuations,

though with her constant innuendoes ringing in his ears, he did wonder about Eileen and Damia but could never bring himself to ask outright. Now he confined himself to, 'I don't see Damia here tonight.'

Colette ran her hand over the top of a black leather chair. 'Eileen's terrified the reporters might get hold the story. Splash their relationship all over the papers.'

'Some occasion your gallery opening must have been.' Jack returns the photograph.

Eileen allows herself a little hum of satisfaction. 'Yes. Though I was nervous of what the reporters would write.' She had been and was highly relieved with their positive coverage. *The Chicago Tribune* describing it as 'a journey into the previously unseen'.

'It must have been the social event of the month. Probably of the season,' Jack flatters.

'Paris never had seasons the way London did. Something to do with the Royal family being in residence, I think.'

'You know,' Jack confides, wondering will he ever succeed in introducing his grandmother into the conversation, 'My great-grandfather pulled every string to have my grandmother presented at the English court. But even his dollars made no difference. I think she ended her tour in Paris. And, of course, you lived in London. Where you presented?'

Eileen gives an amused laugh. 'I declined. I suspect my mother blamed my father's influence. She was very angry.'

Asides and comments like these, Jack once again realises, are the stuff of which great profiles are made.

Then Brigid ruins the flow of reminiscence by an enormous throat clearing and a warning, 'Mr Devine.'

Eileen is in a different place, locked into memories.

This has turned into an afternoon of honest recall, triggered by this stranger, Jack. Mr Devine. There is something about him that keeps tickling at her memory with unsequenced fragments from her past.

For one of the few times in her adult life, she has an urge to throw self-restraint to the winds, to talk freely to this young man without watching her every word. Old age must be affecting her brain.

Chapter 10

All those threads of nostalgic memories, which since Mr Devine's arrival have been winding backwards and forwards.

Now it is the turn of the *Siren* on the day it was completed.

As though it were only yesterday, Eileen sees Colette running sensual hands over the chair's body, stroking the little carved sea horse built into its back. Colette brought sensuality to the most mundane of actions. Hard to believe she has been dead for nearly twenty years. 'This one's a real beauty, what's it called?' she enthused.

'Armchair.' Eileen, standing over her, emphasised the word.

Colette, still stroking the chair, protested. 'That's unfair. It's so beautiful, it deserves a special name.'

Simultaneously, they both looked towards the doorway. Gaby Bloch stood there, watching with hooded eyes. She said nothing. After a few seconds, she backed out of their vision.

Gaby was a strange enigma, big and bulky, of indeterminate age, with strong masculine features. She was the daughter of a wealthy German industrialist, who pandered to her every expensive whim, but after discovering her sexual orientation, cut her off without a mark.

Her affair with fourteen-year-old Loïe Fuller brought her to Paris where, acting as companion-manager, she worked hard to ensure that Loïe's erotic dancing became the most popular act in the Folies-Bergère. Soon Loïe was toast of the town.

Such popularity was difficult to achieve and, with fierce competition from aspiring female flesh, it was even more difficult to sustain.

Nightly, ambitious beauties oozing outward charm and inward venom waited their chance to topple from her hard-earned pedestal whoever happened to be current favourite. Dressed in revealing costumes, they paraded like peacocks, strutting their stuff against those romantically carnal back-drops at which French stage designers excelled.

Every type of woman, the male – and, in many cases, the female – heart could desire was represented at the Folies, the Moulin Rouge and in the other successful clubs that had opened up in Paris. The curvaceous Miss Barrington from London, smouldering-eyed Lola from Madrid, ice-blonde Anna Sven from Stockholm and the flirtatious Jody from no one knew where.

But month after month, under Gaby's tutelage and protection, Loïe retained her number one position.

Eventually they became a peripheral part of Eileen's social circle and it was Gaby who introduced Eileen to Damia. Eileen, identifying with Gaby's background, developed a relatively stilted friendship with her but from the beginning she had no time for Loïe. She could not understand her popularity, considered her talentless and described her as small, fat and American.

When Loïe did a flit from Paris and Gaby, after being immortalised as the bronze figure in that famous art deco lamp, the consensus among the gossiping café society was that, given half a chance, Gaby would replace Loïe with Eileen.

Everyone knew that Eileen, as well as being an innocent where people like Gaby were concerned, was kindness personified. Everyone equally knew that Gaby was a professional taker and utterly ruthless when it came to looking out for herself.

Café society was right. Much in the same way as she had become Loïe's manager, Gaby insinuated herself into Eileen's life.

Colette blew a raspberry. 'What's she doing here?'

Eileen ignored Colette's question on Gaby but answered her one about the chair as though there had been no interruption. 'To please you, I hereby name this chair the *Siren*.'

If she had hoped such a gesture would distract Colette from Gaby, she was mistaken.

Colette stretched to her full plump height. 'Gaby Bloch is a pariah.'

'She's only here for a few days. I'm sorry for her.'

'You're an optimist. You'll have a job getting rid of her.'

'It won't arise,' said Eileen blithely, hoping she was right. Already she was finding Gaby's constant presence a strain. Where she was, Gaby was only one step behind. 'If one cuts away all sensitivity, one cuts away a large part of being human.' Eileen meant what she said but she realised that the words sounded sententious.

Colette, seldom verbally bested, riposted, 'You must allow the tongue to speak the language of the mind.'

Damn Colette for being right. But Eileen could not explain

how she felt herself inexplicably mesmerised by Gaby. Rather like a rabbit caught in the light of a lantern.

She needed a break. There and then, with Colette back stroking the seahorse with the intensity of a lover, Eileen decided that she would spend a few days in Saint Tropez. On her own. She loved the peace of the place. The old harbour, the soberly tri-coloured sea, faded pink house façades and sky as milky as the edge of the desert.

It was not until Eileen met Damia that she began to notice that women involved in relationships with other women were quite ordinary. Frequently, they seemed and behaved like good friends. More or less like other people. Really, Eileen knew, more like other people than she was or could ever be.

'Friendships with women are important, aren't they?' she asked Colette, choosing what she considered to be an opportune moment. They were shopping together in the Galeries Lafayette, wafting around in olfactory confusion in the perfume department, giggling on whiffs of scent, sparkles of glass, whirls of bright and pale colours, customers' silks and furs, and saleswomen enquiring, 'Mesdames, vous désirez?'

'Friendship!' She blew an inelegant raspberry. 'Not for me. I'm more into sex. With both sexes,' Colette answered Eileen's question loudly, throwing back her head in an uproarious laugh.

She should have known. Colette rarely missed an opportunity to shock, particularly in public where she revelled in recognition. Moving along the counter, Eileen distanced herself, pretending she was not with her.

The sumptuousness of the store was a balm. Aisles of deep red carpet. Wide gilded staircase. Balconies strung like latticed necklaces between the marbled necks of fluted columns. Her eyes soared up the cathedral heights before receding into a vaulted glassy distance.

She hoped during this afternoon's expedition 'innocently' to bring the conversation around to same-sex relationships, and in the process to pick up some pointers on their protocol.

She planned to keep the subject general, of course. No way would she spell out to Colette her feelings for Damia and their relationship. Colette suspecting was one thing, Colette having her suspicions confirmed was quite another. Quietly buying a flask of Joy, Eileen chided herself for being a coward and decided to leave the matter.

Colette insisted they look at clothes. Women's clothes were on the next floor. White-gloved bell boys ornate in red and gold, guardians of the lifts, drew back their accordion grids to reveal what looked like gilded bird cages. Eileen and Colette stepped in.

Colette loved dressing in the height of fashion. Her target that particular afternoon was the chemise, flat front and back, with gathered pleats under the arms, cut full and belted under the bosom. It was all the rage that season.

Secretly, Eileen considered its much-hyped style ridiculous and she hated the impact of the current flood of newspaper and magazine articles on susceptible women, extolling the chemise, carolling its comfort, grace and economy, suggesting diet and exercise to achieve the requisite silhouette.

'What do you think?' Colette, in strawberry pink, pirouetted plumply out of the changing room.

Eileen, sitting on an uncomfortable gilt chair, answered truthfully as was her custom, 'Not much.'

'Why?'

'Well, the style doesn't flatter the female shape.'

'Does it make me look fat?'

'The chemise makes everyone look fat, unless they're bean-pole thin.'

'Like lucky you.' Colette gave another pirouette.

The saleswoman, all false sincerity in sensible tailored black, clasped her hands and oh la, la-ed.

Eileen disliked the type of assistant who was more into sales commissions than customer enhancement.

Too sweetly, the woman asked Eileen, 'Would Madame herself like to try . . . ?'

'No. Madame would not,' said Eileen shortly.

Each item of her clothing, even, unbelievably, her work smocks, was chosen for elegance, suitability and comfort, rather than fashion. Currently her wardrobe included evening clothes by Poirot – she particularly loved his black and gold theatre coat; several of Jacques's pastel dresses and silk blouses in flower petal shades; her casuals – tailored jackets, skirts and trousers exquisitely cut and in the best of material were by Chanel; and her underwear was fragile fistfuls of gossamer softness.

Colette had no intention of allowing the spotlight to drift from her. She threw her hands wide, looked at herself in the mirror from all sides and concluded, 'Well, I am fat.'

'Mesdames, the chemise has been voted practical, suitable for every age group and perfectly adaptable to the demands of modern life.' The sales woman was determined to make a sale.

'The only good thing about it is its simplicity,' said Eileen. 'As *Le Monde* says, it can be made in virtually any sewing room and worn later with the air of having issued from les Grandes Maisons.'

The sales woman did not comment.

'I'm going to buy it,' said Colette.

'Do.' Eileen laughed to take the sting out of her earlier remark. 'I keep reading how smart the style is, so it's I who am the dowd.'

Eileen made no comment, as Colette enthusiastically added a hideously fashionable scarlet toque with a ruffle tulle neck trim. Claiming utter exhaustion, she then insisted they needed the recuperative sustenance of coffee.

When Eileen presented her with the perfume, she was uncharacteristically soft and grateful. For all her guff, outrageous ways and extrovert mannerisms, she had few real friends, and despite her regular spasms of jealousy about Eileen's privileged lifestyle, she truly loved her.

'So what's all this about friendships with women?' she asked quietly. 'Are you taking about yourself and Damia?'

Eileen should have known that Colette would not let a remark with such titillating potential pass unnoticed. 'No, of course, not,' she protested too vehemently and to her horror felt a blush stain her cheeks.

'Oh. Is it Gaby Bloch? The Hun herself?' Colette hooted. 'You can't bear to let her go.'

Eileen wanted to disappear under the table at Colette's insinuation. Never would she tell her – or anyone else – that the other night she had to forcibly eject Gaby from her bed. 'No. It's nothing, really. Just idle wondering.' She made an elaborate play of sugaring her coffee, wishing she had never raised the subject and deciding she would manage without the benefit of Colette's dubious expertise.

'Oh, come on, Eileen. Tell me.' Colette had raised her voice again and Eileen did not want her repeating the question, as she was quite capable of doing, at the top of her voice across the crowded café.

She leaned in across the table and, keeping her tone casual, said, 'I was thinking that in same-sex relationships it's important to be close to someone who's an equal, who isn't too much older or too much younger, or if she is, doesn't try to take advantage of it.' Now that she had said it, Eileen thought her comments sounded contrived and bloodless.

'Friendships like that end up in bed,' warned Colette with a dramatic fluttering of eyelids.

'Bed is only part of the piece. It's like my designing. Or your writing.' She said nothing about Damia's performing.

Colette snorted.

Eileen, leaning in towards her, glanced around to ensure that the other customers were busy with coffee and conversation. 'Every time I work at a project, there's a chance that the material I find under my fingers will be different to what it was before. Then because I'm all the time improving my skills, I discover something new, profound, an idea so true, that it'll frighten, exalt and change me. As love and friendship does.'

'You're in denial. Making esoteric what is purely sex.'

'No. I'm not.' Eileen refused to be swayed from her point.

'You won't face up the fact that both Damia and Gaby are contenders for your favours.'

Eileen ignored Colette's implication. 'Bed should only be one part of it. Like working a design. What happens in bed ought to be love and love ought to be real, not done for show or pay or anything but truth.'

'Ah. You virginal Irish. You drive me to distraction. You're all talk, no action and no experience,' growled Colette, hitting so close to the mark that Eileen blushed.

Damia. The green-eyed singer who had won Eileen's heart. She was born Marie-Louise Damien, one of eight children of an impoverished gendarme. But now she was taking Paris by storm, her records were selling in their thousands and posters displaying her in her signature sleeveless black v-neck dress, with outstretched arms, were all over the city.

From their first meeting, Eileen had fallen under Damia's spell. Beneath the singer's veneer of sophistication lurked Jung's 'gross sensuality' which Eileen found irresistible. Primed by the *in flagrante delicto* acted out before her childish eyes on that night of the shadows, as she labelled the occasion, her own sexuality was more stirred by 'rough' than 'refined'. It was a preference which up to now, she had kept to herself.

Where others had failed, Damia succeeded in enticing her from her self-imposed solitude at the drawing board. Initially Eileen was a willing participant in the frivolous world of fashionable restaurants and night clubs, and even acquired a wardrobe of evening clothes from Poirot and boxes of hats from Lavin.

Eventually she grew tired of the frenetic socialising. She introduced Damia to walks in the Forest of Fontainbleau and quiet evenings in the apartment, which despite Gaby's frequent presence, Damia took to with enthusiasm. Together, they smoked, drank wine, watched Damia's pet panther romp with Eileen's strays and listened to her collection of records, which included as well as her own racy selection, English hits like, 'Just a Little Drink', 'Foxtrot with Jack Hilton' and 'A Cottage for Sale'.

Their deepening relationship had Eileen dazed and incoherent with joy. It was as though they were enclosed within a rich and fragile bubble. Yet still she insisted on time for herself, of space between them. Damia wanted to go public. But Eileen's cautious nature and reluctance to commitment asserted itself. She clung to secrecy, claiming to Damia that to move too boldly might burst their bubble. And despite Eileen's own free-thinking lifestyle, she was constantly sensitive to her family's position.

Damia loved lacquer and, to ease her disappointment, Eileen showered her with presents – a brown and silver framed mirror; a black armchair with gold figures; a table with a pagoda design in black and red.

The ultimate gift was a hideaway in Samois-sur-Seine which included a small island. A private place where they could be themselves. The house, decorated Spanish-style, had a large living room, several bedrooms and a big studio with a sizeable refectory table.

There, in the silence of the long hot summer days, they lunched under trailing mauve wisteria.

When seeking the ultimate seclusion, they rowed across the river to picnic on the island where they made love slowly and calmly, drunk with the scent of nature, without a past, without suspecting the future, with just the incredible richness of the present in which they stared at each other, smelled each other, kissed each other and explored each other's bodies.

'I need you. I want us to be together. Always. Not just at weekends.' Damia murmured, turning to Eileen. 'Can we?' They were wrapped in the whisper of the wind and the lapping of the river.

Eileen wanted to laugh, wanted to cry, wanted time to stand still. She turned to Damia, burying herself in her breast, and

Damia stroked her shingled hair to smoothness, looking down at the top of her head in wonder.

'Perhaps,' Eileen said. They had reached that moment of greatest intimacy which had Damia in garrulous high spirits, reaching for her cigarettes and more wine. But for Eileen, as always, orgasm echoed of loneliness and a foreknowledge of death. The little death, the French called it.

Invariably, their days drew to an end, with twilight blurring their edges of soft womanhood, Eileen drawing by candlelight, Damia stretched out on the sofa, trailing cigarette smoke and listening to music.

Idyllic as their Samois-sur-Seine retreat was and despite the growing closeness of their relationship, on Monday mornings, Eileen was eager to return to the monasticism and working routine of her apartment but each week Damia groused at having to leave.

'But we must return to Paris,' Eileen insisted, kissing Damia's closed eyelids and tracing the curve of her lips, 'To our work, our life.'

One afternoon, Colette brought around to 21 rue Bonaparte Roger Giles, Paris correspondent of *The Times*, who politely requested an interview.

'I don't do interviews, any more,' Eileen said to the earnest young man who was immaculately turned out in stiff collar, dark suit and gleaming boots, while she was shiny-faced in her working gear of voluminous smock and woolly socks.

Initially she had been grateful for the amount of newspaper and magazine coverage, her lacquer work received. She talked freely about *Le Destin* but was more circumspect by the time Jean Désert opened. Now, it seemed, her every move was of interest to the press. Despite his denials, she strongly suspected Jacques's promotional hand.

But her insistence on keeping a low profile was beginning to have insidious and far-reaching repercussions. The very reporters who initially lauded Eileen for her innovative, experimental and ground-breaking designs now took her lack of response to their requests for features and articles as arrogance.

Their golden girl had tarnished.

And they were not shy about pointing the finger of failure at Jean Désert.

'Nonsense,' said Colette. 'Of course, you'll give him an interview.' To Roger, who stood awkwardly clutching a notebook, she encouraged, 'Don't worry. She'll talk to you.' She pulled Eileen aside, 'For a reporter, Roger is a real gentleman. Give him a chance.'

'I'm a fan of yours,' Roger said to Eileen. 'I know a little about lacquer.'

'You do?' The reporters who had interviewed her knew nothing, except what she told them.

'Yes. I've done a lot of research into it. I've even interviewed Monsieur Jean Dunand.'

'You have?' Eileen was impressed. Jean Dunand was the lacquer king. She admired not only his work but also his low-key attitude to publicity.

She had no talent for self-promotion, no skills in attracting or dealing with clients, no ability nor wish to gear her social life around boosting her sales. The more her reputation grew, the more she shied away from the public razzmatazz of the kind of promotion that went hand in hand with the decorators' world. Flamboyant lifestyles. Moving in the right circles. Courting the rich and famous. Entertaining actresses of the like of Sarah Bernhardt and Ellen Terry.

Roger Giles was not a typical press man. In him she recognised a man of quiet ability who reflected not only her natural shyness but also her determination. As Colette had said, he was a gentleman. She gave in to his request and they spent a mutually rewarding day together.

Charmed with each other.

Sitting in her workroom with jacket off and tie loosened, he described his life as a reporter which he obviously loved and took seriously. Eileen, being Eileen, was fascinated and asked about his childhood, training, first job, how he prepared for interview, his favourite personality. Questions to which he responded openly, finishing with a deprecating, 'In case you're thinking otherwise, I wouldn't be regarded as successful.'

'Why?'

He gave a little smile. 'Not aggressive enough. I don't intrude into private lives or break confidentiality.'

'And should you?'

'So I understand. Stories that do are more newsworthy. It's the way reporting is going.'

Convinced of Roger's integrity, she relaxed into the best interview of her career.

Chapter 11

Eileen was so delighted by the freshness and accuracy of Roger Giles's write up that she invited him and a small group of friends for an intimate supper. Domestic life was easier since Brigid's arrival: she was cheerful, a quick learner and her Irish charm entranced the guests.

The afternoon of the party was heavy-weathered and humid. Gaby was still around. Despite Eileen's hints – which granted, were polite – she showed no sign of moving out.

Gaby was so distracting. In and out of the workroom while Eileen put the finishing touches to the drawing of a chair. A once-off, a rush job for a private client which should already be in production.

Eileen's thoughts drifted to the dressing of tonight's table. Royal blue linen, white Spode china, silver cutlery, Waterford glass and, she thought, a centre piece of floating yucca flowers. Dozens of beeswax candles and strategically placed incense sticks.

She sighed. This was a difficult client who demanded the almost-impossible.

Eileen's sigh was Gaby's cue to press home advantage, tiny plump hands fluttering expressively and excessively – if Gaby was not using her hands to emphasise a point, she kept them firmly clamped in her pockets. 'You have such style.'

Eileen dipped her head in acknowledgement of the compliment.

'It must be difficult working for people without taste.'

Eileen shrugged. 'How do you know?'

'I've heard you say so often enough.'

'Did I really? How indiscreet of me. But you're right . . . these women and their whims.'

'Wanting you to adapt your designs to their lack of taste.' Gaby lowered her voice sympathetically. 'It must be awful.'

'I suppose. I don't think of it that way. Just doing what I know will work. And I take on very few private clients.'

'Still, an assistant acting as a front person would free you up.'

'Sounds tempting. But I wouldn't be sure it'd be feasible. Clients would still want to liaise with me.'

'It worked when I managed Loïe.' Eileen failed to find any comparison between herself and Loïe but said nothing. Gaby continued, 'I'd help, I'd love to be involved. We could operate a multi-purpose business. A showcase for you and your work, a design consultancy and the work of other selected designers.' Gaby's voice pitched high in desperation. She was without a franc to her name.

Eileen turned around from her drawing board, unnerved by the amount of thought Gaby had put into her proposition. In her plumpness she might look soft, but she had a will of iron. Instinctively Eileen recoiled from her palpable neediness. And yet, Gaby had the resilience of an India rubber ball. Eileen had seen her bounce back, apparently unperturbed by rude and hurtful comments.

Facing Gaby, she said, 'Nice offer. Thanks. But not for me.'

Now was hardly appropriate to bring up tonight's supper. Eileen hoped Gaby had another engagement, that she would not be around. She was into extravagant highlife, clubbing, risqué amusements and rowdy dinners which went on until dawn. Right now, Eileen was not optimistic.

For the first time, she noticed the minuscule drops of perspiration clinging to the fine dark hairs of Gaby's upper lip and the hideous way she dressed her hair. Parted in the centre and combed straight back from her forehead.

Gaby was not easily put off. 'Which are you refusing. My idea? Or me?'

'Both,' Eileen answered. Gaby's toadying was amplified by the humidity. She got up from her drawing table and walked out of her workroom. It was a terrible state of affairs to have to resort to her bedroom to escape a house guest who had out-stayed her welcome.

Jacques was delighted to receive Eileen's invitation to supper. At last she was recognising the power of the press and the importance of publicity.

But he should have known better. Eileen had a different agenda, one where she was taking a back seat. She had asked Colette to read aloud some of Roger's writings and was using the occasion to promote his career.

Colette, flamboyant in yellow and orange, standing with her back to the fireplace, as usual enjoyed being centre stage. Raising her wine glass, she toasted Eileen and Roger. She had dramatised and edited the readings.

'This,' she said with a flourish of her arm, 'is the way Roger, a reporter of repute, sees Eileen's work. Now all of you, listen carefully. "Dark lacquered wood of great beauty, decorated with lightly engraved lines made luminous, in some cases, with a sparing use of mother-of-pearl."'

Colette paused for reaction.

'Hear. Hear,' went the guests.

'And he further writes, "Her red lacquer is understated except by its own colour and flawless surface, but with deep brown she achieves furniture of great beauty that would be extremely restful to live with."'

Colette paused and, with hand on heart, dramatically stated, 'Yes, but, perhaps, he should have added, "without Eileen, whom one could hardly describe as restful".' This comment was greeted by enthusiastic clapping and gales of good-humoured laughter.

Damia, elbow on table, chin cupped in hand, was listening intently to Colette. Eileen meeting her eyes across the table felt that rush of near perfect happiness.

'"In one magnificent screen, this artist has produced a deep transparent blue lacquer like the atmosphere of a clear dark night." And that clear blue, ladies and gentlemen, as you may or may not realise, for years confounded the international experts, but not our Eileen, who as we all know, once she gets an idea, never gives up.'

The evening progressed into the small hours of the morning. Roger, his inhibitions unleashed, proved himself to be a wicked mimic.

Damia was in particularly high spirits. Her name and raucous voice had become synonymous with louche tragedy. On her return to Paris after a sell-out tour of America and since opening Concert Damia, the size of her audiences was legendary. Her latest coup was an invitation to sing the Marseillaise for the film *Napoleon*.

That evening, shutters thrown wide to the sound of birdsong floating up from the courtyard, replete with good food and wine, the atmosphere was mesmeric.

Singing directly to Eileen, Damia gave her signature song 'Le Fou' her all. And Eileen remembered the day she had taught Damia to clean lacquer. The antics they got up to with the oil.

Throwing herself to the floor and, to rapturous applause from the others, Damia finished her song kneeling pleadingly before Jacques.

Neither Jacques nor Eileen were party performers and they were both slightly embarrassed, yet hugely honoured, to be singled out for Damia's dramatics.

As for Gaby, she sat, dressed in her uniform black, between Jacques and Colette, saying little, taking all in, seething at what she perceived as the injustice of her situation. Jacques, who wondered might she be feeling left out, kindly asked, 'Do you've a party piece?'

'Not actually a party piece,' she answered. 'But there's something I'd like to say.'

Colette held her breath. Jacques, knowing Gaby, cursed his untimely question.

'I put a proposition to Eileen this afternoon. An offer which would turn Jean Désert around from loss-making to profit.'

Despite himself, Jacques was interested. He never could resist business.

Gaby detailed the incident in that monotonous voice of hers. It wasn't quite how Eileen remembered but in the interest of peace and her position as hostess, she allowed her to continue uninterrupted.

'Which she turned down,' finished Gaby flatly.

For a moment there was an embarrassed silence around the table. Jacques looked at Eileen, aware of how much she hated talk of Jean Désert. Her eyes were cast down. Damia glanced in her direction too and cocked an elegant eyebrow. Roger sat back relaxed, watching, listening and wondering at the innuendoes which were being aired.

Colette fractured the mood by laughing loudly and rudely. 'I've to hand it to you, Gaby, you've nerve.'

The party broke up shortly afterwards.

But for Eileen the evening had been ruined.

As she got ready for bed, standing in her bare feet on the chill marble of her bathroom, cold creaming and splashing water on her face, brushing her teeth and sliding into a silver-grey silk night dress, she wondered at the complexities of revulsion and guilt which lurked in her attitude towards Gaby.

'She has to go,' Jacques had advised on his way out.

'Get rid of her,' Colette insisted spiritedly, shrugging into a voluminous cape.

Damia had not commented.

From the business-like look of Jacques, Eileen knew he had more on his mind than social pleasantries. He sat down, accepted a café au lait from Brigid and, as was his way, got straight down to business.

'So how's the gallery doing?' he asked bluntly. It was coming up to the third anniversary of its opening.

'I don't really know. I hardly spend any time there.'

In Jacques's opinion the result of this self-imposed low profile was that the people who bought Eileen's furniture, lacquer work and animal rugs largely ignored the person who had created them. And Eileen had done a fine job in alienating the press.

'What are sales like?'

'All right, I suppose.'

'Are the books balancing?'

'If you mean making a profit, no.'

Despite all the hype and glamour and yards of press coverage surrounding its opening, and a list of clients which read like a *Who's Who* of French public life, from the beginning Jean Désert had not realised its potential.

Granted the beau monde considered the place drop-dead elegant and came in their droves, Jacques often thought, just to see and be seen. They looked, fingered and admired but, with the exception of the animal rugs, they did not buy.

Once the gallery reached its publicity-fuelled pinnacle, it teetered for a few months, after which it was downhill all the way. During the first year of trading, Jacques had been horrified to discover that takings only amounted to nineteen thousand francs, hardly enough to pay the rent, the saleswoman and Eileen's workers. The latest figures, he suspected, were even worse.

Lack of profit did not worry Eileen. She had no financial expectations from this or any other of her ventures. But, in introspective moments, she admitted disappointment to herself.

'I consider myself and the gallery a failure.'

Her factual cut-glass statement tore at Jacques's heart strings. He recognised and identified with her shame and would like to comfort her by contradiction but he would not diminish their relationship by falsehoods.

'Sell it,' he said. 'As a going concern. Cut your losses and get out. Before you lose any more money.'

'No. I won't,' she stated in that categorical way of hers. And he knew there was nothing to be gained from pressing her.

Why, Colette constantly nagged, is Gaby still with you and how do you put up with her? Eileen avoided replying because she did not know, though she often wondered why she felt this strange commitment towards Gaby.

The answer came one dawn before she was properly awake, niggling, wobbling on the periphery of her consciousness. She found sleep to be an extraordinary state. Parts of the brain resting, other parts working a busy night shift, putting together all the little bits and pieces that the conscious mind had been unable to sort out in the daytime.

Gaby, heavy-breasted, bulky and sweating, her unwelcome house guest, was her atonement for that night of the shadows. It was she, Eileen Gray, who had set in train the sequence of events which resulted in madness and subsequent death.

Kaleidoscopic impressions of that awful night had dominated her life. What her childish-eyes and mind had half-seen and half-absorbed may have been incomprehensible, but it haunted her. Would it never stop?

The raw lust that penetrated every corner of the shack became aphrodisia to her young senses. An aphrodisia from which she recoiled and which in adulthood had her scouring the writings of Jung for answers to the un-answerable.

The pieces of the puzzle of her ambivalent and confused sexuality were finally falling into place.

Thinking time.

She got up, threw a silk wrap around her shoulders and

walked to the window, her bare feet making soft fleshy plops on the wooden floors. A few rugs, strategically placed, would not go amiss on the chilly dawn boards.

It had been a wet, damp March and early April. Then suddenly the weather had changed, grown hot. In just a few days the parks and gardens had gone from a brown mat to a seething tangle of colour.

Lilacs and wisteria and azaleas burst into blossom. Tulips, daffodils, irises drove spear-like up through the moist earth. A heady blooming saturated the air, seeping in through open windows, infiltrating every crack and cranny, empowering all within its path.

A delicious lawlessness infected everything, including Eileen.

Time to make changes. To take control.

It was only recently she had grasped the relationship between lust and reason. Reason and lust. The contradiction between them was like being torn asunder. She hated this feeling of being trapped between the two. Colette's insinuations were correct. Both Gaby and Damia wanted her.

Gaby no, never. Damia yes. For always and ever, she hoped.

In some deep subconscious part of her psyche Eileen knew that when she allowed her creativity full rein, it harnessed her erratic emotions, kept her sexual desires under control and brought discipline to her life.

It had happened during her apprenticeship to lacquering; while she worked on *Le Destin* and again during her refurbishment of Jean Désert. The lust which disturbed her she could curb, keep under control by the conception, birth and implementation of her designs.

Damia was more than lust. Much more. Their relationship was deep and meaningful.

When Eileen thought of lust, it put her in mind of that time she had come across Padso and Bessie Rossa. All her life, she had tried, without success, to come to terms with that incident. Then, without understanding the implications of what she was seeing, she had both recoiled from and been excited by their animal physicality.

Her abiding image of love related to an evening on the last occasion her father stayed at Brownswood. Peeping through the dining room door, she saw him carry his place setting down the length of the table to where her mother sat.

She looked up pink and flushed as he bent protectively over her. In a sweeping, square-handed gesture, he loosened her hair while her long white fingers re-set his cutlery and dishes. She laughed at him and his expression was so full of love that Eileen shivered. Young as she was, she recognised the sacredness of that moment between her parents.

Close physical relationships on a permanent basis, Eileen had long ago decided, were not for her. She needed personal space, which is why Damia and she were so compatible. Both were independent with their own careers, lives and friends.

Eileen was frightened of dependency but even more frightened of commitment. She was equally frightened of the way invariably, perhaps inevitably, tenderness lost out to lust.

She could not deny Gaby's stormy accusation of a few weeks ago that she loved animals too much to love people. She never turned away a stray. Her dogs came with permanent limps, chewed ears and festering eyes. Her cats arrived jumpy and nervous, with moth-eaten appearances. Under her ministrations, not only were they restored to health, they thrived.

Gaby would have to go. Now that she understood, accepted and had done her penance, she had no compunction about her decision.

Still, it was several days before she plucked up the courage to turn from her drawing board and to say, with Gaby irritatingly hovering at her shoulder, 'It's time you left.'

Gaby's big dark bulk seemed to crumble in on itself. 'Eileen, you don't mean it.'

Eileen's insides were shaking. She had suffered enough rebuffs as a child never to want to be instrumental in meting out rejection to another human being.

She resisted the urge to turn back to her work and to leave their current situation stand. She had coped for so long, surely a little longer would not make any difference? No – Gaby had to go.

She kept her gaze calm, centring on a point between Gaby's overgrown eyebrows and the droplets of perspiration gathering momentum on her top lip. She was sorry but suspicious of the sincerity of this woman whose face had grown red and whose eyes threatened to overflow with tears.

Eileen determined to stick to her decision. She affirmed, 'I want you to leave, Gaby. By tomorrow.' The few words were delivered in sorrow and spoken with tenderness.

Gaby, hands wedged in her pockets, stood mute, as though gathering strength, before turning on Eileen and spitting out, 'You'll be sorry. Mark my words, you'll be sorry.'

A shiver of premonition ran down Eileen's spine. She shook it off as nonsense. The time had come to consign Gaby to the shadows of the past, while she and Damia lived in the present. Her concentration would be on the light of her future which right now was focused on the purity of design. What could be less exotic and more proletarian?

As a child in times of fear, she found solace from her moon-boat in the sky.

However, since her love affair with aviation, whenever she could, she sought refuge and peace in the solitude of the clouds. She booked a flight for that afternoon.

Up in the blue of the sky with the roar of the engine all around she could be honest, allow tendrils of doubt to drift and to linger around the edge of her consciousness. Sometimes these tendrils took on a life of their own that had separate voices clashing, warring and laughing back and forth across the tundra of her brain. But always by the time she returned to earth, she had reached some sort of resolution.

When Gaby left the following morning, Eileen, metaphorically rubbing her hands, considered her decision to be a good day's work. It was only later, much later, that she learned of its far-reaching repercussions and realised what Gaby had meant by her parting shot.

It hurt and amazed her how she was the last to know. All Paris, she was sure, was aware before her.

Forgetting that officially they had not known, that, at her insistence, her relationship with Damia was shrouded in secrecy, she felt betrayed that none of her friends told her.

Jacques said he did not know, that he had no idea, and she believed him. He had the male attitude of listening, listening intently, but when it suited him not hearing and if he heard and the information did register, he could be lazy and indifferent about analysing for repercussions. Anyway, ostrich-like, he had always ignored her relationship with Damia.

It was Colette who plucked up the courage to tell her.

They were sitting on opposite sides of the fire in Eileen's workroom, nursing hot whiskies which were Brigid's current pièce de resistance. Eileen stretched back, drawing lingeringly on a cigarette. She was feeling good, at peace with the world.

Whiskey went quickly to her head and she giggled, 'See the chair you're sitting in?'

'So?' Colette shrugged.

'What does it remind you of?'

Colette twisted around. 'Nothing.'

'Think. Who, so?'

'I don't know.'

'Gaby.' Eileen kicked her feet up in the air in a childish gesture and burst out laughing. 'I got the idea for the shape from the advertisement for Michelin tires, but the *Bibendum* has always reminded me of Gaby.'

Colette knew then that Eileen had not a clue of what was happening behind her back.

'Have you heard from Gaby?'

'Thankfully not.'

'Have you been out anywhere? Parties? Dinners? Clubs?'

'No. I've been nowhere. Seen nobody since coming back from Mama in London after Easter. I've not even seen much of Damia, but then she's busy preparing for another tour.'

'Where's she off to?'

'Germany and Switzerland, I think. She wanted me to travel with her. But I prefer to stay here.'

'You don't know, do you?'

'Know what?'

'About Gaby.'

'No, and I don't particularly want to know anything about her. She's good riddance.'

'There's something I must tell you.'

'Sounds serious.' Eileen plucked a clove out of her glass and sucked on it.

Colette hated being the one to shatter her euphoria. 'Gaby has moved in with Damia.'

Eileen sat immobile.

'She's acting as her manager.'

Slowly and deliberately, Eileen placed her glass on the hearth.

'They're a couple around the restaurant and night club circuit.'

Eileen looked into the fire.

Colette ploughed on. 'Where Gaby, no doubt, in the interests of promoting Damia, is indulging in her passion for luxury and high-living as though it were going out of fashion.'

Eileen smiled a sad smile. 'It's all right, Colette. Thank you for telling me.' For once, her autocratic voice was barely audible.

'Can you believe it?' Colette spluttered. 'They even have a table on permanent hold in the Prunier, a special corner table, together with a bottle of correctly temperatured Tokay wine.'

'I can,' said Eileen.

It was Brigid who picked up the pieces afterwards. Who physically and psychologically held Eileen together during those long, lonely, dark nights of her soul when she hibernated with grief, refusing human contact, refusing to go out, refusing to allow anyone in, refusing to have Brigid answer telephone or door.

During those times, and she had no idea of their duration, she came to understand the true meaning of a broken heart. Strange, she thought, pacing the apartment night after night, trailing from room to room, how you do not appreciate love until you have lost it.

She wished . . . she wished . . . she wished. If only she had known – what attitudinal changes she would have made; how much more open, how less secretive she would have been.

Confusing emotions gnawed at her. Her initial apparent acceptance of the Damia–Gaby situation changed to numbness and disbelief.

That was followed by grief and sadness. Such grief and sadness that she was certain she would either kill herself or die of desolation, a broken heart, jealousy or hate.

Never before had she experienced such a riot of conflict. Never before had she to cast around for labels for her emotions to try to exert even the most tenuous of control.

Eventually, out of all the angst and heartbreak, a modicum of resolution and acceptance came to her. When she re-emerged from self-imposed purdah, fine drawn in recovery, she had a new compassion.

After crossing that mourning hurdle she was less of an innocent, a stronger person. Sometimes, like a tangible asset, she could actually feel her strength and invincibility.

Time heals. That she knew for a fact.

Chapter 12

The box containing the photographs is of inlaid cherry wood and ivory. Jack reaches in and extricates a photo of a handsome building.

'Wow. Where's this?'

'Brigid?'

'It's the old place, Miss.' Brigid makes to take the photograph from him. 'No, Mr Devine. That's personal.'

'It's all right, Brigid. It's our estate in Ireland. Brownswood Manor.'

'Some joint.'

'Joint!' Eileen repeats the word with amusement. 'Yes, isn't it? Some joint! It was on the banks of the Slaney river in County Wexford.'

'You grew up there?'

'Mostly. Though we did the season from our townhouse in Kensington.'

'Such a beautiful place.' There is genuine admiration in Jack's voice. The house is solidly unpretentious, cosily tucked behind a scalloped hedge. A family home that spoke of generations of discreet affluence. 'How could you bear to leave it?'

Little did he, or for that matter anyone else, know how in the circumstances it was easier for Eileen to leave than to stay and, having once made the break, she never returned.

Jack picks out another photo, same house, closer shot. 'Who's this in the foreground? It looks like a man waving.'

'Presumably my father. Brigid?'

'Yes.' Brigid peers closely. 'It's the Master. But Miss Gray?'

'Brigid, I said, it's all right.' Eileen sits a little straighter, steeples her fingers. 'You may leave us.'

Jack hardly dares breath. He so wants to pursue these photographs.

Brigid with a worried look departs.

'My father was probably waving at me. It's the first photograph I took and I wanted a bit of movement, not him standing like a statue. I was so proud of it.'

'I bet you were.' This is more like it. Eileen is beginning to relax, even to allow a modicum of brittle charm to filter through. A few more personal touches like this and he will be laughing. Jack reaches into his pocket, feeling for the On button of the recorder.

It was one of those glorious May mornings, all bright brassy sunlight and short spurts of dark shadows ravelling out from the trees and hedges that bordered the sweep of driveway leading up to the Manor's main entrance. Away in the distance lay patchwork fields in all the shades of green.

Eileen would be ten in August. At last a two-figure age, like her sisters and brothers and real grown-ups. From the time she heard Dada was coming home from Italy, she thought of herself as ten minus a quarter, rather than just nine and three-quarters.

As James Maclaren Smith, the sleeves of his fine cambric shirt rolled up, set up his latest toy, a camera, he was in a jovial mood. Except for this name-changing nonsense, the atmosphere around the old place was unexpectedly pleasant.

He found himself relaxing into his home in a way that a few years ago he would have thought impossible. The older children were relatively biddable – when they were around, they spent much of their time at tennis parties and summer balls. The weather was good, with a promise of real warmth. And Eileen, his youngest, had become his constant companion, trailing behind him asking incessant questions as he walked the land or investigated changes in the household. Such unconditional admiration was a boost to his ego.

Eveleen had a new softness about her too and on occasions was almost wifely. She was the only woman who had ever touched the core of his being. He could not imagine life without her. Despite his various and frequent peccadilloes and the dashed hopes of his marriage, he always returned to her.

But invariably after a few weeks, the parochial society where it was presumed he would play a squirearchical role and the narrowness of the community, added to the miserable climate of Ireland's south-east got to him as, he felt, such disadvantages would to any red-blooded man.

When they returned from Italy after a year of marriage, he had barely unpacked his bags when he realised why he had fled Scotland for the Mediterranean. Already he had discovered that the coldness and puritanical sexual hang-ups of the Scots were shared by the Irish. When it seemed there would never be a let up from the February frost and snow, he made the first of many trips abroad. Ostensibly to paint. In reality to live.

The only note of discord to this homecoming was the move, instigated by Henry Tuffnell Campbell, youngest son of Lord Lindsay, and his eldest daughter's future husband, to have him – James Maclaren Smith – accept a royal licence to change his name.

Even the idea had him choleric. The deal was that and he would be known as Smith-Gray, his children take the surname of Gray and his wife become Baroness Gray.

'Over my dead body,' he had told Eveleen a few nights previously, their eyes meeting in the oval looking-glass on the wash stand, as he watched her shake loose her splendid hair. 'I want what's best for the children,' she said, turning around to meet his gaze, her expressive eyes troubled.

Her life's work had evolved to limiting the damage done to her children by her marriage and by trying to redress her husband's place in the social hierarchy. This change of name was a once-off, an opportunity unlikely to occur again and much too good to pass up on.

'It's snobbery. I won't have it.' James said. 'And, anyway, what's wrong with my name?'

'Nothing.' She was touched that he was simple enough to think that it was only his name that was under scrutiny. She turned away and busied herself brushing. In the early days of their marriage, James used to sit behind her and draw the strong black bristles for a hundred strokes through the soft brown of her hair.

'That young pup,' he sneered. 'Betrothed to Ethel. And without my approval.'

'But you weren't here,' his wife said mildly, deciding not to mention that when asking her to marry, he had not sought her father's consent either.

James feared that the granting and implementation of this licence would herald the final disintegration of his marriage. For now, he decided to let the matter rest. He and Eveleen were on the brink of a major row, another of those gut-churning affairs that starts off over little and can end up dragging in issues that he considered best left unspoken.

He hoped to lie with his wife tonight. Rowing would not further his cause.

James positioned the tripod, set the camera on top of it, added the black hood and, well pleased, stood back to admire his handiwork, liquid sunlight catching the red gold of the fine hairs on his arms, playing with the picot-edged ruffles around his neck.

Eileen stood watching her father's every move. She held, by one arm, her beloved Belinda, of the constantly smiling porcelain face, dark curls and cloth body. Girl and doll were inseparable.

'Now, my special pet, I'm going to take your photograph. Come over here and stand still.' He pointed to a spot by the urn in front of the steps. 'Yes, just like that. Good.'

Eileen loved when Dada called her his 'special pet' and she basked and preened in his praise, infrequent and minor though it was.

He returned to the camera, fiddling at it, standing back, scratching his head, trying to remember the operating instructions which at time of explanation had seemed so easy. James, who was creative rather than technical, refused to be daunted. He examined the various knobs and levers and came to the conclusion that their sequence of operation was incomprehensible.

Last month in Tuscany he met a New Yorker who told him about an American bank clerk named George Eastman who, working into the small hours of the morning in his mother's kitchen, had perfected a fool-proof box camera and roll film which he assured, within a few years, would make uncomplicated photography available to the masses.

James looked forward to simplification of this current complex process but in the meantime, he refused to be beaten. Photography was tipped to become an acceptable adjunct to painting and James liked to think of himself as someone who wholeheartedly embraced invention and innovation.

Much and all as she adored her father and wanted to please him, Eileen was easily bored and she started jigging around, swinging Belinda, as much to catch his attention as to hurry him on.

Asperity in his voice, he commanded, 'Stay still. I won't be a minute.'

'Belinda's making me move.'

'Tell her to behave.'

'I did, Dada. And she's trying. We both are. When will you be ready?'

'Soon.'

'You've had lots of soon.'

'Didn't you ever hear that the best things in life are worth waiting for?'

'Photographs aren't a best thing. They're boring and you're taking ages doing it.'

'I must have your photograph. To make sure I don't forget you while I'm away.'

Immediately Eileen was on alert. Her father's infrequent comings and seeming all-too-frequent goings were the catalyst by which she judged her happiness. 'But you only came home on Tuesday two weeks. Tuesday, Wednesday, Thursday and today's Friday,' she counted on her fingers. 'Only twelve days. You can't be going away again.' When James made no comment, Eileen jumped up and down, 'Promise. Promise me you won't. Please.'

'Never ask a man to make a promise he can't keep,' he said, though with the atmosphere so amenable, he planned to extend his visit, to keep an eye on that royal licence business. Perhaps, stay on until autumn.

To escape Eileen's pleadings, he stepped behind the camera and ducked beneath its black hood. Still, no obvious inspiration as to how to take the photograph struck him, though through the view-finder he could see Eileen jigging around. His temper shortening, he re-emerged. 'Do stand still.'

Eileen tired of this whole photography business and while not distracted from the possibility of her father setting off on his travels again, she was interested in this new concept of men and promises.

'Can I ask promises from a lady?'

'I can't answer for the fairer sex. I confess they quite baffle me.'

'What does baffle mean, Dada?'

James breathed a sigh of relief. He hated upsetting his favourite Eileen, conceived on a rare night of passion when his wife had responded to him with the abandonment of his various mistresses.

Afterwards, he was optimistic, thinking that bout of love-making heralded a new era, that it could be the salvation of their marriage, but Eveleen's burst of passion turned out to be a once-off.

He still remembers her scent, the tumbled rumple of bed linen; her hair wild, her curvy white body and long sinuous limbs; the sensation of being cocooned in their four-poster with November's foggy light filtering through the long windows and the log fire in the small black grate making short cheerful cracklings.

He felt a gathering of more love than he thought possible then, a love against which he had no time to measure. He held her tightly, tasting the salt at the edge of her eye and she murmured his name over and over again into his ear. Afterwards, as they lay in post-coital entanglement, it began to rain against the window, delicate drops, like the tapping of a baby's fingers.

Thankful that Eileen appeared to have lost interest in his travel arrangements, he answered, 'That's my clever pet. Always ask if you don't understand. Baffle means confuse. But we'll look it up in the dictionary when we go back indoors.'

Dada was a great one for looking up words in dictionaries.

'I'm lonely when you're not here,' Eileen confided, standing shadow-still and making sure too that Belinda was not moving.

'Nonsense,' he said, retreating again behind the hood to pull levers and to press buttons. A few seconds later, to his amazement, there was a blinding flash, a smart explosion and all around turned a brilliant white, then seemed to flare into splotches of darkness.

He emerged triumphant and surprised at actually having taken a photograph and Eileen gasped at the cleverness of her father.

He kept his victory casual. 'How could you be lonely here. With your Mama and your brothers and sisters?'

From the look of her, he suspected she was about to start into him again about going away. Her could not bear it and forestalled her by suggesting, 'Now, how about you taking a photograph?'

'Me? Dada, can I? Really? Really? All on my own?' Eileen thought she would burst with excitement. 'I'll take a photograph of you.'

Despite over-explaining the mechanics of the process, to anyone listening with even the slightest knowledge of photography, his instructions were senseless, but Eileen nodded. The operating sequence made sense to her. Young and all as she was, she knew Dada was unfamiliar with the process of photography and she loved him all the more for his adult vulnerability.

'Where do you want me to stand?'

His question gave Eileen an unfamiliar sense of power. Where would she place him? She relegated Belinda to the ground, while she thought, pacing up and down.

'Here at this bush?' he asked. 'By these nice yellow flowers?'

'That's forsythia,' she supplied. She soaked up information like a sponge. 'No, not there,' she said. Where Dada stood would be her decision. 'In front of the steps. In the middle,' she ordered and when he obeyed she had a moment of triumph, though she did not like his stillness. He, who was so alive and vibrant, appeared lifeless, inconspicuous and unimportant in front of the bulk of the building. 'Don't stand so still,' she said. 'Move.'

'I can't. The photograph will be blurred.'

'You don't look real.'

He was amused. 'How do you mean, not real. And me lord of the manor. What do you want me to do?'

'Raise your arm, as though you're waving. And leave it up.'

'If nothing else, it will be a photograph with a difference. Which arm do you want?'

Eileen had trouble with right and left. If she were a Roman Catholic, her nurse Sadie told her, she would not have to worry. Didn't the whole world know that Catholics blessed themselves with their right hand.

'The right,' she called.

'My right or your right?'

She hardly missed a beat, 'Yours.' Perhaps if Dada got holy he would not go away again.

She took the photograph and emerged from behind the camera bursting with pride and a new sense of accomplishment.

He swung her up on his shoulders. She tucked Belinda into the back of his neck, put her arms around his forehead and she thought she would die of happiness. 'Now let you and I enjoy the remainder of today. When I was little in Scotland do you know what my grandmother used to say?'

'No.'

'That the only time we have is now.' He gave an enormous grunt. 'And if I don't put you and Belinda down, I'm going to die of a heart attack.'

Eileen slithered briskly to the ground. He terrified her with his regular talk of dying. The thought of anything happening to him was more than she could bear.

Routinely he announced he was going to drop dead after climbing the stairs; that he had escaped death by a hair's breath at the hands of the local poacher; or nearly drowned while swimming in Lake Como.

It was not until she reached adulthood and discovered

Jung's conviction about difficulties being necessary for man's health needs that she realised the only way her father could tolerate his life was by investing it with non-existent danger. And he certainly was healthy.

He did not understand that, as a child, she found his reeling-on-the-edge of constant disaster unnerving. His dramatic recounting of near-death experiences, brushes with mayhem, descents into lunacy while he looked for missing cologne, lost collar studs or the sheath for his cut-throat razor had her terrified.

He lit his pipe and said, 'I'm proud of you, my pet, the way you speak your mind. I suspect, one day, you'll leave your mark on the world.'

'What does leave a mark mean?'

'Be well-known. Famous.'

'Like you? And your paintings?'

'Och, no. I'm just ordinary. Always have been and always will be.'

For as far back as Eileen could remember, she thought it magic that her Dada could make pictures with a brush. The best coloured pictures ever of trees and fields and mountains. And sometimes he painted beautiful ladies.

Initially his honesty, humility and awareness of his own limitations had been much admired by Eveleen. But they were not long married before she began to hold his acceptance of his mediocrity against him. She wanted a husband she could be proud of, and if he insisted on being a painter, then the very least he could do was become well-known, famous, like all the men in her family, she explained, her earnestness turning to fury when he laughed at the idea.

'But you . . . You're different,' James told Eileen, brushing to the back of his mind the hurt of that and of his many other spats with Eveleen. 'Promise me one thing.'

Eileen nodded.

'That you'll always remain true to yourself.'

'Yippee.' Eileen gave a little hop, skip and jump. 'Does that mean doing what I want to?'

'I suppose that's one way of putting it.'

'Last time you were away, I made a toboggan out of the top of my old pram and I went all the way down the hill in it and I wasn't a bit afraid,' she gabbled.

'It's all right to be fearful. It's a sensible emotion.' He took another puff of his pipe. 'We've all known fear in one form or another. And we're not much of a human being if we don't acknowledge it.'

Eileen liked when he talked to her as though she were a real grown-up but, surrounded by the rich tobacco aroma from his pipe, she wished she could believe him.

'No. It isn't,' she had to get this off her chest. And other than Padso who lived in the woods and who Mama called a hermit and had forbidden her to visit, Dada was the only person she could tell. 'It's not all right to be afraid. Not when your family goes back to the fifteenth century. Did you know that the first Lord Gray was master of the household of King James the second?' she asked.

'Well really. No, I didn't,' he lied. By now he was heartily sick of the antics of his wife's distinguished ancestors.

'And Ethel says I'm a cowardy when I sleep on the corridor outside Mama's room.'

'Balanced on two chairs, from what I hear.'

'How do you know?'

'I've my sources,' he tapped the side of his nose with his

index finger, grasped her around the waist and swung her in a huge circle. 'And choosing to be so uncomfortable. Now that takes courage.'

He carried her up the steps of the house, laid her across his knees and tickled her under her ribs, her tickliest place and then he tickled Belinda's tummy. Eileen could not make up her mind who giggled the most, her or Belinda.

'Hold me tight, Dada. Hold me tight.'

It was the nicest feeling in the world when her father held her close. Until this visit, James had paid Eileen scant attention. Her brothers and sisters, as though taking cue from their parents, to her howls of terror often pretended that Eileen was invisible or, worse, that she did not exist.

That morning, her nose pressed against the cambric of his shirt, there was a new edge to her awareness which made her heart beat faster. Something was going to happen, she knew. And it was a terrible something. So terrible that it had left an advance imprint on the atmosphere, an indelible mark of such intensity that even the sunshine could not obliterate.

'What a wonderful childhood,' says Jack admiringly. 'While you were talking I couldn't help thinking that you've lived through the most exciting era of our times. When you were born Queen Victoria was on the throne and within your lifetime, men have flown to the moon.'

'Yes, my childhood was quite wonderful,' she said. No, it wasn't, she wanted to scream to this sympathetic stranger, it was just awful being an unwanted, unloved afterthought. 'But really quite ordinary.'

Chapter 13

'I guess your childhood and where you grew up played an influential part in your work,' Jack remarks. 'In the States, childhood experiences are regarded as formative to creative development.'

'And was yours a good childhood?' Eileen asks politely. She has never lost her interest in people.

'Yes, of course,' he answers quickly on reflex. 'The sixties were my heyday.'

'Ah, the sixties,' she says with a little clap of her hands. 'The wonderful sixties. The decade when in your country Martin Luther King and Robert Kennedy were gunned down. When body bags were shipped home from Vietnam in their hundreds.'

Quickly, Jack picks up on her humorous sarcasm. 'When France flirted with revolution and British troops went into Belfast. And your future king was created Prince of Wales in a mock Camelot.'

'Touché,' concedes Eileen. 'The first heart transplant was achieved. And a Czech student publicly burnt himself to death in Prague in protest at the Russian occupation.'

Jack tops her reminiscences with, 'And we all sang "Hey Jude".'

'So we did.'

They look at each other, laugh together and Jack feels the further creation of a slender bond.

Eileen knows that, like herself, this young man did not have a good childhood.

Of course, my childhood was wonderful. Of course, it was, Jack's head hums.

Childhood is a happy time.

No mine wasn't. No mine wasn't, sings his gut.

And the old belly flutters of memory are back. Promptly he tries to relegate them to his subconscious.

There are some subjects on which he prefers not to linger. Primarily, his parents and their unintentional ability to dole out raw, abrasive hurt. Ridiculous, isn't it, at his age to still feel that hurt?

I've always been caught between my parents and sisters. Existing between the rock and the hard place, he jokes with his friends.

His mother Patsy, restless and flighty, forever on the go, as though constantly seeking but never finding, paid her children scant attention. He says he is used to it and from the time he first understood such matters, he has made a point of laughing off her attitude.

Irish Famine damage, Jack quips about his father, aware from toddler-hood that his primary interest in him was to mould him to his own image and likeness.

Enough of wallowing in that misery. He has plenty of happy childhood times to counterbalance the not-so-happy ones.

The best were the summer vacations he spent with his grandparents. The joy of swapping city skyline for seascape.

The sense of freedom at escaping the confines of the dark narrow-fronted brownstone family house.

Each year on his arrival at the old whaling town of Bellport, he felt as though he had come home. The first thing he noticed was the taste of salt in the breeze and the smell of the sea.

He loved the magic of the rambling fisherman's house sprawled on the watery lowlands, with its warren of rooms, watched over by the gimlet-eyed Captain Tuthill from the parlour chimney breast.

His grandfather Mick, a great bear of a man, with haystacked hair and crinkly eyes, had a roar that could be heard from one end of the lowlands to the other. His grandson was the son he never had, but his disapproval of Jack's lack of interest in the usual boyish pursuits of American youth was patently obvious.

Not only, he would bellow at anyone who would listen, was Jack a reluctant swimmer, but even with Mick's specially commissioned baseball mitt, he was a hesitant catcher and Mick could not believe that he preferred to walk rather than to ride the specially-ordered Raleigh bicycle, complete with drop handlebars. And as for Gaelic and hurling, under gentle pressure from Belle, Mick had long given up.

During weekends, shiny-faced in white cotton trousers and an open-necked check shirt, a baffled frown lending a bewildered cast to his features, Mick urged Jack to sporting feats in which he had no interest.

His grandmother was little different to now, except younger. Fragile and dainty, like a humming bird, with high cheekbones and translucent skin. Protectively, hovering in the background or sitting in a red-and-white striped deck chair, canopy down to shield her face, some magazine or other open on her lap, whimsically keeping the peace between grandfather and grandson.

She had a way of ruffling Jack's hair and of hugging him to herself that brought his grandfather's athletic antics into humorous perspective.

In her company, Jack basked in the unfamiliar security of unconditional love and approval.

During those long, hot, silent summer weekdays after his grandfather had returned to New York to his latest hobby of playing the stock market, the beach became Jack's kingdom and he a benign ruler with mystical powers. The water was crystal clear, turquoise near the shore, further out shading to amethyst.

When he screwed up his eyes and looked at the sea's greyness, Jack could see magic colours: the deep, almost black-blue that glittered and paled through every shade of blue until it became green, a thousand greens and browns and even turquoises until sea met the silver line of the horizon.

Squatting among the rocks, with their glistening calligraphy of seaweed, encircled by the music of what was happening around him, he collected treasures for the royal coffers – delicately edged scallops, mussels with their dark iridescent casings and encrusted white oyster shells.

And every night after feasting his eyes on the pumpkin yellow sunset, he watched as the moon, riding high in the velvet of the sky, made long cones of kingly light on the black of the sea.

Still Mick's sporting determination paid off. Despite himself, Jack became proficient at swimming, baseball and tennis, even boxing. In his teens, in between dating quantities of girls with indiscriminate enthusiasm, he flirted with playing the drums and enjoyed a brief and successful relationship with chess.

And developed an abiding passion for antiques.

'You'd a privileged childhood,' Theodore Splash – 'call me Theo' – told Jack during his third semester at Columbia University. Placing himself in the hands of a therapist had taken a lot of courage but at the time Jack was confused and desperate enough to grasp at anything that might help.

Theo was a herring-thin man who wore black mohair suits, gleaming white shirts, and who owned an eclectic collection of jazzy ties. He came highly recommended by the campus student counsellor who also happened to be his girlfriend.

At the time, seething with teenage angst, Jack saw his problem as simple. But, in his case, it was a simplicity overridden with guilt.

Around the age of fourteen, he had become interested and then fascinated by antiques – modern antiques – and decided it was the area in which he wanted to make his career.

'A nancy-boy business,' Paddy shouted the first time Jack broached the subject, before stumping out of the room in disgust, followed by Patsy who threw a hurt and bewildered look at her son.

Jack did not dispute Theo's professional opinion of his privileged childhood. Yes, he had so many material things, some necessary, some wanted, more needless and dispensable, that sometimes his life seemed surreal.

Top schools and colleges. Junior membership of the best country clubs and appropriate designer gear. An almost-new open-topped car for his seventeenth birthday and the latest in stereo equipment. All supported by a healthy allowance.

Only too well could he imagine his parents' respective reactions if they knew the percentage of the same allowance currently going on therapist's fees rather than on the heavy boozing and wild partying which his father believed would make a real man of him and knock that antique nonsense out of head; or making contacts, cultivating useful people and dating the right girls, the skills with which his mother hoped he would emerge from college.

Neither appeared to place much emphasis on him obtaining his degree.

Patsy would be all fragile and touchy at the idea of her son needing a therapist. Jack could clearly see her, in their big glass room, sipping at bourbon and coke and blowing smoke rings, surrounded in sympathetic clucking attendance, by her fund-raising friends.

Aloud, she would wonder where she had gone wrong, probably shed a silent tear, and leave gaps in her monologue for her friends to reiterate, as they could be guaranteed to, on the exceptional quality of her mothering.

His father would do his brooding alone and in isolation in his office, pacing the thick, dark-green carpet, his face shuttered, thumbs pinging his wide suspenders in furious symphony, wondering where they had got Jack from, muttering about how in his day, men had none of this namby-pamby nonsense.

The Irish men who survived the Famine and made the journey across the Atlantic to tame this hostile land were tough. They had little choice but to work hard, seven days a week. Using shovels, crowbars, pickaxes and their own muscles, they laid railway tracks across the prairie at the rate of two-and-a-half miles a day. Jack could recite his father's story verbatim.

It was not that his parents were cruel. Jack knew they loved him – in their own way – and wanted the best for him. So why did he always feel like this square peg in a round hole, he asked Theo during their sixth session.

Theo smiled in that knowing therapeutic way of his but, as usual, did not answer.

Unlike Sigmund Freud and his preoccupation with infantile sex, Theodore Splash operated from the broader and more modern canvas of the therapy of talking. The talking cure, he called it reverently. The theory being that after his patients were, as he put it, 'all talked out', they would be able and willing to take responsibility and to make the appropriate decisions for their own lives.

In principle, Jack had no trouble with Theo's *modus operandi*, except that he hoped for guidelines on how to put his viewpoint to his parents and to achieve his objective without starting world war three.

'I want a career in antiques and fine arts. My parents want me in the family newspaper business,' Jack spelt out slowly during his first session.

Theo tut-tutted sympathetically, examined his nails minutely and during their third session asked, 'So what do you *really* see as the problem?'

'I've told you,' Jack kept his voice steady.

'So?'

'As I said.' Irritation crept into Jack's voice.

'I see.' From the tone of voice it was obvious that Theo did not. 'You do realise, don't you, that we're better living in solutions rather than problems.'

'Dammit, I know that. I've always bloody known it. It's why I'm here. On my fifth session. Looking for the solution.' Jack's voice was raised.

'Anger accomplishes nothing. And what do you see as your solution?'

'You aren't listening.'

'Ah yes,' says Theo, intent on easing back the cuticle of his pinky finger with the pad of his thumb. 'The antique business. But how do you propose to go about it?'

'That's where you're supposed to come in.' Jack, on his sixth session, shouted and thumped at the desk.

Theo did not look up from his DIY manicuring, but did comment, 'On occasions anger can be good. Cleansing.'

'And that,' Jack told his grandmother during the Easter vacation, 'was that.'

'Paris during the twenties must have been wonderful.' There is a wistful tone in Jack's voice that touches Eileen.

'It was,' Eileen assures. 'Everyone of creative note seemed to pass through at some stage or another. It was vibrant and full of life. We nurtured our artistry and planned to put the world to right.'

Even as she utters the words she wonders could anyone ever put the world to right? Were people born fragile or did they become so?

What is that phrase about nature or nurture that runs around in her head? Daft words that Brigid read out from one of the Sunday papers. That is the problem with newspapers today. They are too full of all sorts of ridiculous hypotheses, written to pack the available spaces.

Amazing how this afternoon, one memory is triggering another. It is a long time since she thought about *The Magician*. How enraged she had been, feeling every finger pointed at her and laughter behind every hand.

'Have you read Somerset Maugham, Mr Devine?'

'Just *The Moon and Sixpence.*'

'Ah, yes. Gauguin's life. He also wrote a novel featuring a young lady who came to Paris from London to study art.'

'Was that you?'

'He denied it but nobody believed him.'

'That must have been fun.'

'Fun?'

'Yes and flattering. Being immortalised by a writer of Maugham's calibre.'

Eileen bites back what at the time had been her standard retort, instead saying, 'Then, I didn't think of it quite the way you put it.'

Jack is curious. 'So, how did you react?'

'I found offensive the idea of me and my work being diminished to popular fiction.'

'Surely, even then, being fictionalised was worth thousands of dollars of advertising.'

Eileen blinks. A frisson of déjà vu shivers down her spine. For a moment it is though Jacques is present. This is the way he went on. Never letting up on the power and importance of publicity.

The imaginings of old age.

What a curious young man this Jack Devine is and what an unusual outlook he has on life.

'I've never lived in the States,' Eileen says. 'Perhaps, an Irish childhood is the exception that proves the rule to creative development. I wouldn't have thought my childhood had any bearing on my adult life. Except to make me aware of my roots.'

'Roots are important,' Jack agrees. 'Were you a close family?'

Eileen's voice is almost inaudible. 'Very.'

'Let me guess. You were your father's favourite.'

'"My own pet," he used to call me. It was from him that I got the courage to be different. To plough my own furrow, as they say in Wexford.'

'Plough your own furrow. That's a good one.'

Lying in bed, Eileen felt safe. Everywhere was silent, except for the familiar big old house creaks and the soft sound of Mama playing the piano.

It was Eileen's favourite tune, 'Au Clair de la Lune'. 'By the Light of the Moon'. Since receiving her royal blue frock, as a gift all the way from Paris from one of her godmothers, she loved anything French.

The frock, in the finest of wool, was cut simply with a full skirt which had two large pockets trimmed with navy braid, long sleeves and a round neck. Her sisters, Ethel and Thora, jeered the dress's plainness but, even though it was still too big, it gave Eileen an unfamiliar sense of confidence.

But, more importantly, on the day she first wore it, Mama, pausing from writing letters about land purchase for the tenants, said that a lady always knew when less was more and that Eileen had an innate taste.

Eileen did not know what Mama meant, except that it sounded good.

From then on Eileen wished she were living in France where it was obvious that this less being more, and this 'innate' taste which by accident she possessed was a matter of course. When she was grown up, if only she did not love Brownswood so much, she would live in Paris. Just herself and Dada.

Then Mama started singing, her voice so soft that it did not drown out the music. As the notes drifted up the staircase, gentle as snowflakes, Eileen hummed softly, picturing herself on the flying moon boat that she could see out her window, drifting hither and thither on the blue clouds of sea.

Without warning, music and singing stopped, only to be replaced by the rumble of her father talking, occasionally interspersed by a comment in her mother's lighter voice.

Eileen held her breath for so long that she thought she would burst. No raised voices. She expelled in slow gratitude.

A worrier, she constantly assessed the mood of the household, particularly the relationship between her parents. All in all, it had been such an unusually peaceful few weeks that Eileen dared to hope Dada might remain for ever at Brownswood and they could be a real family.

She settled more comfortably under the patchwork quilt which represented their family history. Everyone was in it, except for her. So desperately did she want to be included that she would readily sacrifice a pocket from her Paris dress. But there was no space, the quilt was full.

When Sadie was in a good mood, she would point out the lilac sprigged cotton of the frock Mama wore during the summer she spent in Italy; stroke the delicate ivory silk of her wedding dress; run her rough fingers across the rectangle of mulberry-coloured velvet, taken from the outfit on her first Christmas home as a married woman.

Then there was a strip of glinting gold brocade from Dada's waistcoat; a fragment of linen from one of his shirts; even a piece of the dark serge of his jacket. Eileen's brothers and sisters were represented too, with a scrap of moleskin from Lonsdale's baby breeches; the square of white muslin from Thora's petticoat; a sliver of material from Ethel's yellow party dress and a substantial square from James's first tennis flannels.

Eileen settled more comfortably under the quilt, loving its colours and patterns and the pictures she could make in her head from its squares, rectangles, triangles, circles – and even hexagonals. Sometimes she wondered, when Sadie was stitching it together had she forgotten to include her, or just not bothered.

'I don't care that I'm not in the quilt,' Eileen told Sadie one afternoon. She was hanging around the kitchen hoping for a wedge of freshly baked griddle-bread.

'How could ya?'

'What do you mean?'

'How could ya be in it?'

Eileen tossed her head defiantly but she could not keep the quiver out of her voice, 'Everyone else is.'

'Well. Ya couldn't be.'

'Why?'

'Sure, wasn't it sewn and finished and on the mistress's bed long before you were even a twinkle in the master's eye.'

For a brief moment, Eileen felt herself surrounded by happiness fairies, delicately fluttering around her head on gossamer wings, playing hide-and-seek in her hair, curling up to sleep in her ears. She had not been left out of the quilt on purpose. And, even better, she had been a twinkle in her Dada's eye. She wished she could remember what it felt like to be a twinkle. 'Can I have a bit of the bread?'

Sadie, her face red and her pepper and salt hair worked loose from her bun, took a swipe at her. 'No, you can't. And out of my kitchen.'

Still tuned in to the snatches of conversation drifting up from downstairs, Eileen snuggled Belinda.

Chapter 14

Eileen was almost asleep when the timbre of the voices below changed. Mama and Dada rowing again. She felt her stomach constrict. She wanted to be sick. No, she needed to use the commode. But she was too frightened to move, too full of fear with all those shadows ravelling around her room and all that shouting coming up from downstairs.

For as long as Eileen could remember, she had been afraid of the darkness of the night, but it was Sadie who had taught her the power and the fear of twilight.

When she was very small, Sadie used to lift her up to look out of the nursery window. Together they would watch the light fade and greyness blanket the fields and trees.

'This is the heebie-jeebie time of the day,' Sadie confided, always shivering. Even when it was not cold, Eileen, copying Sadie, shivered too.

'Heebie-jeebie,' she repeated again and again, arms clinging to Sadie's neck, legs wrapped around her waist, hanging off her like a skinny monkey, wishing she could stay there for ever, enjoying the warmth of Sadies's ample body and the sound of the words rolling around in her mouth and off her tongue.

'What's heebie-jeebie?' She was always asking questions and she loved when someone, anyone, paid her attention.

Sadie explained in creepy detail and acted out with scary spider fingers this heebie-jeebie feeling, moving aside Eileen's ragged hair to whisper how during the death of each day, the soul died a little too. Then she would devoutly make the sign of the cross and, watching her big-eyed, making sure to use her right hand, Eileen copied her movements.

After Sadie left, closing the door and creaking down the stairs, Eileen had to remain alone in the nursery which suddenly was full of ravelling shadows and grunting noises.

She would not think of shadows or grunts now, she would think of the solstice. She ran the word around and around in her mouth, sliding it off her tongue and onto her teeth, she loved the sound of it.

Padso had told her about the solstice. 'It's a special day,' he said. 'A time of mystical powers.'

'How do you know?' she asked. She was always wondering how people knew so much.

'There are more things in heaven and earth . . .' he began mysteriously.

Because she did not know what he was talking about, she became scared.

Then he explained, 'In olden times, the solstice was when sacrifices were made.'

She and Belinda were perched on a large stone in the lee of the hawthorn bush that grew outside his shack. The bush had lost its honey-scented clouds of delicate white May flowers. During the past weeks, its leaves had become tough and shiny and its thorns long and lethal.

'What's a sacrifice?' The shadows of starlings burst upon the clearing, the paper flutter of their wings suspended in the air for a moment.

He scratched under his beard, carried away at the rarity of a captive audience, explaining in broad strokes of colourful language, 'Sometimes if the gods so demand, human sacrifices have to be made.' He was oblivious that it was a child hanging on his every word.

Eileen's white face looked at him with shocked intensity and she clutched Belinda more tightly. 'People?' she asked.

'Yes.'

'What kind of people?' Eileen's voice was breathless.

Padso, realising that he had scared Eileen, tried to remedy the situation without compromising truth and fact. 'Some people were born to be sacrificed, others had to be.'

'People like me?'

'Oh. No. Not like you, at all,' he assured heartily, hating to see Eileen upset. He loved her as deeply as he loved the animals that fed from his hand. She was such a sad wee scrap of a thing.

Squatting down beside her, with a stick, he drew a series of interlinking circles, in the dry brown-grey needles that covered the ground.

'There's this place called Newgrange. Not too far away from us in the county of Meath. It has tall blue stones which, during summer solstice, are aligned with the moment of sunrise.'

She did not understand about aligned, but thought it sounded like magic and she asked if he had ever been to this Newgrange place to see the solstice.

Yes, often.

Would he take her next time?

If there's a next time.

Before she had a chance to put her request more forcibly, he said that the solstice rested in Gemini.

She thought that too sounded beautiful. A resting solstice. And then she asked about Gemini.

Naturally, after that, they had to discuss her birth sign. Leo, the lion.

And when they had exhausted Leo, Padso reverting to the solstice, told her how it is so powerful that the tides in the sea ride high before it, particularly if there is a full moon.

She thought about all of that now and about the moon-boat she had seen earlier through the window. Strange how the solstice, which sounded so friendly with Padso and was a lovely lolly sound in her mouth, had become a night-time monster.

But the voices from below had stopped and for that she was grateful.

She began to cry. She often did to keep herself company and to hold the shadows at bay. If she cried noisily enough Sadie might come. That she would in all likelihood get a clip across the ear was preferable to drowning in her miserable loneliness.

She started slowly. Deep sobs under the quilt. Louder sounds with her head out from the quilt. Then she sat up, and holding Belinda tight, tried again. Nothing happened. Nobody came.

When she screamed, really screamed, a shouting scream, nobody heard, or if they did, they did not care enough to come.

Eventually she gave up, climbed out of bed, tiptoed across the room and used the commode. Sadie must be downstairs in the kitchen, probably drinking that black porter stuff. Over the thin cotton of her night gown, Eileen wrapped a shawl and dragging Belinda by the arm made for the door.

But the voices from below had started again. They sounded nearer now. And angrier. Her mother's shrill English. Her father's rough Scots. Irish voices were soft. Even Sadie at her crossest had a gentle lilt. These voices were so loud and so angry that she could make out the word 'adulterer', as Mama screamed it. Then Dada roared about frigid women and her mother screeched back about American harlots. Eileen ran all these new words around in her head.

She did not know the meaning of 'frigid' or 'harlot', but she thought they sounded bad. And as for Americans, judging from Mama's tone of voice, they must be bad too. An adult was a grown-up, she knew that, and an adulterer must be something to do with being grown-up. Nothing wrong with being an adult. She could not wait to be one.

If she were an adult maybe her sisters would let her into their special world. Instead of telling her to run away. That they were busy. Not to bother them. Or, worse of all, pretending she was invisible.

Ethel and Thora. The resilient Gray girls. For as long as she could remember, they had boyfriends, dance cards, invitations to balls and tennis parties. They declined Latin verbs – amo, amas, amat – with the clipped, dedicated arrogance of queens. Sitting close together on the bed, they cut each other's fingernails and smoked cigarettes, coughing and laughing in a camphorous nicotine fug.

Tangles of dark hair, long arms, long legs – one daughter, two heads.

You know Ethel Eveleen and Thora Zelma Grace? So

wonderful, so unassailable. Particularly when joined by their brothers, James Maclaren Stuart and Lonsdale. Always just the four of them. There was never room for Eileen.

And now Ethel was getting married to that horrible Henry Tuffnell Campbell. Weedy and shifty-eyed, Eileen heard Sadie describe him.

In the darkness, the idea of returning to bed was scary.

But what else could she do in the middle of the night?

Have an adventure.

But what kind of an adventure could you have in the dark?

Inspiration struck.

Padso. She would visit Padso.

She knew the way. Despite being forbidden, she spent long hours with him – Mama, thinning her lips, said he was not suitable company. She thought finding a place in the dark could not be too unlike finding it in daylight. The most obvious difference was the scariness. But then Dada said she was full of courage and this adventure would prove him right.

With her parents below, she could not go down the main staircase. And even if she used the back stairs, she would not get through the kitchen without being seen by Sadie.

It would have to be the bedroom window, which was already raised a few inches and its sash unlocked. She eased it open further and looked out. The night was a velvet black which after a few minutes of looking reassembled itself to varying shades of charcoal.

Putting her arms through her cloak, she wrapped it firmly around her and tucked Belinda into her pantaloons. As an afterthought she wedged her feet into her boots and half-did up the laces.

From previous attempts, she knew the difficult bit was getting a secure grasp on the ivy. But as Sadie had told her when she fought against working on her sampler – she hated the boredom of cross stitch, hemming, satin stitch and chain stitch – practice made perfect.

That morning while Sadie was off bustling about her other chores, Eileen took her words to heart. Instead of sitting on the stool with a straight back, working with threaded needle on her latest grubby square of cotton, securely anchored in the embroidery frame, she practised shinning down and climbing back up the ivy.

It was practice which paid off.

At first try, she gripped a thick hairy stem and before she knew it, she was on the ground and pointed in the direction of Padso's. But she was unprepared for this charcoaly darkness which breached the night with the sounds of little creatures shuffling in the undergrowth and she had not known that she would be accompanied by those fluttering black rag shadows from her bedroom.

To keep up her courage, she kept up a running commentary with Belinda.

Padso had instilled in Eileen his love of animals and nature. He spoke to rabbits and badgers, fed foxes and robins from his hand and nursed the injured back to health by his fireside. When she visited together they collected pigeon eggs, field mushrooms, lovage, wild garlic and cow parsley.

He healed her too, dressing a small wart on her right thumb with dandelion milk; rubbing the blister from a nettle sting with dock leaves covered in his own spittle; wrapping a spider's web around a cut and applying cooled boiled daisies to the sty in her eye.

When she had a sore throat, he presented her with a 'hairy Molly', with the instructions to place it in the foot of one of her stockings which she was to wrap around her neck while she slept. But, on the way home, Eileen tenderly removed Molly from her pocket and placed her on a carefully chosen leaf. Being confined to bed with a throat fever for the next three days, she considered a small price to pay for the caterpillar's freedom.

Eileen loved Padso with the blind love of innocence. She was unaware of his unwashed wildness, unruly locks of hair, trousers held up by rope, blackened nails and cracked boots. Nor did she know, nor would she have understood nor cared, about his reputation around the town for women and drink.

It was ghostly out. After a while, as her eyes adjusted, it seemed as if the charcoal light had been sucked out of the night, leaving a sepia-tinted photograph and the ground was covered in dry pine needles that crunched against her boots. Scary. Spooky. Scary. Spooky. Scary . . . She recited the words over and over again, like a litany.

A tree which had come crashing down a few weeks previously looked as though it had torn open the woods and weak grey moonlight fell through the gap as if exhausted by the journey. There was just enough light for Eileen to make out the rust-coloured bark and saucers of fungus, like some evil malevolence, sprouting in the joints between branch and trunk.

She clutched Belinda tighter.

Relieved, she spotted the outline of the shack. 'Padso, Padso,' she called, expecting him to appear instantly, as was his custom.

There was no sign of life, but as she drew closer she could

see a flickering light. By now she was exhausted. Her legs ached, her feet pained, even the muscles and skin in her face felt tired.

Something made her pause on the threshold.

Slowly she pushed at the door and stepped inside.

The light of the tilly threw malevolent shapes and shadows around the room. Later she would think of that night as the night of shadows. Shadows in her bedroom, shadows in the woods and the shadows in Padso's.

For a moment she thought the place was empty. Then she became aware of movement from the settle bed, tucked into the alcove by the fireplace. Heaving movements.

She could make out Padso's shirted back and his trousers down around his knees. She wondered why. Why, too, he was wearing his boots and cap in bed. He was jerking up and down, making the most awful grunting noises and she thought he was sick, perhaps even dying, and his stories of the human sacrifices of the solstice came rushing back.

'Padso, what is it?' she called, stepping closer.

His momentum did not falter. He kept going. Jerking and grunting.

She called again. Louder this time.

As he turned around, Eileen saw her. The woman lying beneath him. A mass of tangled black hair spread out below a picture of Christ crucified.

The woman's shift was around her waist. Torn and filthy. Huge flabs of breasts flopped under her arms. Eileen thought this was it. It was Padso who was killing her. That this woman was the human sacrifice of the summer solstice.

'No. No. Stop,' she called, dropping Belinda to the floor.

When Padso jumped up, Eileen saw his full nakedness,

before he pulled up his trousers, settled his cap more firmly on his head and took a stance beneath the picture. Droplets of blood dripped from Christ's crown of thorns and the silver nails that secured his hands and feet to the cross were huge.

Christ and Padso stared nowhere and everywhere.

The woman sat up, looked around and rose majestically from the settle, tossing back her hair, pulling up the shift, without shyness or embarrassment, easing her breasts into position, smoothing her skirt into place, pushing her feet into cracked boots.

Magnificent in her sexuality, she exuded the strength of natural woman and with a flash of childlike clarity Eileen knew, but would not have been able to give voice to her knowledge, that this woman standing on the mud floor was more real than either of her sisters. Or her mother.

It was then she recognised her as Bessie Rossa from the town.

In the dim light Bessie, heavy-breasted and sweating, looked from Eileen to Padso and back again.

Eileen wanted to rush at and smother herself in the comfort of Bessie. Instead she bent down, retrieved Belinda from the ground and held her against her chest as tight as she could.

Dragging a shawl across her shoulders and without saying a word, Bessie left, easing open the door open on rasping hinges, banging it closed behind her.

Padso stood, scratching at his head under the cap, looking at Eileen, sideways and with downcast eyes.

Shifting from one foot to the other, holding Belinda tightly, warily Eileen watched him too.

Their relationship was for ever changed. A new awkwardness full of unspoken explanations had sprung up between them.

Then Eileen went for Padso. Impelled by an unknown unfamiliar force outside of herself.

Shouting and screaming.

Tearing at this shirt and his face.

Kicking at his shins with her boots.

Thumping his chest with her fists.

He stood still. Not making the slightest effort to defend himself.

She never visited him again.

Chapter 15

Eileen remembered nothing more of that night. But she must have returned home, probably climbed back up the ivy, because when she awoke next morning, the light was still grey and Dada was bending over her.

'Shush,' he put his fingers to his lips. 'Don't make a sound.'

Eileen sat up. He was wearing his travelling cloak. And carrying his small leather valise. She could smell his cologne and, even in the dimness, see the pores of his skin and his goldy hair curling at the back of his collar.

She sat bolt upright, the tendons in her neck pounding, taking in everything, realising the implications of his dress.

'Where are you going?' As she spoke the horror of last night returned. Dada and Mama fighting. Padso and Bessie. She did not know what they were doing but she knew enough to know that it was bad.

'Shush. Back to Italy.'

'You can't. Don't go, Dada. Please. Please.'

'I have to.'

'Then take me with you.' She scrabbled under the quilt for Belinda. She could be ready in a few minutes.

'I can't.'

For the second time within a few hours, Eileen was annihilated, her world tumbling down around her. 'Don't leave me here, please, Dada,' she implored.

'Remember, you're my special pet. Don't make an awkward situation any more difficult than it already is,' he whispered. He was back treating her as though she were an adult. It gave her hope.

'I just want to be with you,' she whispered back.

'And I want you with me, too. But in this life, we can't always have want we want.'

'You can, you're an adult. You can do anything. An adult-er-er,' she enunciated clearly, recalling with pride her mother's most raised-voice word of last night.

She had the whole of her father's attention now, so much so that he even forgot to whisper, 'Where did you hear that word?' he demanded.

'Mama said you were an adult-er-er. I heard her.'

He looked flustered, dropped his valise on the floor, sat heavily on the bed beside her which made the springs ping and creak and said, 'Oh, dear. I can't deny it. We were discussing, in a not too-civilised manner, the matter of adultery.'

Eileen did not question him about this adultery. 'You were fighting again?' she accused, hoping her father would reassure her that it was not so.

'Not really fighting,' he said. 'More disagreeing. Your mother and I think differently on various subjects.'

'It was a shouting disagreement?'

'I suppose you could say that. Perhaps I did raise my voice.'

Eileen relaxed a little, glad to have her father's exclusive attention. 'It was Mama I heard shouting. Not you,' she fibbed and felt awful once the lie was out of her mouth. 'What's a harlot?' For a moment, she had a wild hope that Dada would gather her up in his arms, carry her to the library, take down the big green dictionary and together they would sit at the reference table and look up this word 'harlot'.

The way they had looked up the word 'snob'.

That morning had began again with her father's shouting and ranting about the 'snobbery of English titles and this ridiculous nonsense of name changing'. She had heard him from the landing the previous night. Now his tirade trailed out from the dining room in angry gusts, along with the wafting aroma of kidneys, liver and bacon. When Dada was home, he insisted on the family eating breakfast together.

Upset by the raised voices, she decided to skip food and she watched and waited with Belinda, peeping out from behind the hall stand until her mother, her sisters and her brother James emerged from the dining room and marched along the hallway one after the other, like the ducks from the pond in the meadow.

After a while, feeling a slow return to calm, she crept to the open dining-room door and there was Dada sitting, as though he had not a bother in the world, at the head of the table, surrounded by the silver chafing dishes from the sideboard, taking bites from a large slice of bloodied liver which he held in his hands.

'Come.' he said, mopping with a napkin at the pink dribbles running down his chin, 'It's all right. The black Celt has returned to his hiding place.'

When Eveleen had refused him access to her bed last night, he had made his point about this name change with quiet intensity and, this morning, he was still making it, though now vociferously. No way would he condone it. He was certain he would win, that his powers of persuasion would sway not only Eveleen but officialdom. Tucking into breakfast, a meal of which he was inordinately fond, he was feeling excessively pleased with himself. But then James Maclaren Smith was, if nothing else, an optimist.

Eileen climbed into his lap and he fed her morsels of liver which she hated but ate. After a while, she asked him what the word 'snobbery' meant. He dashed his napkin across the table, jerked to his feet, almost tumbling Belinda and herself from his lap, said, 'Come,' and with her running her fastest behind him, he strode to the library.

He wheeled the steps to the section where the reference books were kept and lifted Eileen on to the second highest rung. She took down the heavy tome with its dark green cover and the words *Oxford Dictionary* written in faded gold lettering. Seated at the library table, her father helped her turn the pages but encouraged her to find the word on her own.

'I have it, Dada. I've found it.' She was triumphant.

'Go on, read,' he urged. They were so close that she caught the drift of his special cologne and his hair cream. Eileen loved all her Dada's various smells, particularly what she called his night-shirt-morning-smell, the strong one which was only there until he had washed and shaved.

She began, 'Snob. N.'

'That means noun.'

'A shoemaker, shoemaker's app-ren-tice . . .' She spelt out the last word carefully syllable by syllable.

Her father started laughing. Great gusts of laughter. 'Show me. Let me see.' He looked at the dictionary, laughed some more and said he was not surprised that 'snob' was a Scots word. Then he read aloud something further down the page about 'ridiculous value set on social standing.'

'What's so funny, Dada?' Her moods see-sawed to match the family's moods, but over the past weeks, she was particularly swayed by her father's various humours. She loved when the happiness fairies danced about the place, settling on her head like these haloes which surrounded Sadie's saints. This morning, despite her father's laughter, she did not think he was particularly happy and she certainly was not aware of any dancing fairies.

'Pretension,' he said. 'Pretension.'

And though she did not know what it meant, just then it did not seem appropriate to question him.

That night when getting ready for bed, she tried Sadie, who told her to make sure to wash behind her ears.

Eileen remembered the word and on Friday evening she lingered in the hallway, waiting for Lonsdale who was coming down from Dublin for the weekend. She and Belinda occupied themselves by jumping the black-and-white tiled floor, taking heed of Sadie's warning care to avoid the cracks so that they would not burn for ever in the fires of hell.

'What's pretension?' she rushed at Lonsdale even before he had properly removed his cloak. He stood for a moment, drinking in the atmosphere of home, handsome in his brass and braided military uniform.

She waited quietly, rubbing her shoe up the back of her leg, while he stroked his moustache and thought. He was more into action than words. His explanation that it meant 'what Father wasn't' was oddly comforting and wholly informative.

Briefly James wondered at the damage he and Eveleen had inflicted on this child. 'Harlots are not your concern.'

'Are they always American?

Instead of answering about harlots, American or otherwise, he said, 'Ladies don't shout. And your Mama's a lady. A great lady. Always remember that.'

Eileen would do anything to keep him talking, to keep him here with her. 'But you're not a gentleman?'

'No, I'm not,' he agreed. He laid his mouth close to her ear. 'It'll be our secret. I never tell anyone I'm not a gentleman.'

'Mama knows,' Eileen whispered back.

'Are you certain?'

'Yes. I heard her tell Ethel. She said, "Your father's no gentleman." That means you, doesn't it?'

''Fraid so. And you remember, Mama's always right. And now, my pet . . .'

'No, Dada. No. You can't go.'

'I have to. But I'll send for you as soon as possible.'

'Send for me? You mean you're not coming back?'

'Not this time. But while I'm waiting for you, I shall post you the photograph, the one you took of me, so you can remember what I look like.'

'I don't want it. I don't want to remember you. I hate you.'

He ignored that. 'I'll be living in Italy. And your Mama and I've agreed that you'll spend lots of time with me. How does that sound?'

With the perversity of childhood, Eileen whinged, 'But I don't want to live in Italy.'

'You won't be living there. Just spending your holidays

with me. We'll have a wonderful time. Together. Just the two of us.'

She sensed a rushing static all around her, sealing her off, so that his voice seemed to reach her from afar, as though he had already left.

The prospect of that future started her crying. This upheaval to her life was more than she could absorb. First Padso. Now Dada. She refused to kiss him and it was only during this visit that he had started kissing her.

She slid down the bed, right under the quilt and, clutching Belinda, turned her back on him as he put his arms around her in an awkward cuddle.

When he left the room, she sat up again and listened to the heavy sound of his steps along the corridor, down the stairs, out the front door. She climbed out of bed then and stood at the window which was open since last night. The dog-cart was drawn up at the bottom of the front steps. Mattie, Sadie's husband, held the reins.

Her Dada, tall and handsome, came down those steps and moved away from the house to look up at the nursery window. But she shifted back into the shadows. He raised his hand as if to wave, then let the gesture fall to his side.

She looked out at the hedges hooped with briars, sheathed and limned in morning mist. Crows rising, scudding, then trotting along the grass like sturdy young turkeys. Over to one side, an unbroken belt of trees meshed together in a plum-coloured haze, and beyond them stretched miles and miles of trees with new leaves.

She did not care that Dada was gone. She had Brownswood and its land. It couldn't get up and go. To her childish eyes, her home was perfect. She knew its every nook and cranny and she loved its aura of familiar comfort, reinforced by its shabby gentility, worn carpets, mis-matched furniture and faded walls.

Brownswood land stretched further than her eyes could see. Even when not allowed outside, she escaped confinement by looking out the nursery window, over the fields peppered with domino cattle, and beyond the woods resting on the horizon, to the great green immensity of space rolling into hills and mountains that wore the shadows of the sky. The more she looked, the larger and more extravagantly remote landscape and sky became.

James Maclaren Smith took his leave of home and family in a single glance – unconsoling, unaccepting and unreconciled. Then he turned and walked towards the cart. He did not look back, nor did he look upwards again. And Eileen did not call after him.

He never used the new version of his name which in the end was changed without his permission.

Chapter 16

From the window of her bedroom, Eveleen also watched James leave Brownswood. Outwardly, she appeared self-controlled; inwardly, she was in a turmoil. Her life was over. Pride was a terrible sin. But not as bad as lust. And now that James had confirmed his liaison with this American, there was no going back.

Eveleen Pounden had been raised in a stiff Anglo-Irish atmosphere in Daphne Castle, just outside Enniscorthy. An obedient, docile girl, she had no personal ambition beyond conforming. She never disputed that her life would follow a similar pattern to her mother's, which would include a matched marriage to a man chosen by her parents, producing children and running a household.

Somewhere along the line, though, like all young girls, she hoped for romance. She and her cousins were consumed by the idea of this mysterious love.

Full of imaginings, they posed in front of the mirrors.

Creamy white shoulders.

Graceful arms.

Up-thrust breasts.

Dissecting love.

Aping the sensations of palpitating, fainting and blushing.

Dressing each other's hair with feathers, flowers and jewellery.

Swapping gowns.

Gorgeous untouched creatures in lace-trimmed pantaloons and tightly laced corsets.

Who knew nothing, yet firmly believed they knew it all.

Despite all those theoretical preparations, Eveleen was unprepared for the impact when love found her in the form of James Maclaren Smith, while she and her aunt holidayed on the Italian Lakes.

James, a handsome, womanising Scot of middle-class background, was something of a dandy, and augmented his living as a landscape artist by seducing and painting for quite exorbitant fees wealthy young matrons, who were bored by life, by too much money and with having too much leisure time.

As easily as tossing away the stone from a peach, a fruit of which Eveleen had grown inordinately fond, on meeting James she threw caution to the winds and quickly followed it by the twin concepts of discipline and duty on which she had been reared.

From the beginning, James, too, was smitten by Eveleen. Her freshness and lack of side he found stimulating, and her rather dour and dutiful attitude to life was familiar. He ignored both his other conquests and his painting to concentrate exclusively on wooing her.

Within days he had charmed her chaperoning aunt with posies of wildflowers and lavish compliments into allowing him to take Eveleen picnicking, a pursuit he loathed, though he delighted in Eveleen's coltish grace and loosened hair when he could persuade her to race him along the shore. Of course, he made sure she always won.

He never tired of watching the way she sat so prim and

straight-backed on the uncomfortable gilt chairs during those interminable evening recitals in the hotel. But any discomfort he suffered was more than compensated for by the promise-laden glances from beneath her lashes and, to the jealousy of all those disgruntled matrons, he visibly melted when she smiled her slow smile.

Eveleen was in love. Really in love. Having a suitor, she was one up on her cousins. Unlike them, she could discuss love from personal experience and did when she returned home in September, bubbling with excitement at James's proposal of marriage. That he had asked her outright, without even requesting her father's permission, in her eyes, confirmed the depth of his love for her.

With much ranting and raving and choleric outpourings, his cheeks suffusing under the rich ochre of fox-hunting fresh air and port-swollen veins, Captain Jeremiah Lonsdale Pounden refused to sanction the marriage and threatened to cut off his daughter without a penny.

Her mother, Lady Jane Stewart, a tiny woman with empty eyes, herself daughter of the tenth Earl of Moray, adopted a calmer approach by reminding Eveleen that particularly as she was an only child, she had a duty to her lineage, a position to uphold within the community and there was also the matter of family loyalty.

But it was Eveleen's cousins, suddenly and unexpectedly adopting the values of their parents urging her to think again and classifying James, whom they had never met, as an adventurer, who wounded the most.

After all their shared secrets and discussions about love.

She looked at them in hurt amazement, fled to her room and eloped a week later.

When it came to the consummation of their marriage, James was in for a surprise. The unbridled passion he had so patiently waited to be released on their wedding night was never realised.

His bride, stiff and nervous, bore no resemblance to his laughing, rebellious sweetheart. He made all types of allowances and tried all manner of cajolings. But to no avail. If anything, as the months went by, Eveleen grew more rigid each time he approached her to make love.

Uncharacteristically, he remained not only faithful, but tender, solicitous and loving. When she became pregnant, he hoped that motherhood would restore to him the girl with whom he had fallen in love. But that did not happen and, with money running out, at his wife's insistence they returned to Ireland where the Poundens made available to the young couple Brownswood Manor, just a short distance from Daphne Castle.

Eveleen, who had matured from starry-eyed romantic to pragmatic prodigal daughter, was quietly welcomed back into the claustrophobic family fold. She picked up the reins of her old life as though she had never left and even within the inner circle of the family, the subject of her marriage was never broached.

Dutifully she produced four more children and got on with life, publicly loyally supporting James's constant travelling; privately grieving during his absences, waiting in anticipation for his homecomings, hoping that eventually he would settle into Brownswood.

The shame of her last conception lived on. By marrying James, she had brought enough humiliation on herself and her family. The memory of her one occasion of wild sexual abandonment both disgusted and titillated her. She, Eveleen Pounden, had taken wanton pleasure in an act she had been brought up to think of solely as duty.

A gloriously terrible something had snapped in her that night. Her carefully orchestrated emotions of the well-brought-up deserted her. Sometimes, in pensive moments, she allowed herself to wonder at the all-consuming passion which flared between James and herself, and to wonder if that was the love of which James had so frequently spoken.

She disregarded the ensuing pregnancy until it could no longer be ignored. Equally, she disregarded the resultant child and handed her over for rearing to the servants who called her 'the poor craythur' and meted out to her the same rough care as they gave to their own babies.

Over time she pushed the memory to the back of her mind, and gradually her equilibrium was almost restored and the pragmatic matron virtually returned.

But the past few weeks with James had been so happy that she had broken her self-imposed rule of more than a decade and allowed him to lie with her. And more. He was hard to resist. She justified her softened attitude by daring to hope that he was reformed, returned permanently and that they had a future together.

She was so certain he would deny the rumours that she broke another of her rules and asked him about recent gossip. His current liaison, it was said, was with a seventeen-year-old artists' model from America, with golden hair curling down to her waist. For a long time, Eveleen had known of, but inured herself to, James's reputation for mistresses who with the passage of years grew ever-younger.

James had a Scots middle-class integrity. Desperately he

wanted back into his marriage again. Believing the new bond between Eveleen and himself could take the truth, and anyway loving and respecting her too much to lie, he admitted liability, offered explanation and tried to tell her that the liaison had been over from the first night she had allowed him re-entry to her bed.

But instead of listening, something deep and primal within her snapped. Her face was shocked, her mouth a tight angry line and her blaze of disappointment scorched the air between them.

Something that had her shouting words she had not known were in her vocabulary. Something from which there was no going back.

Something from where there was no return.

Something that as time passed made Eveleen understand Bessie Rossa. For whom, also, there could be no return.

Not that the circumstances of that were widely spoken about, though they did get an occasional nudge-nudge, wink-wink airing in shebeens, when after too much porter, the men's tongues became loosened, or at morning mass where they were whispered from behind the women's hands in hypocritical God-help-us gossipings. Even the priests from the altar glossed over the unchristian shame of the punishment meted out to Bessie in the name of the Church.

On moonlit nights, humming the old 'come-all-ye' songs sung in the kitchen of a distant childhood, dirt-ingrained fingers plucking at the stumpy fringe of her black shawl, hair streaming wildly, Bessie Rossa flitting from tree to tree, wandered the woods at the back of Brownswood, always working her way towards Padso's place.

Not that Padso would have anything more to do with Bessie. The look on young Eileen's face that night cured him of Bessie and her like for ever. Without mentioning Eileen's name, in the dark of the confessional box, he admitted his sins to the parish priest, who insisted before granting absolution that Padso would have to make a public confession.

Padso hesitated. Drew a sharp breath. Drew several sharp breaths. Only too well did he know of the ignominy and denigration of public confession, but when threatened with excommunication and the prospect of burning for ever in the fires of hell, he capitulated and he performed the following Sunday from the altar after eight o'clock mass.

Then it was left to the parishioners to enthusiastically fulfil their duty of casting out the woman who had sinned.

The exception was Eveleen who, though quietly grieving the loss of James, insisted that Bessie be allowed refuge in their woods and be fed and clothed whenever she came to the back kitchen door. She was broken and harmless, Eveleen said, unaware of what she was doing, just a poor lost soul, a child of God, who should be respected and left be.

Smug in their self-righteousness, the townspeople muttered about the family in the big house being Protestant, not Catholic, and how there was no accounting for their behaviour. Some ignored Bessie as though she did not exist; others jeered, called her names and threw rotting garbage at her.

Eileen who lived in terror of being got at by Bessie, avoided the woods.

On Christmas morning the following year, Bessie was found naked, blue-lipped and frozen-limbed, un-fragrant in death, under the bare, black-branched hawthorn bush which grew outside Padso's shack. It was silvered with hoar frost and festively festooned with exotically shaped icicles.

Eileen was glad Bessie was gone, dead for ever, though her dreams were constantly haunted by the picture of Bessie and her camisole.

The strangeness of the different faces of love.

By the time James sent the photograph Eileen was ten and a quarter. She looked at it briefly, her eyes filled with tears – the hopes that they would be a real family were for ever shattered. Resisting the urge to tear it up, she put it carefully under her mattress where it was found by Sadie and transferred to a drawer.

As James had promised, they did holiday together, sometimes relatively successfully, other times utterly disastrously but always Eileen returned home feeling empty and deprived. By now she knew the meaning of harlot and adulterer and she had developed an irrational dislike of Americans and all things American.

Eileen was full of black and white feelings and she felt powerful.

Henry Tufnell Campbell was her blackest feeling. How she hated him. He and her sister Ethel were only returned from their autumn honeymoon in Rome when, as Sadie said, 'without a by your leave', he filled the house with builders and stonemasons, tearing at the outside and inside, then he brought in fleets of painters and decorators.

Three autumns later his orders of carpets arrived from England, along with curtains from France, furniture from Germany and tapestries from Belgium.

Eveleen, looking bemused rather than angry at the disintegration of her home, the house that had been in her family for generations, went around in what had become her customary daze.

To no avail, Eileen raged at her mother's indifference.

Ethel, starry-eyed, hung on her new husband's every word and agreed with his every proposal.

Thora, bewailing being left on the shelf, travelled backwards and forwards to Switzerland comforting herself with a ski-instructor.

Lonsdale and James, men of few words and professional dodgers of unpleasantness, avoided visiting Brownswood.

When his renovations were finished, Henry threw a lavish party. The local newspaper was effusive, describing the house as, 'a magnificent specimen of Elizabethan architecture, with a charming parterre laid out in faultless style'. It went on further to effuse, 'The entrance lodge, which has recently been completed, is quite a gem'.

'Gem, gem,' Eileen muttered.

Considering the reporter who had written the story hypocritical, the following day she stormed into the newspaper offices in Enniscorthy, demanded to see the editor and made her complaint.

As far as the editor, a nowhere-man whose fingers constantly worried his moustache, was concerned, the gentry, even the youngest of gentry, were a law unto themselves and he knew enough to listen with sympathetic intent. 'Young integrity gone didactic,' he told his wife that night, equally pleased with his insight into young Miss Eileen as with his command of the English language.

Eileen's eyes began to hold a knowing expression of sadness

and experience. Her childhood was over, her youthful innocence gone forever. Her beloved Brownswood had been taken away from her but she would not let it go without a fight.

She was everywhere, asking questions, criticising Henry's decisions, querying his commands, seeking to undermine his authority. But by now he was entrenched firmly as master and, like the sword of Damocles, he held dismissal without compassion or reference over the heads of the staff.

When he realised there would be no end to Eileen's pesky behaviour, that she would never stop treating him as an interloper, he persuaded Eveleen, now officially titled Baroness Gray, to adjourn to her house in Kensington, pointing out the convenience of being well-established in London for Eileen's forthcoming presentation at court, doing the season and acquiring a suitable husband.

In the end Eileen left Brownswood Manor quietly. Like her father, never looking back.

On Eileen's sixteenth birthday, her mother and herself took breakfast in the morning room. Crunches of toast, clatters from cups re-united with saucers, crackles from *The Times* as Mama, pink-faced in unusual excitement, read aloud from the Court Diary.

'Next year, it'll be your turn to do the Season.'

Now was as good a time as any to make her announcement.

'I shan't be doing the Season.'

'You what?'

'I shan't be doing the season or being presented at court.' The words which Eileen had rehearsed over and over again under the seclusion of her bedclothes, were delivered with considerably more bravado than she felt.

'You will be presented,' Eveleen said, her voice dangerously calm. 'You've to think about making a good marriage.'

This all-consuming business of being presented and doing the season was another of Eileen's black feelings.

'I will not.' Eileen stood firm, eyes locked with her mother whom she blamed for allowing the desecration of Brownswood and for what she regarded as her now permanently homeless state. 'And you may as well know, I'm not going to marry. Ever.'

'You most certainly will,' Eveleen blustered belligerently.

'I shall not.'

Eventually, it was Eveleen who broke eye contact. Icy calm took over from her usual uninterested torpor. 'And, pray, what do you propose doing with yourself?'

'I'm going to be an artist.'

'A painter? Like your father?' Her neck and face flushed an angry red, 'Most certainly not.'

Her mother's reaction took Eileen by surprise. She was increasingly passive, most of the time apparently undisturbed by and unaware of life's happenings. It was as though all hope had cracked with James's departure, splitting her open to her very heart and laying vulnerable and bare all her private dreams and aspirations.

On occasions, she remembered her maternal role and tried to reinforce her authority. Invariably, her efforts turned futilely aggressive.

Eileen's reason for becoming an artist had nothing to do with following in her father's footsteps, as her relationship with him was decidedly disharmonious. It was to fulfil the creative urge which she felt on constant simmer below her surface. Other than painting, she knew of no other medium where she could explore her artistry.

She watched Eveleen finger the cameo brooch on the neck of her white ruffled blouse and, when the cold little laugh she had acquired since the departure of James echoed around the room, Eileen excused herself, stood up from the table and, straight-backed, walked out of the morning room, into the wood-panelled, darkly-carpeted hallway, up the stairs with its gleaming brass rods.

Being on the receiving end of Mama's demands made Eileen feel grown-up. Woman to woman grown-up. That morning she crossed the final boundary from child to adult.

She hated London.

She hated the stiff formality and ponderousness of this house, all dark wood, heavy furniture, drab walls and dreary brocade curtains. Insistent on having her bedroom decorated to her taste, she had supervised the stripping and beeswaxing of the old oak floor boards to a golden sheen. The walls she had painted sunshine cream and she finished off the windows with floaty muslin curtains.

Closing her bedroom door firmly, she rooted around among her paint jars until she found a pot of bright red, a large camel-haired brush and a soft lead pencil. With the pencil, she drew the outline of a large heart on the wall above her bed. Carefully she painted it in.

Romance.

Pleased with her handiwork, she sat at her dressing table and looked long and hard into the mirror.

Her looks, she decided, would do, though she would like a simpler hairstyle – how she wished she could have short hair.

As for her wardrobe, she hated the currently fashionable pastel dresses with their uncomfortably tight waists and awkward over-puffed sleeves. She yearned for dark comfortably tailored skirts and jackets in pure wools, linens and silks. Even better, she wished she could wear breeches and wondered would she ever dare defy convention that far.

She then turned her attention to the grander issue of her life.

So far, it had not pleased her.

With a grateful sigh and a rush of positive white feeling, she said goodbye to the child she no longer was and spread her arms wide to embrace adulthood.

The first unhappy stage of her life was over.

She would keep control of the remaining stages.

Chapter 17

Strolling back with Jacques from the annual motor show held at the Grand Palais, Eileen's head buzzed with images of the latest models, sleeker lines, faster performance and increased roadworthiness.

He cut into her reverie by remarking mournfully, 'I find it difficult to believe that in the space of a few years our wonderful yellow fiacres and coachmen with their shiny white top hats have been replaced by owner-driven automobiles.'

They had detoured to take in the Parc Monceau with its maze of paths and geometric-shaped flower beds, a riot of patriotic red, white and blue, geranium, alyssum and lobelia.

As usual, they were appalled to laughter at the park's collection of neo-antique follies, though they were huge fans of its large lily pond with pink, yellow and white blossoms waiting to burst into bloom.

That afternoon the place had its regular complement of neatly dressed children playing polite ball, perambulated babies in frilled bonnets and gossiping nannies in starched uniforms and navy capes.

'You're an old stick-in-the-mud,' Eileen teased. 'And I suppose you'd still prefer gas to electric lighting. Or even better candles?'

'Now that you mention it,' he laughed. She flicked her glove at him and they walked a few yards further in companionable silence.

'What about rugs?' he asked. 'Ever thought of doing rugs?'

'Rugs. What kind of rugs?' Eileen was still back at the motor show, surrounded by Rolls-Royces, Mercedes-Benz, Citroëns and Bentleys.

'Rugs. Carpets. For the floor, of course. You could design and I'd handle the business end.'

Eileen stopped in her tracks. 'That sounds great. It's something I've often thought about but never taken further.' She gave him an impulsive hug. On the rare occasions when they made physical contact, it was platonic rather than sexual and she liked to be the instigator.

This time however it was different. For no apparent reason the atmosphere between them crackled with tension. Their eyes locked and she felt as if all the breath were being sucked out of her body. Then she dropped her gaze, 'You are clever.'

His recovery was immediate but it did not stop him wondering what was the point of hiding his feelings. He wondered about mentioning marriage. A preliminary probe. He had long wanted to propose to her. Instead he said, 'Hmm. I know I am clever.' He paused wondering would she pick up on his mood. Give him an entrée. When she did not, he continued, 'Rugs are a fascinating prospect. The market is right. I sense in the near future, they're going to be a must-have home and office accessory. With enormous commercial possibilities.'

'I keep telling you, I'm not interested in commercial.'

'Your end would be purely creative.'

'How do you know so much about it?'

'Research. I've been looking into the idea for a while.'

Jack wonders how many minutes of recording time is left. Hand casually in trouser pocket, he has been turning on and off the machine in an effort to conserve tape, while at the same time, attempting to capture Eileen Gray's personality and to catch both the flavour of her conversation and her sharpness of comment.

With every fibre of his being, he is tuned into this woman, her life and her extraordinary career. He has come to know, to like and to admire her. For the first time ever, he understands and can relate to his father's obsession with the newspaper business. In the same way as he knows antiques, he knows he has the making of a superb piece of journalism.

The thrill of the chase. The headiness of capture. The excitement of subjugation. The almost orgiastic fulfilment. The ingredients of a thriller. It is all here unfolding before him.

He itches to write it up.

Eileen tackled rug-making with her usual enthusiasm. To her amazement, she discovered that the few classes and lectures on the disciplines of drawing, painting and the use of colour which she had so reluctantly sat through all those years ago at the Slade transferred effortlessly to the design of rugs and carpets.

Her worry was her eyes. There was constant early morning blurring and increasing difficulty with focusing. Just minor, she told herself, but deep inside, she suspected it was more. Recalling Jacques's words about the unhealthy atmosphere of lacquering, she attributed that as the cause and was pleased to be taking a break from working with chemicals in a dusty atmosphere.

She often thought of the morning she had drawn that red heart on the wall of her bedroom, the day she vowed to keep control of her life.

Despite her much vaunted independence, she would like the warmth, love and closeness, this conforming coupleness which others took for granted. It was not due to lack of opportunity that she was alone. A selection of eminently suitable young and older men and, indeed, women were a constant factor of her life.

Since more or less getting over Damia, she did her best to fall in love with some of them, but once they moved towards intimacy, she found herself withdrawing.

Sometimes, in the blue skyscape of her imagination, she envisaged lost battalions of opportunities with people marching by in regimented lines of two by two.

Not because she was blasé, as Colette often insisted. But because she was afraid and shy. How clear it became to her as she grew older. Only she knew and probably would be the only one who would ever know, that she was too afraid to commit to anyone, too afraid to be hurt.

The exception was Jacques who brought her gifts of chocolate, saw to her welfare, protected her and treated her as though she were as fragile as a china figurine.

In his company, despite Colette's constant innuendoes about the imminence of his marriage proposal, she felt safe and secure. Perhaps, it was because he had never overstepped the boundaries of their friendship, though on occasions, given a modicum of encouragement, she suspected he would. Like that day strolling back through Parc Monceau she was certain he was going to say something. She willed him not to. Then, perversely, wanted him to.

He constantly advised her to be more open, less shuttered.

'Risks are the motors of advance, especially in emotional and intellectual respects,' he said, twinkling eyes lightening the intensity of his words.

The two of them chuckled at the appropriateness of his metaphor. Eileen and her motor cars!

Moving away from her drawing board, she motioned him to sit opposite. 'Well, you're hardly the archetypal risk-taker yourself,' she teased, herself teased by the drift of his private scent, untainted or masked by any form of cologne. Incense of the present in an envelope of aromas.

Jacques drank in this woman who so fascinated him. Tall, slender-bodied and pale-skinned with aristocratic features. Like rare wine, she had improved with maturity. Funny and grave in turn. A heady mixture of shyness and confidence. So talented, yet so unassuming.

Every now and again, usually when he was about to declare himself, his aberration, as he thought of that incident with Bel McDonagh, reared its head.

It was by no means well done. At the end she cried out in surprise and pain. She was pinned under him and she clung to him and bit her lips. There were drops of blood on the embroidered sheets.

He stared at the drops frightened by the feeling of satisfaction they gave him. Virgin-hunting he had always considered a perversion. The kind of thing Willy went in for. But at that moment he understood its attraction. The primal hunter instinct. The blood made Bel his. He had marked her and she had let him, as though it were some sort of perverse ritual, as if she had asked him to tattoo her, to brand her as his and, on a raft of lust, he had obliged. And then left her, disgusted at himself.

An emotion of darkness, animal in relief, an exhaustion of all care superseded his previous feeling of paternalistic protection. This was an emotion which bore no relation to love. It was self-consciousness compounded, possession of what one cannot keep, of what one would not want to keep. Unbridled lust was the nearest he ever came to defining it.

He was glad she was returning to New York on the following day. But he wished she had not pursued him to rue Bonaparte. Not that Eileen ever referred to it.

That one experience all those years ago taught him a lot about himself. Too much. Too much about his motives. Too little about love. His love, he consoled himself, lay dormant, waiting for Eileen.

His voice serious, Jacques continued, determined Eileen would hear him out. 'To love is to risk. To be open to new friendships, new experiences, new challenges and changes, all involve risk. To try new ideas and methods is to risk.'

He was aware of the contradiction between their personalities. Instinctively, he was suspicious of innovation, preferring to root himself in tradition and commercial certainties. Whereas Eileen was open, daredevilish, her passion and interest in all forms of innovation coming a close second to her work.

He saw from the sideways slither of her eyes and the protective way she folded her arms across her chest that he had touched a chord which had made her uncomfortable.

'Dammit, Jacques, don't lecture. I can't bear it.'

'This isn't lecturing. This is conversational fact. As you well know.'

'Conversational fact! If this is conversation, I shall become a recluse. And I do take risks. Aren't I going into this rug business?'

'As you well know, that's not the kind of risk I'm talking about. That's no risk at all. Your success, our success, is a foregone conclusion. No, I'm talking about emotional risk. What I'm really trying to say, is to give yourself a chance to love. And before it's too late, to allow yourself to be loved in return.'

His expression was so full of love that Eileen felt a frisson, the same sort of frisson as she had experienced that May morning all those years ago in Brownswood when she had taken her first photograph. Though, instead of this frisson being an advance imprint on the atmosphere, this was old, a degraded imprint, an indelible mark of such intensity that time had neither diminished nor obliterated it.

She had an overwhelming desire to rise from her chair, to cross the divide and to throw herself into Jacques's arms. Strange. And she had never before spontaneously thought of him romantically. She pulled herself together. All this talk of emotions and love was most upsetting and most unlike Jacques.

'The costs of taking emotional risks are occasional failures and the likelihood of suffering which makes us better human beings.' He was determined to continue, to have his say.

He had been drawn to Eileen from their first meeting. By now he loved her deeply.

'Jacques. Please.'

'But the prizes can be truly glittering,' he finished with a great throat-clearing harrumph and a look that had Eileen again thinking of how comfortable it would be to find refuge in his arms.

But, of course, she did not. Their relationship was based on friendship. A warm, rewarding friendship. She knew only the urbane, sophisticated part of him. Outside the clear, comfortable boundaries of their relationship, on the other side of that barrier, was the unknown territory of the sensual, sexual man, whose existence she was certain they would be imprudent even to mention, much less ever to explore.

She preferred not to know of his various liaisons. They were short-lived, inconsequential. He continually returned to her, as he had all those years ago after being with Bel McDonagh.

Instead of saying anything, she raised her hands in a gesture of defeat, got up, turned away from him, back to her drawing board.

Always there was solace to be found in her work.

It was less traumatic to lose herself in designs. To become passionate about abstract forms rather than human bodies, to enjoy the sensuality of material rather than the sexuality of people.

The rug project was absorbing not only her waking hours, but also her dreams. In her dreams, she and her design concepts were full of courage and adventure. There were no barriers, no places where she would not journey, no impressions she would not explore.

It put her in mind of that so-long-ago winter, when as a nine-year-old, she had converted the top of her old pram into a toboggan and without thought for personal safety, hurtled down the side of the hill. She transferred the exhilaration of that tobogganing experience to her drawing board.

She allowed herself to be drawn further and further into out-and-out geometric patterning, which with a mounting sense of excitement and in an almost dream-like state, she committed to paper each morning.

Striking shapes. Her first courageous steps into the world of abstract art.

Sharp triangles. Elegant rectangles. Generous circles. Neat squares.

Bold slashes of intersecting lines, both curved and straight.

Joyous swirling, swooping, angular arrangements creating arabesques of movement.

Then colours: earthy tones of soft browns, hot oranges, calming green, energetic reds, her beloved midnight blue and, of course, dense black and the lightest of white.

Her conception grew on the object itself. As her mind was uncluttered by theory and preconceived ideas, the line between her original idea and execution was a fine one. But she knew, always, that her critical capacities would become sharpened and honed by the immediacy of the task.

She was never disappointed.

Neither was Jacques disappointed when he saw her preliminary sketches for the rugs and carpets. They were better than anything he envisaged. They reduced him to silence and he knew with the same certainty as he had with *Le Destin* that they were on a winner.

Immediately, he set about putting in place the legalities of their joint operation, the written confirmation that Eileen would design while he looked after the business end.

He offered an abundance of practical support, making the necessary arrangements for them to visit Morocco where Eileen returned to her notebook days of lacquer-learning, as she was initiated by Arab women into the age old skills of weaving and dyeing wool with natural colours.

Next she travelled to England to master weaving and rug-knotting and returned to Paris full of enthusiasm with looms, wool, a teacher and burning determination to succeed.

Nobody was surprised when it was Jacques again who found the perfect location for their rug-making operation – three rooms on the top floor of a dark and narrow little street, still in the Saint Germain district – the building from which Balzac the previous century had run his print shop.

To Eileen's joy, the property even had a small garden. Jacques watched with affectionate amusement as, rug design on hold, she employed a landscape artist to maximise its tiny potential.

The result was a charming paved area of old sandstone slabs, with pockets of wild flowers – cushions of golden primroses, clusters of fragile violets, spears of bluebells, even pink bells, miniature pansies and bunches of lemony cowslips. Her final touches were a strategically placed sundial and a seat in natural slatted wood to catch the midday sun.

The completion of the garden in early May was Eileen's excuse for a celebration and she sent out exquisitely hand-painted floral invitations rather grandly titled 'A Champagne Garden'.

'Wonderful, isn't it?' Eileen, wearing a slim sleeveless sheath of pale blue linen, her arm linked through Jacques's, was as excited as a child, pointing out this, showing him that.

Jacques bit back his question of what would happen when the wild flowers died. He would have used long-term plants.

Something along the lines of sensible miniature coniferous shrubs.

That, he realised, was another difference between himself and Eileen. She lived for the present, while he thought of the future. Together they were a good combination. Pleased with his discovery, he gave her arm a little squeeze.

As Jacques predicted, rugs became the season's must-have accessory for the chic home and stylish workplace. They were easier both to manufacture and to sell than the labour-intensive lacquer objects. With demand exceeding supply, the business took off from the word go. His main problem was finding and training suitable staff.

Within a small area of Saint Germain, a thriving empire of skilled craft workers had grown up. Top-class carpenters, French polishers, Sugawara making lacquer pieces, and, of course, rugs and carpets rolling off the English looms. Experts came and set up shop attracted like moths to Eileen's burgeoning reputation though, as people soon realised, it was Jacques who was the organisational force.

In the face of stiff opposition from Eileen, he insisted on labelling each rug, 'Designed by Eileen Gray'. He determined the rug-making operation would not become another Jean Désert. Currently her best seller was the 'Footit', a fun rug, named after a clown, which retailed for one hundred and fifty francs.

'I went into that gallery with such high hopes,' she said frequently and dolefully. She was haunted by its failure.

'Well, your rugs . . .' he consoled.

'Hardly the products with which to make one's mark on the world.'

'But you've remained true to yourself.'

She gave a bitter little laugh. 'I have that.'

She had, during various stages of their relationship, confided in Jacques parts of her childhood, concentrating on the more positive aspects, such as her father's belief in her. As an adult she identified with James Maclaren Smith and, recognising much of him in her, could understand his way of life. She made peace with him long before his death and was able to remember him and their good times together with affection and love.

Jacques often thought that Gaby had the right commercial ideas about the management of Eileen's work. Not that he would ever say so.

Gaby Bloch was a forbidden subject.

Chapter 18

Initially when Jacques put to Eileen the proposition of re-doing Louella and Eugène Levy's apartment, she refused.

'No. No. No.' She laughed across the table at him. 'You've to be joking. Not Louella.'

'You're constantly refusing me,' he joked back, delighting in her sparkle.

Without a word ever being spoken, Jacques was on constant look-out for suitable projects for Eileen. He had commissioned several pieces from her for his modern collection but he wanted her to expand. He was good at making and following up contacts, whereas she could not be bothered trying to secure business. She still had not developed a talent for self-promotion and the thought of this modern 'networking' horrified her.

It was another of those warm, wonderful June evenings. They had an outside table at one of their favourite restaurants, the unfashionable quayside Les Olivades. Trees leaned out from the downstream wall, their leafy crowns above the quay making deltas of shadow in the lamp light.

Louella had a well-deserved reputation for being particularly difficult. Eileen heard her described as a screaming virago. She selected her private clients with care. Pandering to egos was not in her remit.

With the precision of a surgeon, Eileen lifted the delicate white flesh from the spine of a Dover sole, while Jacques attacked a filet mignon with gusto.

Across the river, Notre Dame's bells rang out bim, bom, boom. 'If you listen to those bells, you'll hear your true love's voice,' Jacques told her.

'I know. Bim, bom, boom. I do listen. Or rather I used to when I first came to Paris. When I was young and naïve and believed. Though I've yet to hear the voice of my lover.'

'That's because you're too impatient to truly listen.' Jacques smiled across the table. I can hear. They're saying Ay . . . Lee . . . N to me. Now you listen.'

A decade ago a reporter had described Jacques as a man who chose to dream the impossible dream. Jacques liked to think he lived out the metaphor.

Eileen was unnerved at an imagination gone so to riot that she almost believed she could hear a distinct Jacques in the bim, bom, boom.

'You will re-consider the Louella proposition, won't you?' Jacques as usual refused to allow the unusual pleasure of a minor flirtation with Eileen to interfere with business.

'No, I won't.' She mopped up the residue of buttery meunière with a wedge of crusty bread. 'You'll have to come up with something better.'

Jacques adopted what she called his muleish look, crimped mouth and sliding eyes, his prelude to a sulk.

'And sulking doesn't work with me,' she warned.

He shrugged. He would ignore that. 'As a designer, it would be good to have the opportunity of putting your own imprint on a series of rooms. You'd be able to use an interlinking scheme, rather than the one-offs you're always complaining about.'

'Oh, Jacques, do stop, you'll give me indigestion,' Eileen groaned. 'Why are you always so damnably and justifiably persuasive?'

'A lot of good it does me with you.' Jacques's smile did not quite take the sting out of his comment. This evening he was in one of his more forceful humours.

As always, Eileen was touched by his interest and often wondered how she would cope without his support and constant presence. She considered him her dearest friend, though she was ambivalent about his increasingly tender and slightly proprietorial attitude towards her. Sometimes she wondered if he felt Gaby and Damia's very public relationship had paved the way for him.

'And you know how Louella talks. She'd be a walking advertisement for you.'

'That's what I'm afraid of.'

Over Jacques's shoulder, Eileen watched a skinny barefoot girl in a skimpy white cotton shift work the street. She was selling boutonnières from a heavy shoulder tray. When she reached their table, Jacques bought the contents of her tray, about twenty small cream drooping roses, petals adhering to each other from the heat.

He gestured to the girl to give them to Eileen and he gave her some extra coins for dinner. The girl's eyes were enormous and wondering but she said nothing, not even thank you. Close up, Eileen could see the rosy burgeoning of her breasts through the grubbiness of her thin shift.

Surrounded by the tiny roses, Eileen looked quizzically at Jacques. 'What was all that about?'

'I like those roses, they remind me of you.'

She laughed. 'In what way?'

'Clean and prickly.' Dodging a sliver of crust that she flicked across the table, he turned around; his arm gestured at the girl who was making her way back up the street, childishly jumping and skipping over the cracks in the pavement, the empty tray bouncing on her shoulder.

'No doubt she'll be back tomorrow and the next night with more roses, but eventually she'll end up on the street without roses. But for now, she's all right.'

'And you're all right, yourself.' In the silence of twilight, Eileen looked at him as though seeing him for the first time. 'And all right, I'll do the Levy apartment.'

Later, pacing her workroom, she tried to make sense of her capitulation. In no way, she assured herself, had she been influenced by Jacques's handling of that little flower girl. He was correct, it would be interesting to impose her taste on a complete apartment.

Well . . . she had found doing up this apartment fulfilling . . . as far as she had progressed.

Only the other day she had come across an old notebook crammed with architectural sketches of the house she was going to build and decorative ideas for her apartment. The house was one-storey, flat-roofed and modernistic. The apartment had silvered walls, a black-and-white circled ceiling, pewter furniture and grey curtains.

So much for the best laid plans.

By the time Eileen set out for her first meeting with Louella, characteristically, she was totally absorbed in the project. The initial sketches and notes of various ideas and materials were in a document folder tucked under her arm. For this job she had allowed her imagination free rein and in her mind's eye she could see the completed apartment.

She moved briskly heading towards the fashionable seventh arrondisement, the venerable Faubourg Saint-Germain, as Jacques joked. Her outfit was by Chanel, a slender calf-length skirted charcoal grey suit with a long lean jacket and elegant court shoes. Despite her client being one of Paris's top milliners, Eileen chose to be hatless. Her shingled hair defined her aristocratic features, though it was the freedom more than the flattery of style that pleased her.

A sky the colour of school ink hung over the buildings. Occasional slanting shafts of sunlight dragged shadows out onto the pavements where Paris café society thrived and intellectual aspiration simmered.

Eileen loved her adopted city with quiet passion. She was still enchanted at the way the misty street lamps marked the Pont Neuf; the imposing Gothic bulk of the Préfecture; the Place Dauphine, that wonderful unique wedge of ancient buildings. And across the river, perched on the Île de la Cité, the way the enormous flaming jewellery of Notre Dame's windows blazed frosty and glittering in the rain.

Louella, a soignée brunette, received her in the dim, suffocatingly hot and over-crowded reception room where she held soirées on the first Friday evening of each month. This morning, devoid of the artists, writers, actors, politicians and people from the fashion industry with whom she surrounded herself, to Eileen's amazement, the room looked even more cluttered.

Rising from a chaise longue deep in the shadows, Louella, waving her signature ebony holder complete with Black Russian cigarette, greeted her. 'Eileen, dahling.'

Her husband Eugène Levy was a wealthy banker, double her age. Smitten from the moment of their first meeting at a convention in Boston, he indulged her every whim, which included keeping her own name, her public refusal to have children and her insistence, before she would marry, that he set her up in the millinery business which he did and which she had made a roaring success.

Eileen held out her still-gloved hand. Louella's staff were notorious for their lack of training. The maid had ushered her into the reception room with discourteous haste and an attitude bordering on insolence. Eileen often heard Jacques and his friends wonder how Eugène put up with the casualness of his household. Colette insisted sex was the reason. Eileen suspected she was right.

Louella ignored Eileen's outstretched hand. Instead she went to kiss Eileen on both cheeks, dramatic social kisses which Eileen ducked. Her natural reticence rebelled against such flamboyance, particularly from a stranger.

After great communicatory difficulty – Louella shouting instructions in her clipped Boston voice – the maid, a blank sullen expression on her pretty face, eventually brought a silver tray, tarnished in places, and the accoutrements of coffee which turned out to be vile.

Louella, after just the one sip and a *moue* of distaste, eased another Sobranie into her holder, lit it with a flourish from a jade table-lighter and settled back. With an airy wave of her hand, she said, 'Now. Do tell me what you plan. Jacques says you're the best.'

Eileen looked around the room. Flocked bottle-green wall-paper, matching heavy velvet curtains, an expensive, good-as-new, too-patterned carpet – Aubusson, she was sure – and an abundance of over-stuffed chairs and couches and tables chock-a-block with ornaments and bric-à-brac.

'Perhaps you'd like to take a look at these.' Eileen opened her document case and took out the sketches.

Louella waved a languid wrist. 'Why don't you talk me through them.'

Eileen wondered how such a passive woman could be so successful in Paris's cut-throat millinery business.

Remembering, as she often did in times of tension, her father's commending her to be true to herself, Eileen knew that even if Louella were an angel, she could not work around the room as it existed. 'The apartment needs to be emptied,' she told Louella, presuming the other rooms to be equally cluttered.

She had her attention now. 'Emptied? What do you mean?'

'Everything taken out.'

'While you're decorating?'

'I'm re-doing. Not decorating. I don't decorate. Everything has to go,' said Eileen firmly.

'You mean all this.' Again Louella waved an expansive arm.

'Yes.'

Louella bristled. 'No, it's not possible. These are heirlooms. Belonging to my husband's family. My husband's a very important man.' Everyone knew of Eugène Levy's importance. Everyone equally knew that if Louella wanted the heirlooms disposed of, disposed of they would be.

'It wouldn't work otherwise. You know the kind of interiors I do. You've seen examples.'

'Yes. But I thought . . .' Louella's voice trailed off. Eileen and her designs were the talk of Paris and Louella determined to have her, only her, do the apartment. But she knew that Eileen could, and did, pick and choose what appealed to her. She suspected she was only here as a favour to Jacques Doucet.

Louella had a difficult job persuading Eugène that their apartment, which had been in his family for the past fifty years, needed re-doing. Personally, she thought nobody could be expected to live in such a tastelessly put together place. Not that she said so, or would ever even hint. She had not pulled herself this far up the social ladder by being outspoken.

She had an even more difficult time assuring him that in no way was she casting aspersions on his mother's obviously excellent but outdated taste and style, as a man of his discernment and intelligence must surely realise.

When he remained unconvinced, she journeyed across the cold pink satin expanse of their bed to stroke his forehead and to coo into his ear. 'A successful banker, like you, dearest, deserves an environment worthy of your position.'

Last night's expedition had paid dividends and she wanted to get the project moving before he had an opportunity to change his mind.

'Show me.' She injected a note of enthusiasm into her voice and held out her hand to Eileen for the sketches.

Immediately she was impressed. Whatever else about Louella, she knew the importance of design. Even from these preliminary sketches, she recognised that this was design with a capital D. Impact making and innovative. 'Talk about "rationalist concepts",' she murmured.

The luxuriousness of style was masked behind simplicity and yet Louella picked out an unprecedented rigour in these preliminary sketches. The Levy apartment would be a work of art. A showpiece, the like of which up to now, even in Paris, was unprecedented.

Louella liked the idea of breaking new ground. Of being at the helm of innovation. Still she hummed and hawed. It did not do in the initial stages of negotiation to be seen as too eager or too enthusiastic.

Eileen, making no pretence at drinking the coffee, watched as Louella flicked through the folder and made an occasional jotting in a small leather bound notebook. Every now and again, Louella looked up as though trying to gauge Eileen's reaction, which registered nothing but calm pleasantness. Eventually, after checking her man-sized wrist watch, Eileen rose.

'I've another appointment. Thank you for your time.' Her voice cut-glass crisp, she held out her hand for the folder, relieved that she would not have to work with Louella, though disappointed not to be executing her plans.

'I'll keep it.' Louella insisted, also rising, dusting ash off her morning dress. 'To let my husband have a look this evening.'

'My designs remain with me.' As a child Eileen had clung to Belinda, as an adult she was reluctant to be parted from her designs.

'But I want to go ahead. As soon as possible.' Eileen's apparent indifference to the project removed any lingering hesitancy on Louella's part. She knew it would take a lot of journeys across the bed, hours of pillow talk – and probably more – to bring Eugène around to Eileen Gray's designs, though not for one instant did she doubt her powers of persuasion.

When Louella moved, she moved quickly. Within a fortnight work was started. For the hall walls Eileen used four hundred and fifty brick panels, lacquered in black and texturised with eggshell to give the appearance of a lattice screen.

The walls in the salon were panelled in dark lacquer, decorated with wave-like motifs of tarnished silver, the idea for which, Eileen later told Jacques in a fit of giggles, came from the tray on which was served her first and only cup of ghastly coffee in the Levy apartment.

Thick black carpets punctuated with abstract motifs borrowed from Cubism and its rhythms covered the floors. The lighting was muted. And the majority of the fittings were in glass and chrome.

The specially designed furniture included a black lacquer desk, a daybed with carved wooden feet, a dressing table of sycamore and ivory, a low armchair in red and yellow lacquer with arm-rests formed like serpents, and the *Pirogue* sofa, shaped like a dug-out canoe, stuffed with matt gold cushions, whose lacquer resembled the pelt of an otter.

Never even in her wildest imaginings did Louella Talbot dream that her apartment would create such a stir, that the furnishing and fittings would cause such a sensation and be so widely reproduced in national and international newspapers and magazines.

She was particularly impressed at the long feature run by *Harper's Bazaar* though, she confided to friends, she would have liked more about her and the apartment and less of Eileen.

'The last word in interior decoration demands walls of lacquer and furnishings to match. Paris is still however ahead of the English capital for it possesses Miss Gray, admittedly the master of her difficult art. Her style is thoroughly modern although there is much feeling for the antique . . . She was the first in the field to show an unusual perfection of workmanship . . . Take the double doors. The framework is of black lacquer encrusted with gold while the long panels are of black. The walls might pose as studies from the latest Cubist exhibition. At least one panel might be *The Nude Descending the Staircase* . . .'

As Eileen had drafted the preliminary drawings for the apartment on rue Lota, never for one moment did she suspect the number of titled Europeans, American millionaires, Argentinean beef-barons and Indian princes who would intrude into her life to clamour for her designs.

Jack has to be almost out of tape.

If only he can get Brigid out of the room – despite Eileen's request that she leave them alone, she is in and out like a yo-yo – he will be able to slide the recorder from his pocket and turn the cassette around without, he is certain, Eileen being any the wiser.

'Some more wine, Mr Devine?'

'Thank you. No, but if it's not too much trouble, I'd love a glass of water. Flying is so dehydrating. Positively parching,' he adds. Even as he speaks he realises he is overdoing the dramatics. Why is it that lying, which should be sparse on words, invariably employs an over-abundance?

That both women seem unsuspecting of any ulterior motive does not make him feel any better. Brigid returns the wine to the tray and leaves the room.

Jack strolls across to the window.

The pattern of his movements – an impressionistic cat lick shadow – niggles at Eileen. She gropes for recall. But the image she seeks remains elusive, flirting on the periphery of her mind.

This is another opportunity to mention his grandmother.

Not to do so is deceitful. Again, Jack says nothing, but is uneasily aware of how uncomfortable he is with this out-of-character, duplicitous behaviour.

The weather has deteriorated again. The rain returned, thickened and steadied, and evening glimmers off the slicked cobblestones. In the distance he senses the volcanic rumble of the city. But here in Saint-Germain all is quiet, the district's village-like atmosphere all-pervading.

He is right, the tape has run its course and, as though to remind him of why he is standing by the window, it gives a gentle beep. Guiltily he looks around but Eileen Gray sits motionless, her eyes inscrutable behind the thick lenses.

As he reaches into his pocket to turn off the machine, it gives another beep. Impossible. But sounding louder this time. As he fumbles, she moves, restless shoulders settling the grey cardigan foursquare, knees activating under the rug.

'Mr Devine, what's that noise?'

He turns towards her, still scrabbling for the switch. 'I don't hear anything.'

Another beep.

'There. Now do you hear it?'

Needing to keep his distance from her sharp ears, he leans nearer the window. 'Perhaps something outside,' he concedes, willing the batteries to run down. Anything to stop her inquisition.

Her voice is even more definite as the machine gives another beep. 'No, it came from inside here. Over towards the window. About where you're standing.'

At last fingers and switch connect, just as Brigid re-enters with a bottle of Perrier and a glass.

Now that the immediate danger of discovery has passed, he is full of courage again, plotting as to how he will insert a fresh tape.

'Your water,' Mr Devine.'

He had forgotten. He pours it over the slice of lime and drinks.

'Brigid, did you hear anything?' Eileen queries.

'No. What sort of thing?'

'The sort of sound, I presume, a tape machine makes when it has run out of tape.'

Talk about sarcasm – the weapon of the educated, according to one of his professors at Columbia or, as Jack read somewhere, the lowest form of wit. He dares not look at either woman. Emptying the remainder of the bottle into the glass, he drinks as though his life depends on it.

'If I didn't know better,' Eileen says, 'I might have thought it was yours.'

'Couldn't be, could it?' As he utters the slick lie, Jack is washed with self-disgust.

Sitting back opposite Eileen, the only way he can justify his behaviour is by assuring himself that his profile will enhance Eileen Gray's professional reputation.

Eileen frets about Jack Devine's familiarity.

What is it about him? Why can't she bring it to the surface?

What is it that keeps calling from the labyrinth of her neural wiring?

Why can't she drag it into consciousness?

What link is her id aware of that she is not?

It was during the autumn dinner party thrown by Louella and Eugène Levy to celebrate the completion of their apartment that Eileen first heard Jacques hold forth on the power of twilight. In his own way he was as bad as Sadie and her heebie-jeebies. 'We humans are made for twilight,' he insisted, 'which is why we're so comfortable in this room.'

Louella was being her more-than-usually brittle self. She was seething, furious, though she dared not voice her feelings.

Paris Match wanted a centre-page photographic spread of her apartment, for which she granted gracious permission. The stipulation that it would focus on a profile of Eileen Gray came later. When, point-blank, Eileen refused, Louella invited the editor to lunch. He accepted with alacrity, designated the Hotel Meurice and, chin dribbling blood from the largest fillet steak on the menu, laughed heartily while dismissing her – Louella – as an alternative interview subject.

Oh, the shame of it.

And, as if that was not bad enough, Louella subsequently discovered, Eileen had also declined to answer a series of questions put to her by *Vogue*.

When Eugène came upon Louella crying, he worried that she might be ill. Living in dread of anything happening to his wife, he was highly amused on hearing the cause of her tears but refused to become involved, as had Jacques when she approached him.

Eileen looked around. Jacques was right. She had not consciously set out to create a twilight decor. But if she had, this was it. Amazing how Jung's responsibility of the unconscious popped up again and again.

'It's only when light is reduced and the pupil opens that feeling goes out of the eye as touch, and then we really plumb space with the eyes. It's a very sensuous act. Twilight is a very sensuous time. Eileen, after creating this,' Jacques's arm swept the room, 'wouldn't you agree?'

To her consternation, Eileen felt a blush starting at her waist and creeping the whole way up her body, she could feel the heat through her camisole, radiating out from the silver and grey bias-cut sleeveless gown which Jacques had presented her for tonight.

Everyone had to be aware of her discomfort. She bent her head and made a big production of enjoying the wine's aroma.

Jacques who, with Eileen by his side, was in his social element, cut a sliver of Camembert and popped it along with a green seedless grape into his mouth. 'That's why it's so natural for us to be comfortable in the twilight. We make love in reduced amounts of light, and then we're really feeling with the eyes as well as our hands.'

Dear Jacques, how often she wished she could reciprocate his feelings. Even pretend, as she knew other women did. How simple life would be. But deception, as her parents had recognised from an early age, was not Eileen's way. Regularly Colette brought up the subject of Jacques and her suitability. She had even, on one occasion, admitted to jealousy of the purity of their relationship.

'Could I use the bathroom?' Jack is uncertain whether the word 'bathroom' is correct. Restroom is American. Perhaps he should have said toilet or gents, cloakroom or even the latest vulgar 'loo'.

Brigid nods and leads the way out of the salon, her comfortable bulk swaying from side to side down the corridor. For a horrible moment he wonders will she wait outside. But no. He hears the squelch of her shoes in retreat.

The bathroom echoes what he had expected of the whole of Eileen Gray's apartment. Here is the heady combination of minimalism and opulence. Black, white and silver. Delicate marble, gleaming chrome. A great tub of a bath. A generous shower with an enormous shower head. Functional streamlined fittings. Luxurious white towels monogrammed in black with EG parading around the walls on slender rails.

With a sigh of relief, he sits to empty his bladder. There is a comforting something about carrying out this body function sitting rather than standing.

Exciting and all as getting this interview may be, he finds himself drained. On second thoughts, he is not, he thinks, cut out for this nerve-racking cloak-and-dagger business. He wishes he were not caught up in this tangle of lies.

The last thing he expects to see as he sits relaxing, trousers around his ankles, is the photograph. Colette, he is sure. Staring down at him from a lofty position over the door. A black-and-white profile study, with a knowing look, eyes that have seen it all, cupid's bow lips smiling in delicious anticipation and halo of wild curling back-lit hair.

The photo strikes an uneasy note of incongruity in an otherwise harmonised and sanitised setting.

Jack flushes the toilet, replaces its chrome lid and turns on the basin's mixer tap which he leaves running at full strength while he inserts a fresh cassette into his machine. Taking no chances he also replaces the four slender batteries. Then he rinses his hands under the pounding water, turns off the tap and dries his hands on the thickest, fluffiest towel he has ever encountered. Slipping the tape machine into his pocket, he makes sure the switch is accessible.

The ticking clockwork of rain accompanies him back to the salon.

Chapter 19

With Jack out of the room, Eileen's thoughts drift to Brigid. Wondering what she would do without her, how she would cope. She sits more upright. Gives herself a little shake. What is wrong with her? Is she going soft thinking like this? She does not need anyone. She could manage on her own.

After all, Brigid is just a servant. No, she realises – this is an afternoon of consciously streaming bitter-sweet memories – Brigid is more than a servant, she is a loyal companion, a constant non-judgemental kindly presence.

Her arrival was a happy day for Eileen, though knowing her brother-in-law, she was suspicious of his uncharacteristically generous offer of sending out, fare paid, a servant from Ireland. Knowing Henry as she did, she was certain he had to have an ulterior motive.

A year later she was proved right when he demanded Brigid returned, to replace her mother, he insensitively wrote, but only after ascertaining that she was trained. She was trained, all right. Well trained. She had trained herself.

Eileen felt it only fair to give Brigid the option. Paris or Enniscorthy, she asked, and was ridiculously pleased when Brigid chose to stay.

Round one to Eileen. Albeit a minor victory. But one which went a little way towards vindicating Henry's desecration of her home. And she does like having an Irish voice around the place.

Carrying a tall black glass vase filled with Jack's roses, Brigid is all indignation on her return. 'I don't trust that Mr Devine. Wanting to use the lavatory, indeed. He's up to no good.'

Eileen laughs. Brigid and her character analyses are based on the most ludicrous of hypotheses. 'What have you there?'

'Mr Devine's roses.' Brigid places them on the mantel.

Eileen peers and asks incredulously, 'Are they cream coloured?'

'Yes. Small and wishy-washy.'

Cream roses.

Strange the way the brain makes random connections between unconnected incidents and unconnected objects.

'Thank you, Brigid.'

'What, Miss?'

'Thank you.'

'For what, Miss?'

'For everything.'

This is the first occasion in a long time that Brigid remembers Miss Gray ever thanking her for anything, much less everything. From life she learned that the gentry are into giving orders, not saying thanks. Still, it gives her a lovely warm glow. She has an urge to put her arms around her lady but, even though it is years since they have touched, she fears any such gesture could be again misconstrued.

Back then, it took Brigid a considerable length of time to work out that Miss Gray was neither eating nor sleeping and going around with blotched red eyes because Fräulein Bloch had moved in with Mademoiselle Damia.

Initially she did not believe that what she was thinking could be possible, but gradually, by interpreting Cook's pursed lips and throw-away remarks, she pieced enough of the jigsaw of that relationship to work it out. Women together. Never had she heard the like of it. Never either had she realised the hornets' nest of emotions that were released by what she intended merely as a gesture of comfort.

Still, all that is water under the bridge now.

Then she was innocently naïve. But she learned hard and she learned fast. And in the process of learning, she lost her ability to be emotionally open, to be able to say what was truly in her heart. 'But you're having a good visit, Miss?' she says in her kindly but controlled manner.

Eileen is thinking the opposite. All these memories have her disturbed. She thought they did not matter. That her past had no place in her present. But she was wrong.

She wishes she had not been so stubborn, insisting on welcoming this Jack Devine. She envisaged their meeting as a golden cameo, a reminiscence of the glory days, a stretching back into projects of times gone by.

She should have known better. Outside the pages of Colette's fiction such happenings do not occur.

She wonders has she tipped into second childhood?

Or, in her case, could it be third?

How she hates and rails against the decrepitude of old age, part of her wanting it over and she dead and buried; another part of her wishing not only to stop the clock, but to wind it back, but back to where, to which point in her life, she can never decide.

In contrast to her sight which deteriorated more slowly than even the various consultants had anticipated, her ageing process was neither gradual nor gentle. It seemed to rush up to her, push her over and then run off jeering.

Strange how each hour of the vanilla afternoons of her childhood seemed to stretch for ever but now whole years flicker past in the briefest of time before eroding into black treacle nights.

When she is gone, her work must leave her mark on the world. It is her reason for living.

Equally, she must continue to ensure that all traces of her personal life and relationships are erased.

'It's still raining,' Jack remarks on his return from the bathroom.

'Yes, cats and dogs,' supplies Brigid, who having grown up with the soft rain of Ireland, abhors the heavy, greasy French rain, the way it engorges into slow drops and zigzags down the windows.

'It rains in Paris like nowhere else,' Eileen contributes.

Jack looks down at Eileen, gives a slight shrug, throws his hands wide. The fans of laughter wrinkling at the outer corner of his eyes work overtime.

Now that he has the recorder back working, his resolve is firmer than ever. He injects a note of mock humour into his voice, 'What am I doing going on about the rain when there's so much I want to ask you? When we've so much to talk about. Is that a picture of Colette in the bathroom?'

'Yes. And it was she who insisted it be put there. Who hung it herself.'

Colette, cynical writer with a heart of gold and a conveniently flexible set of morals. Eileen considered herself lucky to have had her friendship.

Over the years, what a lot of experiences they had shared. She was lively and unpredictable. The things she said. And even worse, the things she did. Always on about Willy.

Worse than the Irish with her matchmaking.

For ever quoting Machiavelli about fortune being the arbiter of only half of our actions. Waiting for somebody to ask the obvious question. And when, invariably, they did, expansively insisting that the other half was their responsibility.

Constantly turning up like a bad penny, as old Sadie used to say.

On the day that Eileen was consciously trying to come to terms with her failing eyesight, she heard her calling from the courtyard below.

For too long, unable to face up to the reality of probable blindness, she had made excuses about her sight. Now, it could no longer be ignored. She was frightened. So frightened. The process of acceptance was painful. And impossible.

Blind. Blind. Blind. She hated it. It was a terrible word. She had even looked it up in the dictionary. 'Without sight,' it said. Without sight. She said the two words over and over again as though giving voice to them would bring acceptance. But it didn't. If anything, it made it worse.

''Allo. Anyone in? Come on, Eileen. Brigid. Open up. I'm here to see Mademoiselle Gray.' No asking was Eileen in, no wondering was it a convenient time to call. What Colette wanted, she wanted now. And invariably got.

Wafting from below, Eileen heard Brigid's gentle but firm Irish voice, 'It's not possible. Miss Gray is in her workroom. Busy. And she is not to be disturbed.'

Brigid had been a fast learner, the perfect protection from unwanted callers.

Not that Colette would be put off. 'Nonsense, Brigid,' her voice sailed upwards, 'Your mistress won't mind me. I've some very important news.'

'No, Mademoiselle. She is busy.'

From the sounds of shuffling, Eileen presumed Colette had prised past Brigid. Her presumption was proven correct when she heard Colette's heavy footsteps and heard her call indignantly, 'Eileen, Why can't you be on the ground floor. I'm utterly fatigued . . .'

Eileen came out of her workroom and leaned over the banister. Colette was but a colourful blur. Today was one of her bad sight days.

'To hide away from interruptions like you,' she riposted down the stairwell, knowing there was no getting rid of Colette and realising that she could do with a break from the angst of her thoughts. For a while, anyway, she would be guaranteed to forget her problems.

Colette arrived on the landing. Puffing dramatically, a hand clutched to her heart, her red hair in a flagrant frill from under a purple cloche, her physical discomfort in no way hampering her speech. 'Rumour has it there's someone with the initial D who you wouldn't mind interrupting you.'

Eileen led the way into her studio. 'Really, Colette, I wish you wouldn't gossip about my affairs.'

'I wasn't gossiping, I just happened to pick the information up in passing,' said Colette virtuously.

'You shouldn't be listening, either,' said Eileen crossly.

Colette put down her handbag, a capricious affair of purple and pink suede panels and a jingling gilt chain and chortled wickedly. 'Doesn't all Paris know you're putting together a collection for Jacques Doucet? Nobody – well hardly anyone – wonders if you're lovers. And of course, I'll neither verify nor refute. It's not my business. And I say so to anyone who asks.'

Only too clearly could Eileen imagine Colette's antics. Flushed and flustered, she replied weakly, 'I wish you wouldn't.'

'Wouldn't what?'

'Tease.'

'Doesn't everyone know of your influence?'

'What do you mean?'

'That you were the one who persuaded Jacques of the benefits of modern against his beloved eighteenth century.'

'I didn't persuade him. It was his decision.'

'Has he sold off yet?'

'What?'

'His collection.'

'I don't know.'

'You don't know?'

'Well, some of it, I think.'

'Well I heard that while he was off playing golf the sale from part of his collection fetched thirteen million francs. He must be worth a fortune. I hope he's paying you well for all the work you're doing.'

'I wish you wouldn't.'

'Wouldn't what?'

'You know, talk, like this. Go on about money. It's Jacques's business. And mine,' she added as an afterthought. 'Nobody else's.'

Colette guffawed. Her plump figure with swinging legs was uncomfortably accommodated on the work table.

Eileen hated when Colette teased. From past experience she knew that invariably she came off second best.

'Of course it's everyone's business. You're in the public eye. Everyone wants to know what you're doing. For whom. And with whom.' The last three words were spoken so low that Eileen wondered if she had imagined them. One look at Colette's smirking face confirmed her worst fears.

Colette hitched up her cerise-coloured skirt a little further, held out her silk-stockinged legs all the better to admire them and the curve-heeled, navy pointed shoes with the delicate buttoned bar across her instep. Colette had great legs, knew it and enhanced them with the most expensive hosiery and shoes.

Eileen gestured defeat, 'All right. Pax. Now that you're here, have a look. See what you think?'

Colette eased herself off the work-table. Hands behind her back, she prowled up and down the workroom, giving occasional appreciative grunts, stopping every now and then to run her hands over a piece. She paused at Eileen's drawing board, leaned across and lifted a sheet of paper resting against the wall. 'Now what's this?'

Eileen was halfway down the room, standing with her back to the fire. 'What?

'This sketch.'

'Hold it up.'

'I am. Can't you see?'

Eileen's heart missed a beat. Whatever Colette was holding up was just a vague blur. She was not ready. Nobody must know yet. Not until she had come to terms with her failing eyesight. She walked towards Colette. Subterfuge had become a way of life, but one which she found increasingly difficult.

She put a note of irritation into her voice. 'Of course, I can see. No need to be so dramatic. The sun was blinding me, that's all.'

'There's no sun today, Eileen. Hasn't been much this April.' Colette's voice was quiet, matter-of-fact. 'What's wrong? Is it your eyes? I know you're having trouble with your sight.'

Eileen injected a false note of incredulity into her voice. 'More rumours?'

'No. Not rumours.'

'Don't fuss. It's just a momentary blurring due to creative exhaustion.' Lightly she laughed, 'It's all these interruptions, they're so stressful.'

Colette shrugged, threw her arms wide and raised her eyebrows.

Eileen burst out crying. 'Irreversible deteriorating eyesight,' she sobbed. The relief of giving voice to her diagnosis was instant. The message was the same from the opticians she had seen over the past month in Berlin and Zurich as it had been from her man in Paris.

'How long?'

'None of the consultants can give me an answer.'

For once Colette said nothing. She came over to where Eileen stood and put her arms around her. Colette had never seen Eileen cry before. The two women stood quietly, body to body. After a while Eileen dropped her head to Colette's shoulder and after another space of time Colette tentatively stroked her short thick hair.

She waited motionless until Eileen moved to disentangle herself. 'Please don't mention this.'

'It'll be our secret. I swear,' assured Colette.

Eileen gave a short laugh, 'Imagine me or anyone entrusting you with a secret.'

Colette gave a gusty sigh, threw her hands in the air and put on her hurt look. 'Well, if you feel that way . . .'

Eileen rushed to assure she had meant no offence and Colette knew the intensity of the moment had passed. Sometime, when Eileen was ready, they would talk about her sight. But it would be later. Probably much later.

'So what's your news?' asked Eileen. As Colette had known, she was glad to have the spotlight off herself.

'Can't you guess?' asked Colette, arms spread wide, face puckered, dramatising misery.

'Complications with a new lover?' hazarded Eileen.

Colette sighed. In the circumstances, she determined to milk every ounce of drama from the telling. Anything to take Eileen's mind off her problems, even for half an hour. 'How well you know me. He's not all that new. But we've to be discreet.'

Eileen laughed incredulously. 'You discreet?'

Colette shook her head solemnly, her doleful expression ludicrous under the humorous cloche. 'It's Bertrand.'

'Bertrand who?'

'You know, you've met him.'

'The only Bertrand I know is Henri's son.'

Colette held up a finger to her lips.

'Not your stepson?' Eileen was astounded. 'Tell me it isn't?'

'It is.' Colette knew Eileen well enough to know that for now she was wrapped up in this latest drama. That was Eileen, even at the height of her own troubles, still interested in others.

'You and him?' Eileen could not believe she was asking this question.

Colette nodded.

'You're mad.'

Defensively Colette justified, 'We're madly in love.'

'And you think being in love justifies flouting convention?'

'Always,' Colette waved her hand, 'Toujours l'amour. Nobody shall part Bertrand and me.'

'You said the same about yourself and Missy. What if Henri finds out?'

'I'll have to make sure he doesn't, won't I? Oh, dear. Enough of that. The thought of it depresses me. Discretion is so bourgeoisie, don't you think?'

Eileen did not reply. From early childhood, the twin attributes of discretion and convention were an inherent part of her life. Instilled in her by her mother and maternal grandparents. More by unspoken than spoken words.

But she had defied convention. Politely refusing to conform to familial expectations of duty and marriage and children, quietly and determinedly she opted to live the lifestyle of her choice. But, in deference to both the living and the dead, she had always tried to be discreet. 'Is this your important news?'

Colette clapped a hand across her mouth. 'Imagine, I nearly forgot. But then I find love much more exciting than business, don't you? *Chéri* is to be published.'

Eileen was genuinely delighted. Colette told anyone who would listen, even total strangers in cafés, on the Metro and while shopping, about the joys and tribulations of her personal and writing life, particularly with regard to her difficulties with various publishers.

'Congratulations. From what you've told me, it's a very sensitive story.' She gave her Mona Lisa smile. 'These days, Paris could do with a little sensitivity.'

'It's plenty sensitive. No doubt about that. But the publisher is worried about litigation. Look at all the fuss *Ulysses* created. Written by that fellow countryman of yours.'

'That's a wonderful success. Such a success that I'm calling my new range of autumn rugs Ulysses.'

'Well, let's hope James Joyce doesn't find out. From what I hear, humour's not one of his strong points.'

'Wait until you see, *Chéri* will do as well as *Ulysses*. The story of an ageing courtesan's love affair with her friend's son. An in-depth study in feminine psychology. What could be more current.' Jokingly she finished, 'You'll be toast of the feminists.'

Colette held out her legs for further inspection, turning her ankles this way and that. 'I don't see Gertrude and co. being overly impressed by a true romance.'

Eileen gave a little laugh. '*Chéri*'s hardly that.'

'Oh, but it is. It's a true romance. Based on fact.' Colette looked triumphant, a small child having achieved a naughty objective. 'Your friend James Joyce maintains that all fiction is fantasised autobiography – though in the case of *Chéri*, I have to say, there's not all that much fantasy. It's more reality.'

Eileen was thunderstruck as she realised implications. 'Colette. You never have. You couldn't. Tell me, I beg of you, the book's not about your relationship with Bertrand?'

'Yes, it is. Quite delicious, isn't it? I had to tell someone. Imagine my publisher – thinking it fiction and still worried about litigation. If only he knew. I doubt he'd even have paid for my publicity photograph. And that has turned out brilliantly.'

'How could you?' Eileen groaned. 'What have you done?' She was constantly unnerved by the chances Colette took, as well as by her dramatic lifestyle.

'Forget about *Chéri*. Wait until I tell you about Man Ray. He's quite delicious. He has this tiny studio near the Eiffel Tower . . .'

'Hmm. I know. A wonderful photographer. Who knows how to get the best out of his subjects.' A thought struck Eileen. 'Did you wear that hat?'

'Of course I did. It's this season's latest.'

'I know. But for a photograph.'

'While Man Ray considers cloches the ultimate in fashion he had me remove it for the photograph.'

'Well, I'm glad one of you had taste.'

'You wouldn't believe the amount of taste that was displayed during our session.' Colette had such a wanton look that Eileen suspected more than photographs had taken place in the studio. 'I shall make you a present of a copy. But only if you promise to display it in this new bathroom of yours.'

Eileen laughed. 'Done. I shall supply you with hammer and nails so that you can hang it yourself.'

After Colette left, Eileen sighed and not for the first time wished she was more light-hearted. After being in Colette's company, she was acutely aware of her own shortcomings. Mainly her secretiveness. She was quite intolerant of any form of intrusion into her interior life. This attitude characterised her relationships, be they sexual, platonic or work-related.

Thinking about this led on to worry about her eyesight, translating to terror that she would be unable to work, and circling back to disappointment at her achievements. Oh, she may have executed brilliant designs, been toasted as a success and had considerable newspaper and magazine coverage.

But she knew. She knew the truth.

Knew what it was like to have initial disappointment sour to outright failure. Blasé as she might appear, not a day went by that Jean Désert did not gnaw at her insides.

With sight-time running out, there was a renewed urgency to consolidate her life, to ensure she left this important mark on the world.

So much to do. Probably so little time.

In an intuitive flash she knew where she must start. She would take Jacques's advice, cut her losses and sell the gallery. The relief at having made the decision was enormous. She would pass it to the property agents for a quick sale. At this stage Jacques had no need to know.

What next?

What else but the house. She even had the preliminary drawings and sketchings.

A house for herself. Her own home. To her own design. Why had she waited so long?

For generations, her family had owned property, both in Ireland and in England. Property was in her blood. She had the Irish hunger and passion for land and bricks and mortar. She still felt the pain of Henry tearing Brownswood from her. Neither the family home in Kensington nor her apartment here in Paris had assuaged her loss.

From start to completion, the house would be hers alone, handled by herself. From foundations to roof. Exterior landscaping and interior furnishings.

It was a project which would allow her to remain true to

herself. It was a project which, for now, she would keep secret.

Four days later she and Brigid were in the South of France.

After three weeks of frustrated searching up and down the Côte d'Azur, she took a day off. That particular morning she drove up from Menton towards Roquebrune-Cap-Martin, parked her car next to the little railway station, took her swimming costume and towel from the back seat. The pleasure of a refreshing swim before the sun climbed too high, rather than land purchase, occupied her.

She walked down a path which she hoped might lead to the sea but a few minutes later, it fizzled out. Intrigued by the isolation of the area, she clambered over crumbling walls, through the scattered Levant pines and bushes of wild rosemary and euphorbia, before coming on a small, natural terrace cut into the rocks.

To the west lay the massive rock of Monte Carlo. South and east there was nothing but sea.

Swim forgotten, she stood on a site of breath-taking beauty. The perfect site on which to build the perfect house. Private. Tucked away between the Provençal hills and the Mediterranean. With a long wide vista. Rugged and robust.

Her search for a site may have been over. But her problems were only beginning.

First, hampered by being a woman and, secondly, for holding a foreign passport, to secure the land, she had to overcome the convoluted French legalities and the bureaucracy of officialdom.

Before she could build, the bureaucrats – all four of them,

small and overweight, dressed in dark suits and starched white shirts and with fast blinking eyes – warned that her design must both enhance and maximise the site's natural environment and potential.

She did not foresee any problems there. The site was perfect for the design which had lain dormant all those years. Over the past weeks it had taken further shape in her head.

Her sight pattern was variable. Some days good, some days not so good. But with strongly lensed glasses and her magnifying glass, for now she could see well enough to work. Nobody mentioned driving.

Chapter 20

When Colette called to number 21 and found it closed up and without a sign of life she was uneasy. Eileen had said nothing about going away the last time they met for a glass of wine at the Café de Flore. Her neighbours had neither seen nor heard of her for weeks, they said.

Rue Bonaparte was the sort of place where people kept to themselves. Colette much preferred her home on the more bohemian rue Jacob, a thronging street, where all human life interwove and where people took an active interest in each other and in their comings and goings.

Eileen often disappeared unexpectedly, sometimes on her own, frequently with Brigid in attendance and, on occasions, she could be gone for weeks. Brigid had become an adept travel administrator with an uncanny knack of smoothing out rough edges and paving the way for Eileen's comfort.

But this absence, Colette felt, could be different. Although flight from reality was not Eileen's style, she was facing the prospect of blindness and without sight she could not work. Design and creation were her raison d'être.

After a few days of no contact, breaking her sworn word, Colette took Jacques into her confidence.

They became instantly close, drawn by shared anxiety, eating together morosely, either haphazardly off the corner of Colette's kitchen table or elegantly in the dining room of Jacques's apartment, well-publicised as a temple of modern art on avenue du Bois. They settled to little and, as usual, they sparred off each other, although their decision not to notify the gendarmes was mutual, mainly because neither wanted to be on the receiving end of Eileen's anger should their worries prove groundless.

Eventually, on a Sunday morning several weeks later, unable to bear the strain of not knowing and the frustration of doing nothing, Jacques, with a box of Eileen's favourite chocolate truffles tucked under his arm as a sort of talisman, went around to her apartment.

To his amazement, the windows and shutters were open.

When, apprehensively, he knocked on the door, it was thrown wide by a radiant Eileen. Relieved beyond words, he took her mood as an omen that all was well within her world.

At times it was difficult to know with her.

When absorbed in a project, if she permitted Brigid to answer the bell ring at all, she was quite capable of not receiving whoever had the temerity to call unexpectedly; if one was lucky, she might grunt a greeting before turning back to her work; or on a good day she could be effusively welcoming.

Simultaneously she asked how he was and hugged him hello. Thanking him for the chocolates, she opened the wrapping paper, tore off the cellophane and popped two into her mouth, before passing the box to him.

He waved it away. 'Eileen, we were so worried.'

'Who's we?'

'Colette and I.'

'I should have known.'

'Where were you?'

'Down south.'

'On your own?'

She nodded, her mouth full. 'Well, Brigid was with me.' Eileen still had that habit of eating chocolate with endearing gluttony both when she was depressed and when she was elated.

Nursing the box, she led the way to her workroom. Going to the large drawing board set up inside one of the long windows, she put down the chocolates and pulled out a drawing from beneath the T-square. 'Look. Look at this.'

'What is it?'

'What do you think?' she teased.

'I've no idea.' Now that he had got over his first delight at seeing her and at knowing she was safe, he was annoyed at what he perceived to be her lack of thought and he refused to enter into her high spirits.

'It's the house I'm going to build.' Enthusiasm made her accent even more cut-glass than usual.

'You build?'

'Yes. Well, have built. Exciting isn't it?'

'Hmm, yes. I suppose.' Jacques examined the drawing minutely.

Obsessional application to whatever happened to be her current work project, to the detriment and exclusion of all else, was so typical of Eileen. He should be used to it by now. But he was not. It happened while she was absorbed in *Le Destin*, with the setting up of Jean Désert, when she was designing rugs and while she worked on the Levy apartment.

She had obviously been back in Paris for several days, holed up, engrossed in compiling a set of working drawings, oblivious to the fact that her friends could be – were – worried.

Eileen was Eileen.

There was no point in remonstrance.

He replaced the drawing on the board.

'It's most impressive.' He did not look impressed.

'Oh, for goodness sake, don't sulk.'

'I'm not,' he protested.

'You've heard about my sight?'

He nodded numbly and looked miserable.

She went to him and wrapped her arms around him in a way she had never done before. Close, warm and womanly. There was something inexplicably different about her that morning, a new softness, a sense of completeness.

'Don't worry. I'm told this sort of blindness is gradual and can take years,' she told him airily.

Since accepting the consultants' verdicts, telling Colette, making the decision to sell Jean Désert and becoming absorbed in this new project, her anxiety about her sight had relegated itself to an optimistic second place.

'I want to do this, to build this house.' She pulled out of his arms and looked into his eyes. He had always found it erotic that they were the same height. 'For me.'

'Will you marry me?'

For years he had planned this moment, veering from the absurdly romantic to the ultra-casual proposal. He had tried, without success, on so many occasions, to find the right words. Today, he was annoyed with her. Proposing marriage was the last thing on his mind.

He looked at her intently. But all he was aware of was her sharp intake of breath.

His body scent was wafted towards her on the drift of air coming in through the open windows. Smell, that most evocative of the senses. Her nostrils quivered.

She bent her head but saw nothing. Not the lead pencil she was holding. Not the pearl buttons on the cuff of her blouse. Nor the little 'Footit' rug with its laughing clown face on which she stood.

A real couple. She could be part of a real couple. The kind of couple Colette envied. A couple who were close, talked and cared for each other, who ate, worked and planned together. Nobody but Jacques had ever loved her in such an unconditional way.

When finally she raised her eyes, she saw his gaze was still unbroken and his expression full of the love she had avoided for so many years.

Alarm filled every plane of her face, drawing away the blood from her skin, widening her eyes.

She could not marry him.

Perhaps, because he read her apprehension, he turned his head away quickly, his emotional barometer dropped to its lowest point as waves of helplessness and feelings of foolishness moved through his body. He wished he had not spoken.

She too wished he had not spoken.

Intellectually she wished that she could reciprocate his feelings. There had been moments. Brief moments.

All those years ago in her bedroom in Kensington, she promised herself control of her life. At the expense of companionship and love, she had achieved it and she wasn't about to sacrifice it now.

'I've broken with the traditional architecture of the area,' she said as matter-of-factly as she could manage with her heart beating wildly. 'The houses are all very beau. Too beau. Like an over-decorated wedding cake.' What had possessed her to use the word 'wedding'. She knew she would never answer his question; she suspected he would neither repeat it nor ever again refer to marriage.

'Is beau a problem?' Jacques asked, his voice even.

'It could be.'

Her heart beat slowed and she popped another truffle into her mouth. When she offered him the box, he waved it away with an irritable, 'Surely by now, you know I don't like sweet things.'

Turning his back to her, he bent his head in contemplation of the perspective which was laid out on her work table.

'Remember that interview I did with *L'Architecture Vivante*?' When Jacques did not turn around, she continued. 'I said that a house is the shell of man, his extension, his release, his spiritual emanation, a living organism in which each inhabitant should find, as well as independence, an atmosphere of solitude and concentration.' She quoted verbatim. It was a belief which was dear to her and on which she liked to expound. But now, she used the words to fill silence.

After what seemed an age, he straightened up, turned around and with his expression well camouflaged behind his beard, said smoothly, 'Good idea to show the house in relation to town, sea and mountain. But what's this?' He pointed to a black dot.

Eileen, relieved to be back on working track, ran a careful index finger along the diagonal line leading towards the dot. She was not yet ready to use the magnifying glass in front of Jacques. Buying it had been her first physical manifestation of her acceptance of deteriorating vision. 'It's the passage of the sun in relation to the ceiling eye – this black dot – in what will be my bedroom. I want to maximise on the sun as much as possible.' She shuffled though a pile of photographs. 'Here, look this is the view from the terrace.'

'It's quite striking.'

'Isn't it? But the real challenge for me is creating a dramatic dialogue between site and house.'

Jacques sighed. 'Lucky you. Dialoguing between house and site. At least they'll do your bidding.'

Over the next weeks and months, Eileen worked tirelessly, dividing her time between Paris, where she completed a set of preliminary working drawings and made a model of her 'little refuge', as she referred to the project, and Roquebrune where Brigid had rented a flat.

Her design which, as agreed at planning stage, embraced and complimented the natural contours of the land, caused not only consternation, but barefaced hostility among officials who refused to negotiate or to compromise. They claimed it was too stark and too modernistic.

'Shuttered ignorance,' Eileen ranted at Brigid.

'How about pay-offs, bribes?'

'What do you mean?'

'Sure, don't you know it's the way things always got done back home.'

'No, I didn't. And certainly not at Brownswood Manor.'

'It happened, Miss. The whole time. You or the baroness may not have been aware. But it happened.'

Eileen gave a short laugh and looked at her maid with new respect. 'On occasions, you quite amaze me.'

Initially dubious, she skirted around the subject of bribery. As Brigid said, and rightly, she would have negotiated with the devil himself if it meant getting moving. She need not have worried. Her tentatively phrased proposal was met by the same four dark-suited, flickering-eyed officials, with back-slapping, hand-shaking, cheek-kissing enthusiasm. She bore the intrusive intimacy of these physical manifestations with a façade of humorous fortitude.

Once she had made the appropriate payments, the locals, encouraged by the officials, became her strongest allies, ensuring that she hired the best of craftsmen. Initially a mason, two assistants and some strong labourers. The project was labour intensive – all the materials having to be transported to site by wheelbarrow.

During the three years of construction she remained on or near the site, cutting as short as possible her visits to Paris. Dressed in a trouser suit, silk shirt and a jaunty bow tie, she buzzed up and down the treacherous mountain roads in her MG roadster, checking on the most minute details, ensuring every aspect of her design was adhered to, refusing to compromise.

The locals too made regular visits as much to monitor progress as to watch the antics of the 'mad Englishwoman', as they described her. The discovery that on occasions she slept on site had them rolling their eyes, throwing their hands wide and nodding in delight at her behaviour confirming their description.

During this time, Jacques was conspicuously absent from Eileen's life. While she missed his company, encouragement, support and his ability to accomplish, she felt invincible. Empowered. Deftly she dealt with finances, administration, sourcing, ordering, manufacture, delivery. On her own. For herself.

Even her eyesight was not causing undue problems. It had reached a certain plateau of deterioration and appeared to be in remission. She was able to adjust her life around it. Her greatest sadness was the knowledge that she would never again take control of a plane and embrace the skies.

Having plunged to the depths of some deep well of peace within herself, she went about each day exultantly, content in her own company. Into this project she poured her soul, and in repayment it fulfilled her every emotional and intellectual need. It was only on completion that she realised how all her creative undertakings had led to this moment.

As well as psychologically, physically her house met all her criteria. Tiered. Carved from rockface. Walls of glass, looking out towards the ever-changing turquoise of the Mediterranean. Seen from the sea, the sensation was of a ship at anchor. The fittings were functional and avant-garde, with a marine theme. Sailcloth membranes on the terrace protected from the sun, life preservers hung from the balcony deck and *Transat* reclining chairs, named after Transatlantique, the ocean-liner company, suggested a cruise.

On land, the design was equally impressive. By using the same floors, walls, shutters and lights, the exterior terrace seamlessly converted to a second living room.

The furniture was chrome, leather, wood, glass and cork. Wall-mounted headboards with compartments and extending table tops aped cabin fittings. There were also hidden areas for storage which spoke volumes of Eileen's habit of stowing away her inner life.

Remembering Jacques's comments on the completion of *Le Destin*, she called it *Tempe à Paille*, a variation of the old proverb. The name satisfied her quirky sense of humour. It was only with this, her refuge, that she felt fulfilled. In *L'Architecture Vivante* parlance, she had reached her 'pinnacle of creativity and maturity of design'.

During the course of an early interview she had said, 'To create, one must first question everything.' It was a design philosophy in which she firmly believed. Now she knew that the life she had spent questioning had paid dividends.

To her disgust, *Tempe à Paille* and she attracted as much interest from newspaper reporters and magazine writers as had *Le Destin*, Jean Désert and the Levy apartment. Likening their circling to birds of prey, she refused requests to view, appeals for interviews and petitioning for photo opportunities.

The idea of offering Roger Giles an exclusive presented itself during one of her limbo periods between sleep and wakefulness. They had remained close, mainly because he never imposed on their friendship, never asked for preferential treatment, never even requested another interview, and she had proof of his understanding of both her and her work.

He jumped at her invitation and within hours was on the night train to Nice.

His feature, with her approval, was syndicated throughout much of the world. He wrote of 'Extraordinary architectural conception'; 'Perfect interaction between the different functions of the rooms'; but her favourite lines were, 'Her lack of academic training has led to a freer and more imaginative execution of her task.'

During the long languid months of late spring, summer and early autumn, she spent her time at *Tempe à Paille* on her own, except for Brigid, sketching and painting, trying her hand at pottery, photographing pieces of driftwood against the backdrop of sea, writing snatches of poetry and, unbelievably, working on a tapestry, during which she regularly sensed Sadie hovering approvingly at her shoulder,.

The place was the perfect natural backdrop for thinking. The sound of the sea washed her thoughts in a gentle musing way which took her into unexpectedly pleasant and, sometimes, unpleasant creeks and backwaters of memory.

She had recognised real love between her parents. But she had also seen that it had neither brought them happiness, nor had it been enough to keep them together.

She had nearly succumbed to Jacques, nearly allowed herself to be taken in by love. Dada and Brownswood went from her. Damia too. Jacques could leave as well. Nobody or nothing, she hugged the knowledge to herself, could part her from *Tempe à Paille.*

The time arrived when she was ready to open her home and again to share herself. But even less of herself than previously.

She sent specific invitations to chosen guests.

Jacques was the first person she invited. She wondered would he come.

When he received her hand-written note, he wondered ought he accept. But he did. They spent a golden few days walking and swimming, absorbing the cool cleanness of the air. Without any planning and without much talk, night after night while sitting on the terrace after a late dinner watching the navy blues and dark greens and listening to the soothing and continuous susurrus of the Mediterranean, gradually they re-built, re-structured and re-adapted their relationship. The subject of marriage was never mentioned.

Eileen's moon-boat rode high in the sky and on occasions she felt the presence of her father radiating approval. She had made her mark on the world while still remaining true to herself.

It was nice, too, to have Jacques's confirmation.

Despite their healing time, the hours they spent together back in Paris, the further projects they worked on and the many vacations they took in the South of France, gradually, as they grew older, they drifted apart, still fond but seeing less and less of each other.

His damned proposal, as she thought of it, constantly hung between them.

And now this Jack Devine.

It is as though she knows him from a long time ago. A ghost from the past? Such consolation does not exist. Sometimes, she regrets the lack of such a comforting phenomenon.

She finds herself relaxing into the *Bibendum*, she and it a harmonious one, as had been her design intention, arthritic joints at ease, a warmth creeping into her bones.

She has changed her mind. A woman's prerogative, especially at her age.

Despite her earlier misgivings, she is glad she allowed him to visit. They have covered a lot of territory and, as she had hoped, re-living her projects has been satisfying. And while she could have done without the crowding reminders of her past, they have brought a new peace.

She feels quite light-headed, drugged almost with the

myriad of delicious, half-forgotten thoughts and seeping memories, as formless and as insubstantial as the morning's whisping grey mist.

'My grandmother knew you,' Jack seems to be saying, his voice coming from a distance.

'Who?'

'My grandmother. Bel McDonagh, as she was then. Before she married. She's now Belle Fagan. Though widowed. You met while she was in Paris. Doing the Grand Tour. In the 1920s.'

'I don't recall.' The denial is out before Eileen realises that of course she remembers the pretty young blonde American. Bel was difficult to forget. She was so obvious. The way she hung on Jacques's every word. And so pathetic that last morning. 'Yes, I do remember her. Why didn't you tell me this before?'

'I don't know.'

'Of course you do.'

Of course he does and he finds himself confessing. Aware of his grandmother's antipathy towards Eileen Gray, he explains how he suspected it could be reciprocated and reflect back on him. He also tells her about the family newspaper business, his father and the interview. 'It was important to me that you liked me, would open up so that I'd get a good interview.'

'And have you?'

'Yes.'

'What will you do with it?'

'I don't know.' He drops his head.

Strangely, what he does with the interview is no longer of interest to her. 'Why are you telling me all this now?'

'Because it's important to me that truth, not subterfuge,

exists between us. Gran didn't want me to come to Paris. Didn't want me to meet you. I think she was afraid.'

'Afraid! Afraid of what? Your grandmother and I had nothing in common.'

'You'd Jacques Doucet, didn't you?'

'What do you mean?'

'I don't know. But he seems to be the link.'

Link. His brain is playing odd tricks.

Link. Her brain is playing odd tricks.

He has always given his brain cells enough room and flexibility to make random associations of apparently unconnected thoughts.

So has she. Random connecting has been an integral part of her creative vision and design strength.

For as long as he can remember he has played linking games.

Link.

He is amazed at the connections these links make . . . He nearly has it. No. It is gone, drifting off.

She is dragging behind him, her mind off on another tangent. 'I see,' she says. But she does not see, she does not understand. 'You remind me of somebody.'

'Who?'

'I can't quite place . . .' Silence stretches between them. Then . . . 'Oh, Jacques, I wish I could remember.' She holds out her arms in supplication, the robe across her knees moving in sympathetic agitation.

At that moment, she reminds him of his dying grandmother. He goes to her side, drops to one knee and touches her cheek with the flat of his palm. It feels like dried paper.

It is then that she catches his scent, that same natural scent from decades ago.

The happiness fairies are all around. Her effortless self holds her and Jacques in thrall, in an ambrosiac way, like a tiny puff of opium lifting her ever so slightly off the surface of her world. It is enough.

'I should have married you when you asked.'

'Why didn't you?'

'Afraid. I was too afraid.'

'Of what?' Hunkered before her, he holds both of her hands in his.

'Being left again, I suppose. Losing control of my life. And commitment. Total commitment to another human being. That's hard.'

Her reasons are not difficult to say. Having voiced them, her sense of relief is enormous.

Jack's brain cells flow randomly. Then stop, causing one of those inexplicable shifts in the drifting brain that delivers a revelation to a vacuum.

Similarly, Eileen's cells move towards disclosure. She pulls her hands free. Replaces them under the rug. 'For a moment, I thought you were someone else.'

Jack's revelation comes in the form of three unspoken words. Jacques Doucet's grandson. His mother Patsy is Jacques's daughter. The knowledge has arrived in his mind with such clarity and making such sense of his life that he cannot understand why he has not known before.

'For a moment I was that someone else.'

'Yes,' she answers. 'You were.'

At last his life makes sense. The square-peg-in-a-round-hole syndrome explained. His relief too is enormous. It is like coming home, the way he felt each summer when he arrived at his grandparents' house at Bellport.

He will never tell his grandmother of his discovery. It is the way, he knows, she would want it.

He will never see Eileen Gray again.

He will write up this interview, the story of his meeting with her as honestly as he can.

Not for his father.

Not as a profile for publication.

As a treasured memoir for himself.

But his priority is to find Elvira. Forgiveness, commitment and love. Relating and linking. For always and ever. He has changed. The gesture was effortless. And he has more than enough love for both of them.

Author's Note

Although *Time & Destiny* portrays real people and in many instances is inspired by actual events, it is a work of fiction. But the actions, thoughts, words and feelings attributed to the characters are the products of my imagination, as are the liberties I've taken with locations and time sequences, such as the date of first publication of *Ulysses*. In as far as my research informed, I have tried to remain true to Eileen Gray's projects and to her work philosophy.

Eileen Gray (1878–1976) grew up in Enniscorthy, Co Wexford and Kensington, London. She was the youngest child, on her mother's side of a wealthy Anglo-Irish family with royal connections and her father was a Scots painter. Ethel, her elder sister, did marry youngest son of Lord Lindsay whose renovation of Brownswood Manor Eileen deplored.

She lived most of her adult life in Paris where she made a name for herself as a designer and lacquerist.

I have 'borrowed' the site, drawings and furnishings of E.1027 for Tempe à Paille. Tempe à Paille built in Castellar was her second house.

Her sight failed and she became reclusive, though still working.

When in 1972 Yves Saint Laurent bought her lacquer screen titled, *Le Destin*, her work enjoyed a new revival and she became a reluctant icon.

Before she died she destroyed her personal papers. Throughout her life she had relationships with both men and women, but never a long-term liaison.

Colette, Sidonie-Gabrielle Colette (1873–1954) was married to Willy (Henry Gauthier-Villars) who claimed her Claudine books as his and did have a penchant for sex with young children.

As well as the *Claudine* books, Colette is best remembered for her news coverage from the front during World War I, her later novels *Chéri* and *Gigi*, her plays and the many outrageous scandals that surrounded her. She lived and worked in Paris.

I did not come across any proof that she and Eileen ever met.

Couturier Jacques Doucet, was so impressed by Eileen Gray's lacquer work that he bought *Le Destin* and commissioned several other pieces. And he did sell off his eighteenth-century collection to concentrate on modern.

He and Eileen Gray never had more than a formal and disharmonious working relationship.

Damia, Gaby Bloch and Loïe Fuller appear more or less as themselves as does Bruce Chatwin.

Louella and Eugène Levy are loosely modelled on M. and Madame Mathieu-Lévy; as is Marcel Dubois on Paul Léautaud.

Belle Fagan, her grandson Jack Devine, the remainder of that family and Roger Giles are all figments of my imagination. As are Sadie, Padso, Bessie Rossa and Brigid (Eileen Gray was cared for by Louise Dany from 1927 to her death in 1976).

Acknowledgements

Thanks to Peter Adams for his informative biography, *Eileen Gray, Architect/Designer*; to Judith Thurman's *Colette*; *And God Created the French* by Louis-Bernard Robitaille. I am indebted to Dr Patrick F. Wallace, instigator of the Eileen Gray permanent exhibition at The National Museum of Ireland, Collins Barracks; to the French Embassy for their help, to the National Library and Pembroke Library for their unfailing patience; to Donal P. O'Sullivan who whetted my appetite to make that train journey to Roquebrune. And, of course, Xavier who walked with me in the footsteps of Eileen Gray, and also Suzanne and Peter for their comments. Finally to the wonderful team at Hodder Headline Ireland, especially Ciara Considine for her sensitive editing.